CHASING NIRVANA

Ellyn Oaksmith

Find out about new releases!

Sign up for Ellyn Oaksmith's newsletter!

WHAT CRITICS ARE SAYING ABOUT ELLYN OAKSMITH'S BOOKS:

"A rare combination of incisiveness, sensitivity, and humor." –Judith Arnold, USA Today Bestselling author.

"LOVED, LOVED, LOVED this book! Great characters—hysterical dialogue—spot on teen angst—BRAVO! A funny, tender, poignant book about family dynamics and how the ghosts of the past haunt us in the present."

–Christa Allen, award winning author of Since You've Been Gone

"Funny, laugh-out-loud, women's fiction, that will touch the heart and leave you thinking about your own life!"

–A Tasty Read Book Reviews

"A story full of honesty and perseverance...funny and truthful."

–Brooke Blogs

"I would recommend this to anyone...a joy to read."

–Racing to Read

"This is a great story to read and one than explores cracks in a family unit that were just waiting to appear."

–Mrs. Brown's Books.

CONTENTS

CHAPTER ONE

"They laugh at me because I'm different.
I laugh at them because they're all the same."
Kurt Cobain

FRAN

Nikki flies out of the girls' locker room, barely able to contain herself with what she's heard on the soccer field. She heads to me like a homing pigeon, all long legs and flying wet hair, a stretched-out version of her kindergarten self with boobs. Normally she dishes out gossip as she drives me home. We stop for fries if we have money. She drives and we dissect the day, speculating about who is pregnant, who got accepted to what college, and who is a first degree burnout destined for jail. What I don't know is that this time the rumors are about me. They're true and terrifying and are going to change my life.

Nikki and I have been best friends since kindergarten when she sidled up to me at playtime with her arms crossed, sniffing at the babyish scene. Her thick brown hair was braided, tied with matching red bows. "See that kid over there?" She pointed to a boy with a suspiciously bulging nostril. "He has a Lego stuffed up his nose."

I'd already spotted a tiny girl carefully licking her fingers at the craft table. "That red-haired girl is eating glue." Nikki didn't care that my sweater was threadbare and missing two buttons or that my hair was a nest of snarls. A friendship sparked and grew. I basked in the glow of her unclouded family life, gobbled the square meals she took for granted. I was her willing audience, the person along for the crazy, adrenalin fueled rocket of Nikki's life. She can't wait for anything, ever. I am always the first to know.

In fourth grade Nikki marched right out of Mrs. Lainley's class, down the hall into my classroom. "Kyle Parder peed his pants. It went all over the floor and touched Lisa Steeney's shoe." She hugged herself in delight, waiting dramatically to unveil the deliciously disgusting finale. "She barfed." After a mighty bear hug, she whispered, "I won't see you at recess. I'm going to get busted for leaving the class. You're my bestie forever." We linked pinkies and said our solemn goodbyes.

It's senior year and no, she hasn't changed all that much.

She's perfect.

Sure enough, when she reaches the bench where I always wait for her after yearbook, Nikki blurts, "Someone nominated you for prom queen 1993." The last three words are very dramatic, as if it's the name of a Broadway show: Prom Queen 1993. It would be totally funny, this dramatic delivery with me sitting on the bench and her dripping wet from a hasty shower. Aberdeen School is behind us, as grey and dismal as the cloudy late spring day. But nothing about it is the slightest bit amusing because she's talking about me.

"Totally hilarious. Not." I hoist my backpack as we head to the senior lot. Every day after soccer and yearbook she gives me a ride home. It's always the best part of my day.

"Totally true. Totally funny and by the way, like totally freaking awesome."

I study her face as we walk to her car. "Wtf? You serious?"

She nods. "As a heart attack." This part she sings. "They posted the announcement right after third period. Taylor Davis was a mess at practice. Going on and on about how you don't even care and she does and how it's not fair. I automatically love anything that pisses her off."

I'm not listening. I'm too busy working myself into grade A panic attack. My palms sweat, my heart flips. I have survived high school like a barnacle clinging to the edge of a deepwater reef, hunkering down. People could and will talk. When you're popular, like Taylor, you don't mind because most of it is sheer jealousy. In my case, it's poisonous darts aimed at my exposed hide. Nikki, with her epically normal family, of course, doesn't get this. "Why would someone nominate me?"

She frowns, balancing on me to take a rock out of her fancy Nike slide. "Um, because you're like freaking awesome?"

Right. There is a small fringe minority that when pushed, might call me, at very best, nice. But the majority of the school actively despises me. As in, if burning at the stake were still a thing, they'd whip out their Zippos. "Nikki, they're doing it because I'm gay and they think it's funny. It's like nominating a whale for mayor."

She sighs. "Another really good idea. Who cares, just do it!"

Nikki is this horrible living, breathing Nike ad. She never dwells on the negative because an obstacle is something she effortlessly sails over or dies trying, bashing her head against it like a deranged water buffalo until she finds another goal. When I was first slapped with the word "gay," she didn't let me moan or complain or feel sorry for myself unless we were otherwise occupied in something she deemed positive, like doodling mustaches on fashion magazine models or having a two-person MTV dance-a-thon in her living room. Although it's seriously irritating, she's my lifeline. She's the Ernie to my Bert, the Charlie Brown to my Lucy. Nikki's parents are people who protest, people who believe in causes; people who think their opinions matter. Nikki inherited their oppressively optimistic genes. I don't even want to think about what I've inherited.

"Taylor thinks prom queen is hers, signed sealed and delivered." We reach the student parking lot. Fat raindrops flop onto the pavement. On the Washington coast, we don't have weather. We have rain. "She'll kill me."

Nikki rakes through her backpack for the car keys. "Not if we kill her first."

"Now you're just scaring me."

"Which is exactly why you need to run." She struggles with the car lock. If all the rust in the world suddenly vanished, Nikki's mom's Volvo would collapse. "If there ever was someone who needed an opponent, it's like Taylor Freaking Davis. Who says she has to win?"

She's a little too thrilled about this. Also, she has her own reasons for hating Taylor Davis. "Is this about you and Taylor on the soccer field?" *Or Paul?*

"No," she says a little too quickly, followed by, "Although it was a brilliant idea." *It's about Paul.* "Look, I know you think this is about me and Taylor." *Um, no, I think it's about Paul.* "But who says you don't have a right to this thing?'

God help me she has that look. "Taylor Davis will win prom queen. It's written in stone somewhere. Her birth certificate says Taylor Davis, future prom queen, class of 1993."

Nikki gives me a long, loaded look. "Unless you win." If you want Nikki to do something, tell her she can't.

"There isn't going to be a Big Gay Prom."

She puts the car in reverse and guns it backwards without a glance. Luckily there is no one behind us. Nikki's attitude toward driving is the same as her attitude about life: look out world, here I come. "I totally would have dropped this until you said big gay prom. I can see the posters now. It's going to be totally freaking awesome."

NIKKI

My dad was the first one to point out that Fran and I make a great team. "Everyone needs a linebacker to run interference." I'm Fran's linebacker. I can ease the way and also, bring her into the conflict. Like running for prom queen. See, Fran's whole life is about not being noticed. The one time she was caught off guard and shared something personal it led to her being outed in the most brutal way possible and since that summer in 6th grade, she's been shrinking into herself. She's this human sinkhole that has been slowly but surely caving in. I figure it's my job to make sure that doesn't happen. Not on my freaking watch.

Did I mention I'm very good at getting my own way? Maybe I learned it from my dad, who is a public defender. He loves arguing with me about everything, even stupid things like do eggs really need refrigerating or if I deserve to drive after those dumb neighbors said I came too close to their stupid kid and the other one who ratted me out for running over their boxwood hedge. I'm like a dog in a fight. I just go for the neck and hang on like hell until I wear my dad out. Most of the time, it totally works.

When we turn into her driveway, Mrs. Worthy's latest live-in loser staggers outside, bellowing at Fran, telling her to get inside for dinner, she's late. Except he doesn't say, "Hey Fran, come in for dinner," like a normal person. He says, "Get inside for fucking dinner. You're fucking late." Totally classy.

My mom says Fran's mom never quite left high school, which is just about the scariest possible thing I can freaking imagine. Fran needs to get out of here. Fast.

Winning prom queen is the first step. And no, the fact that Paul is dating Taylor has nothing to do with it. Okay, well, maybe a little. If Fran won and Taylor was denied prom queen that would make me happy dance from here to Seattle.

Did I mention that I hate Taylor?

There. I said it.

I hate Taylor.

She's mean. And tiny. And beautiful.

Also – she's dating the guy I've been in love with for like, eons. The only thing worse than seeing the really nice guy I love dating someone else is having that person be Taylor. Maybe I can blame my college situation on Taylor. Maybe I've been so distracted by watching Paul stick his hand in her back pocket that I have screwed up my life. Maybe that's what I'll tell my parents. When I tell them.

Did I mention that I hate Taylor?

PAUL

The last thing Dad said when he ditched us was, "Son, I sure as hell hope you understand women better than I do because they are a foreign species."

Of course, Dad didn't leave a forwarding address or much of anything else so if I did puzzle anything out in that department, I wouldn't be able to contact him. But no, I cannot figure women out, least of all Taylor. You'd think after chasing a girl for year and dating her for three, you'd know more than you did at square one. Nope. Doesn't work that way.

Taylor is yelling at me because Fran Worthy was nominated for prom queen. When I first heard about it in the locker room I didn't think much about it. Yes, Taylor informed me sophomore year that as her boyfriend, I would be prom king but honestly, who cares? You stand on stage like a moron with a crown on your head. Your friends, who would trade places with me in a white hot second if Taylor crooked her perfect little finger, will make fun of you unless you break the stupid crown in half, which will piss off Taylor. It's all just high school drama.

I have legit concerns, like keeping my turd brother from drinking all the grocery money.

Taylor sees it as the culmination of working four years to stay at the head of the pack. Ninety-nine percent of the school wants to bed her or be her. Popularity is her drug of choice and honestly, living on Planet Taylor is exciting. Sometimes though, I wonder. Dating her is like a full-time job.

As far as I know anyone is allowed to be nominated for prom queen but that's not the way Taylor sees it. She's pacing up and down in her kitchen, screaming about how Fran can't just waltz in and steal this from her, really getting herself worked up. By the time her mother comes in and drops her purse on the kitchen table Taylor is full on screaming.

"Paul! Do something!" Taylor's mom yells like I know how to control her daughter. Nobody talks Taylor out of anything, least of all me.

Not only have I not figured out women, I have not figured out Taylor. When I heard she wanted to go out with me it was like being struck by a meteor. For one thing, she's gorgeous. Also, she's rich. Her dad is an orthodontist and their house looks like something out of a magazine. When Lyle Dennam told me at soccer practice that Taylor wanted me to ask her out, I kind of freaked. A girl like Taylor could have any guy she wanted. Why in the hell did she want me?

By the time Taylor's mom has calmed her down, we're all sitting at the kitchen table drinking Diet Cokes. Well, Taylor's mom is drinking wine. After the first glass, she's up to speed.

"She doesn't even care, Mom! Whoever nominated her meant it as a freaking joke!"

"Don't swear honey, it's vulgar."

"Freaking is not swearing. Tell her Paul, it's not swearing."

Mrs. Davis glares at me so I mumble something.

"Paul, stick up for me here. Why are you being so quiet?" Taylor snaps, crunching her ice.

"It's not really swearing."

"I meant about Fran!" Taylor coughs as she accidentally swallows some ice. "Whose side are you on? I swear to God I'm going to start screaming if you don't show me more support."

I know it won't do any good to point out that she's already been hollering pretty much nonstop since we entered her house. Her Pekinese dogs trail her around like yapping wind-up toys. Between them and her screaming I have a massive headache. This was supposed to be a ride home after soccer but she was so upset I came inside even though I haven't showered and it's my night to cook.

I told Taylor all this in the car and yet here I am. Taylor has this way of almost crying that makes her cornflower blue eyes the size of dinner plates. When those suckers brim with tears, I panic, as if someone is dangling a mewing kitten over a vat of boiling water. She knows that I will do absolutely anything to avoid watching her cry. Anything. Because no matter what it is; somehow, it's always my fault. Although it's irrational, it's predictable. Taylor counts on it.

Mrs. Davis is patting Taylor's arm, giving me a cold look like I'm the biggest loser in the world. Like if I were a better boyfriend, I would be coming up with a plan that would soothe her troubled child. They both have this way of making me feel completely useless. As if they got the same manual on dealing with men that includes tips like *Give the man a dirty look when you are dealing with an emotional woman. It will make the man feel like he's not doing his job and you're doing it for them. Then they'll be in your debt, right under your thumb. This is where you want them. Always.*

Taylor likes dating me because I'm captain of the soccer team and she thinks we look good together. I complement her petite frame, making the other girls jealous. Yes, she's high maintenance and makes me feel like an idiot. But when a girl like Taylor likes you, you go out with her. That's just how it works. No one turns down a Super Bowl ring.

Mrs. Davis' diamonds sparkle in the overhead light. The kitchen, like the rest of the house, is blindingly white. Even the dogs look bleached, with matching white satin bows holding the hair out of their beady little eyes. One of them bit me the first time I came over. Taylor said, "Oh my God – isn't that cute?" I'd love to put those dogs outside and see if eagles carry them off. That would be awesome.

Taylor's mom shoots me another look while talking to her daughter. "Don't you worry about a thing, honey. I'll go talk to Principal P. and work this out. He cannot allow a lesbian girl to run for prom queen."

"Why not?" I blurt, like a total moron. I know Fran. If it wasn't common knowledge, I wouldn't even know she was gay. She doesn't look or act different. She's just a pretty, normal girl, as far as I can tell.

Taylor and her mom whip their heads around so fast they are a blur of tawny blonde hair and Chicklet teeth. Identical blue eyes narrow in on me, making me itch with nerves. These are two women I do not want gunning for me.

"Paul are you saying that Fran is a more suitable choice for prom queen than your own girlfriend?" Mrs. Davis doesn't let me answer, just plows ahead, tapping the table with one long nail. "Do you think that it's okay to have a known *lesbian* represent the student body and set an example for the students?" She wrinkles her nose when she says lesbian. I open my mouth to respond but she keeps on. "Do you think the school should uphold that kind of deviant behavior?"

Finally, she stops. Taylor studies me critically. "Paul?" she says, sniffing delicately. "I don't care that she's a lesbian but I do care that you support me." Oh no, she's going to cry. Shit. Better choose my words carefully.

"She won't win. I mean, obviously."

Taylor feels a little bit better but her mother is still blinking her gunky eyelashes. "True. But do you honestly feel I can sit back and let this girl mock my daughter?"

I don't really see the problem. Taylor will win. She'll drag me up on stage wearing some monkey suit and I'll stand there like a jerk, holding her hand. Running against Fran won't change anything except maybe people will talk about Fran, which is what this is about.

"No, I guess not."

Taylor's mom stands, dusting off her immaculate hands. "You guess not?" She tucks her thick hair behind an ear studded with a fat diamond. "Paul honey, you'd better think long and hard about this. There is a right side and wrong side to this issue and you do not want to be coming down on the wrong side. Things could get very ugly for you."

Outside I sit in my car for a very long time. I'd just been threatened by my girlfriend's mother. Things are getting very weird. And they are about to get a hell of a lot weirder.

To make matters worse, when I get home there is a letter on the kitchen table. It's from my dad.

FRAN

Mom and Dwayne both turn to stare at me, when I come in the front door, which is strange. What is even more bizarre is that they are sitting at the little rickety linoleum table in the kitchen like some 1950s family, if 1950s fashion included mullets and acid-washed jeans. We never eat together.

The first time I went to dinner at Nikki's house I automatically carried my dinner into the den to watch TV. I didn't think it was physically possible to digest food away from the television. I mean, sure, I saw TV families eating together but I didn't know it happened in real life. Normally when I come home Mom is glued to the TV in the tiny room off the kitchen with her hand in a box of Wheat Thins. Dwayne is in his "lounge" in carport with the ugly lamp glowing and his bigger, better TV.

The Outdoor Lounge was my mom's idea. One of the many things she didn't think about when she dragged him home was that our house would shrink. Although my whole life we'd lived with an assortment of her boyfriends, we'd had an entire year in this house to ourselves. So, when Dwayne moved in with his big loud voice and explosive farts, there was no place to escape. I could hear every move he made through the paper-thin walls of my bedroom. He'd watch sports late into the night, yelling at the television. Mom convinced him that the carport was an extension of the house, like a den, without walls. But, instead of removing him, the lounge just put him on display, like a Komodo dragon during the rain until it smells meat nearby. When he coated the television with shrink wrap to keep out the moisture it was a proud moment.

Mom came up with the term lounge. I came up with the term White Trash Terrace.

As I stand there studying him, Dwayne puts down his beer and pushes out my chair with his foot. "Drink some fucking milk."

I resist the urge to sneer, "Why thank you Dwayne."

I cautiously sit and peel back the tinfoil from my Hungry Man dinner. Inside is a gelatinous grey substance that could be road kill. Dwayne sees my distaste, adding, "You need to put some meat on you. Maybe you'll grow some boobs." He chuckles as if this is hilarious.

A note about Dwayne's sense of humor: he doesn't have one. Or rather, what he thinks is funny just isn't.

Mom says "Du-wayyyyyne," as if she knows it's weird that her boyfriend just commented on my breasts or lack thereof and yet she's going to put up with it because Dwayne helps with the rent and she doesn't want to live with Grandma June who lives above a biker bar. Once a year, at my request, we have dinner together. Mom and Grandma drink cheap wine. By the time we get to dessert they're telling each other how the other one ruined their lives.

So that's Christmas.

While I'm drinking my milk, Dwayne points out that he chose the Salisbury steaks especially for me, which is ironic because I'm a vegetarian. "Thanks."

When Dwayne moved in two years ago Mom neglected to mention the whole vegetarian thing. The gay thing was off the table too since Mom and I have never discussed it.

Dwayne discovered that I was gay from someone at his uncle's hardware store who had a kid at the high school. I had become known as That Lesbian Girl or That Freak or this year, compliments of PC, That Fucking Dyke. The day Dwayne found out he came home furious, informing me that although it was perfectly acceptable to show girl-on-girl action in Playboy magazine, he wasn't going to live with a "rug munching pervert" because it was "against the laws of nature."

I didn't ask him what laws of nature he was following. Nor did I point out that homosexuality abounds in nature. I just went into my room and listened to *Nevermind* three times in a row with the volume cranked at ten on my Walkman.

There are a couple things in life that Kurt Cobain's wailing voice can't soothe but I don't know what they are. And I don't really care. Summer of 1990 I wandered into Disc Jockey Records in the corn-dog scented South Shore Mall. I had an hour to kill while Nikki and her mom shopped for school clothes. The manager was listening to *Bleach* so I sat down on a milk crate and stayed until it was done. Then I asked him to play it again. After the third spin, I got up the courage to ask him about the band. When he told me that they were originally from Aberdeen I just about swallowed my tongue. The idea that someone from Aberdeen had produced music that was played on the radio blew me away. Not just any album, an album filled with rage and anger, detachment and loneliness. The kind of record I could listen to every single day a hundred times, letting the music sink into my skin until it became part of me.

It was the first time that music didn't just sound good, it sounded like my life. Nirvana's songs cracked me open like a nut. All I wanted was more. More music, more time, more freedom from a life that dragged me down. The manager hadn't ordered any more copies because no one would buy it locally but when I asked, he promised he'd order me a copy.

That record changed my life. Saved my life.

Moving the dripping hamburger patty around, I study Dwayne, knowing he has a scheme. I can see it in his beady eyes when he nods meaningfully at my Mom. "Tell her doll baby."

Doll baby knits her brows like she knows this is a bad idea but also, she likes being able to afford meat. Two summers ago, we subsisted primarily on day-old fruit pies she carried home from work. By the time they reached us, they were smashed and nasty. She told me not to worry. Plenty of girls grow up and marry rich men. Look at Audrey Hepburn in "Sabrina." Also, "How to Marry a Millionaire." Marilyn Munroe knew her stuff. And Eliza Doolittle in "My Fair Lady." If I just paid more attention to her movies, I'd stop being such a silly worry wart. By the end of the month, after we'd spent our food stamps, my mouth would break out in canker sores. I'd beg her to please go to the food bank.

"It's humiliating," she'd mumble, eyes glued to the TV.

I'd point out that since we didn't have a dental plan (or any other plan) we'd better get some canned vegetables or something. Half the town skulked down to the food bank. No wonder so many people in Aberdeen thought suicide was a good exit strategy.

I can tell by the way Mom's eyes pinball around that Operation Saving Fran isn't her idea. Confrontation isn't her style. But she'll go along with it. And if I want a roof over my head, I will too.

Forcing my face into a smile, I listen to their plan to ruin my life.

CHAPTER TWO

*"I'm so happy because today I found my
friends - they're in my head."*
"Lithium," Nirvana

FRAN

"**I**t's called the South Aberdeen Baptist Church," Mom says, keeping her eyes on Dwayne like a robot. "It's Dwayne's church."

I throw the empty foil trays into the garbage. "You have a church?"

Dwayne empties his beer, crushing the can under his boot. "Hell to the yes. Since I was that high." He tosses me his empty.

Mom silently pleads me not to ask when, exactly, this church-going happens what with his busy schedule of calling in sick at his uncle's hardware store, grooming his mullet and watching TV. "We've signed you up for a Teen Life class. It'll be like Billy Holliday in 'Born Yesterday'.

She's this uncouth tough chick and they hire William Holden to smarten her up. He's a handsome lawyer."

"I'm an uncouth tough chick?"

"Dwayne, you tell her." She jumps up from the table, grabs her plant spritzer; racing to her colony of African violets as if they are dying of thirst. Those plants are probably the closest thing to siblings I'll ever get.

Dwayne nods proudly. "Yep. Teen Life." Heavy emphasis on the last word as if I'm confusing it with Teen Death.

We all know Teen Life is aimed at deprogramming me from a gay cult. I don't know who the cult leader is but I bet he's a funny guy with a cool job, who lives in a city and dresses super well. The anti-Dwayne. After some nervous spritzing action, Mom slides over a brochure. On the cover is a basic assortment pack of beaming straight kids with perfect teeth: black, white, Asian and Mexican. The Native American kid off to the side doesn't look very happy. Maybe she's hiding weapons in her backpack. I hope so. When I open the brochure, I'm offered a weekly option and a twice weekly option, which is circled. "Twice a week?"

The poor violets are being spritzed to death. "Yes," Mom says, her rabbity eyes darting between Dwayne and me. I can feel Dwayne pulling her strings. "The twice weekly option will get you ready for life?" To her, it's a question.

There's nothing more to clean in the kitchen so I sit down across from Dwayne. "So, this class will get me ready for waitressing at Plaza Garcia's until my teeth fall out?" I'm a tad bitter that I'm the only one of my friends without college plans.

Now she's dusting her huge video collection, itching to slide one into the player we rescued from someone's trash. "There are much nicer places in Aberdeen than Plaza Garcia."

What Mom really hates about Plaza Garcia is that my grandma got me the job. "But both classes conflict with yearbook."

Dwayne opens the slider, goes out and returns with another Olympia beer. "Who fucking cares about yearbook? A bunch of fags who can't make the football team."

"Yes, but they're my fags." Whoops.

Dwayne's sagging jowls open wide, stunned at my temerity, a word he wouldn't know. He looks at my mom, asking permission to beat the living crap out of me.

She hurries into the kitchen.

Permission denied.

He opens the garbage can, removing the tinfoil platter containing my uneaten, congealed Salisbury steak, waving Exhibit A. "Fucking ingrate." He then launches into one of his three speeches. This one is called "After All I Have Done For You." It is subtitled: You Ungrateful Little Bitch. (Speech 2: "I Could Have Played Pro Ball Except For My Torn Ligament." Speech 3: "I'm Smarter Than Everyone, including Bill Clinton, who should do his own thing and not listen to that Stupid Nosy Bitch Hillary.")

Dwayne storms off, doing his best to slam the sliding glass door, which sticks in the runner which is quite funny. I am smart enough not to laugh. Mom rinses my milk glass, pouring me a half glass of beer. I don't normally like beer but I drink. If anyone needs a drinking buddy it's my mom. "Just give the class a chance. Dwayne is just looking out for your best interests."

"No, he's not."

"I know you can't see it this way but Dwayne is taking an interest in you."

"I know you can't see this but he hates me." I sip my beer, wishing it was orange juice, the kind that comes in cartons fortified with calcium for growing bones, like at Nikki's house. I also wish that my mom was like Nikki's, a registered nurse who embarrasses the hell out of me with brochures on safe gay sex and keeps Chunky Monkey Ben and Jerry's in her freezer with a note: Unless you are Fran, Don't Eat Me.

Televised cheers from Dwayne's Mariner's game floats through the glass. I study the Texas shaped water stain on the wall. When we moved in, it was as small as Rhode Island. Mom lights a cigarette. She opens the window over the sink to blow out smoke before turning to me. "You'll probably end up liking it. Who knows, you might even meet some nice people."

And then it occurs to me. This might be a good place to meet my people. The queers.

NIKKI

I'm already pissed at Taylor from the soccer field so when she snaps at me in the locker room, it's on.

"You'd better tell your friend that she'd better drop out of running for prom queen," she sneers as she comes around the corner with a towel wrapped around her torso, fresh out of the shower. The fact that she looks like a freaking MTV video, with her long, wet hair and fake tan makes it worse, somehow.

It's cold and inhospitable in our locker room, which is attached to the track and field buildings. Most people hustle out of here to get to their homework or fast-food jobs. Taylor always hangs out, gossiping. "Afraid of the competition?" I sneer.

Taylor looks up from applying lotion to her legs. The look on her face means I've nailed it. "As if."

There are twelve girls left in the locker room, all pretending very hard not to eavesdrop. Since freshman year it's been all out war. Two girls like Taylor and me, both aggressive, fast power forwards, were bound to bump heads, although I didn't help matters much. As soon as I realized I'd be competing for captain with She Devil, I was freaking ruthless. The worst part of it is that we're team cocaptains. The two people that are supposed to set the example of leadership despise one another.

I try to stay calm. "She has just as much right to be prom queen as you do."

"Just listen to yourself. You're totally deluded. My mom is talking to the principal right now to see if he'll stop her."

"The principal? Why?"

Taylor's mouth curls into an ugly snarl. "Because she'll embarrass herself."

"At least she's not, like a total bitch."

Taylor's head snakes back and forth like a cobra. "I know what this is about. You couldn't get Paul so you have to get back at me somehow."

The first time I saw the TV show The Incredible

Hulk and that guy morph into a huge green monster I thought—that's me. I get this white-hot rage that bubbles up into my brain, blinding me. And although my parents, coaches, and teachers don't believe me—I have no control. Nobody pushes my buttons more than Taylor.

I've spent four years trying to manage my feelings around her in a never-ending battle to not smash her stupid face. Normally I can control it but right now every shitty thing Taylor has said or done comes raining down on me and I want to freaking kill her. I grab the nearest thing at hand—a Costco-sized bottle of Kirkland brand shampoo and lob it at her as hard as I can. Her stupid blue eyes go wide as she sees the heavy projectile. She turns but not before the bottle nails her face. She's screaming bloody murder, saying I attacked her. Half the team is standing there with their jaws open in total shock.

The other half is rushing to comfort her. Everyone stares at me like I'm a serial killer.

Candy Heller whispers to Dana Juarez. "Did that just happen?"

From outside the cement locker room I can hear Taylor's mom. "Taylor? Baby? Are you okay? It's Mom, I'm outside."

"Mom? Nikki attacked me!" Taylor takes her hand off her cheek. Oh no. There's a long, jagged scratch and blood welling up.

"I didn't freaking attack you!" I'm a little panicked.

"Yes, you did! My face! If you thought you had problems before you had no idea!"

Shit.

FRAN

The basement of South Aberdeen Baptist Church feels like a bunker. Looking up at the grimy rain-speckled windows, I can see the feet of the people from the last meeting: AA people in worn-down heels and scuffed boots. Their smoke floats in through the cracked window. Seated at the long tables formed into a square are a bunch of surly teenagers, plus a kid I know from yearbook named Mike. His nickname is Dirty Mike, given his penchant for talking smut. He's a classic stoner and tonight, true to form, his eyes are glazed to a fine reddish-hued patina. We nod and I glance at the other kids. There is a girl with major eyeliner. A Walkman cord snakes out of her ear.

The song playing in my head is "Frances Farmer Will Have Her Revenge." The soothing thing about this song, besides the lyrics and Kurt's familiar voice, is that Kurt's baby daughter and I share the same name. Yes, the actress Frances Farmer did end up in a mental institution where she received shock treatment for her radical ways, which is tragic but still, it's a nice connection. So yes, I like the song.

A pot-bellied guy in a beige cardigan ushers in stragglers, shaking hands, proclaiming proudly, "I'm Don," as if this is an impressive feat. He has a beatific stare, which lasts a beat too long.

There is a slight commotion by the door before the single most amazing thing in my life happens. In walks the most interesting girl I have ever seen in my life. Scratch that, she doesn't walk, she stomps. Her eyes are behind glossy black bangs but I know they are angry. Her furious stomping is a language I understand. She doesn't want to be here anymore than I do and she's not going to take this sitting down. She's furious and beautiful and exotic in a way that clearly doesn't belong in Aberdeen. I've worshipped her from afar for a year.

Allison showed up junior year and gave me a heart attack in third period.

I was sitting in English lit, time had morphed into a Jell-O like thickness. We were all so bored we were technically dead. A fly was driving me nuts and I wished Mr. Cronner would open a window. The door opened and it was like that moment in the Wizard of Oz when everything turns to color. I wasn't the only one who felt it. The entire class sat up and stared. Allison had this urban cool thing going on, all torn black jeans, a tiny nose stud, and shiny black hair slanting over her almond eyes. New Girl. It should have been written in neon. Transfer students were a big deal but this girl stood out like a gazelle among the clueless meerkats. No one had to tell me she was from a big city. It was written all over her like graffiti.

As Mr. Cronner droned on: "Boys and girls, I'd like you to welcome Allison Kondo, a new student who has transferred from San Francisco..." blah, blah, blah, I fell in love. Yes, I know. It was pathetic and corny and a walking teenaged cliché but Allison had this presence. This 'I'm Just Killing Time 'til I Go Do Something Spectacular With My Life' that you don't see here. Aberdeen is the kind of place to drink yourself to death. In the rain. Wearing polyester slacks.

Immediately after developing a tornado of a crush I hit reality. Hard. The odds of her being into girls was roughly the same as a Great White shark jumping through the window, followed by an asteroid and six leprechauns named Mick. Las Vegas odds would be something like one trillion to one. Not favoring me.

Shit.

"So, Allison, have you read *The Dead* by James Joyce?" Mr. Cronner had asked after his standard waiting-for-everyone to quiet down/fall asleep.

"Yeah, last year," Allison said. "I wrote a paper on James' treatment of women in *Dubliners.*"

Of course she did.

And now, a year later, she's here. In a church basement.

With me.

Causing every cell in my body to come to life, tracking her like a magnet.

Thank you baby Jesus. Thank you Dwayne even though I still hate you.

"Welcome," says Don. "Please sit down."

Allison stares at him for a very long time as if he is an insect she's getting ready to squish. For an awkward eternity, she stands there indecisively, ready to bolt. I'm waiting for her to say, "Screw this," before she flees. If she does, I'll be right behind. We can bond over the stupidity of anything called Teen Life. Or Teen anything for that matter. I'm ready.

She exhales slowly, clomping to a free chair between a kid with Duran Duran hair and eyeliner girl. I'm dying to see the source of this clomping so I sneak a look under the table at her boots. They are Frye motorcycle boots with a thick silver buckle on the side. The kind Peter Fonda wore in *Easy Rider.* They are boots to get stoned in and make love in at the bottom of a desert canyon. They are shit-kicking boots. I add this to the list of things I know about Allison: she has the coolest boots on the planet.

When I raise my head, Allison is seated. She nods with recognition, which is encouraging. Don goes on about how this class is going to teach us how to embrace a Christian, moral life full of values and blah, blah, blah. Allison lowers her chin. Her hair becomes a curtain between us. She puts her hand to her head and makes a gun, pulling the trigger and silently mouths a gunshot noise.

It's the most eloquent gesture in history.

Besides the boots, she's funny. It's like going down a ledge, this falling in love thing. There are degrees of slipping. Just when you think you've leveled out, you're in a deeper.

While Don continues his peppy Way of Christ speech, Allison pulls out her backpack, which is plastered with a mass of Sharpie doodles so insanely cool I want to study them for hours. She dislodges a huge calculator.

Don pats her shoulder. "Sorry, this is time for life talks, not homework." He says Life Talks with capitalization, which is super annoying.

Allison gives him a look so dark, so angry that I want to stand up and applaud. Doesn't he see that she's far too cool for anything that he could ever say? Doesn't he realize that the coolest person in the universe has just graced us with her presence? How could he not bow down to her eloquent indifference?

With supreme boredom and resentment, she shoves the backpack under the table, leaning down to retrieve a Sharpie. She uncaps it and puts it to her nose, sniffing so deeply it's almost obscene. Like she's disappearing into the portal of her mind and has begun the ejection sequence.

A thing for Sharpies: another thing to love about Allison. I open my notebook and right across from the ever-changing, constantly re-ordered list of my hierarchy of favorite Nirvana songs (current favorite: "All Apologies" because, well, 'everyone is gay,' is a great line and fun to think about.) I begin my new lists:

Things I Know About Allison:
Thing for Sharpies and Frye Boots.
She's funny.

Three things.

After Don makes sure that eyeliner girl has stowed her earphones, he claps his hands. "Anyone want a Coke?"

While Don hands out drinks and bags of chips, he begins his sermon, asking how many of us have accepted the Lord Jesus Christ as our true savior. Several kids raise their hands. I immediately label them as ass-kissing suck-ups. Mike grabs three bags of chips. Don makes him put back one, which Mike thinks is a real coup.

Eyeliner girl stares out the window, thinking about whatever tape is in her Walkman. Allison takes a bag of Barbecue Lays. "We're Christian and Buddhist."

"What? Hold the phone!" Don says, holding out the box of chips. Eyeliner girls takes two bags without looking.

"My parents are Japanese and American. I'm both."

Don reaches the front of the room, ripping open his own bag of plain chips. "But you believe in Jesus, right?"

Allison frowns at a chip. Her nails are black and short. "Not really. Just God."

Don stares at her as if she's just sprouted a third eye. "But Jesus is the son of God."

Allison studies the map of Ancient Rome on the wall. "What if he didn't have kids?" she asks.

"Mmmm-hm," Don says, turning slightly purple, pausing to eat a chip, dusting the salt from his fingers. "Well, that's a great place to start our chat." He places a thinking finger on his chin. "Mmmm-hm. You see, Jesus is a vibrant and essential part of guiding us through these turbulent teenaged years. He is the very human embodiment of God himself." He jams in three more chips, washing them down with 7UP. He hums as he speaks, interjecting Mmmm-hm into every sentence. "Jesus is there to see us through the temptations of the physical world because just like you and me, Jesus walked this earth and dealt with the same urges. I know this is hard to believe—" His eyes go wide as if he's about ready to explode. "But Jesus was a teenager." He waits for someone to comment about this shocking revelation. Nobody cares. Mike is so into his potato chips it's kind of obscene.

Don waves a hand around the table. "Our bodies, mmm-hmmm, they are telling us that we want something that is wrong. Temptation is the battle of these formative teen years."

He stops dramatically, trying to maintain eye contact with each and every one of us which comes off as creepy, as if he's trying to drill a pathway into our brains. "Our job is to listen to Jesus, who shows us the path towards self-control, family and faith." He points as he counts each one off, nearly breaking his fingers on a ceiling so low it feels like we're being crushed by the church. "Self-control, even if it means..." His face turns flaming crimson as he studies the threadbare carpet. "Even if it means pleasuring.... alone... which is better than acting on our sinful urges."

Eyeliner girl snorts. Allison doodles. Mike licks salt off his fingers. The smiling dorks grin harder. We're all thinking the same thing. *Is he really telling us to masturbate? Did this just happen? It's day one and that's what you're giving us—masturbation?*

"Even if it means spilling seed without procreation, which is really what sex is all about later. Much, much later. A little private time is good for you boys." He finally looks up from the carpet, blinking sixteen, maybe seventeen times before he says, "I don't know what the girls do but I'm sure you can talk to your health teacher at school."

Allison rolls her eyes. Her sophomore year health teacher must have looked like mine. Mrs. Donfligger is a grey, raisiny black lady who wears comfort-soled shoes that stick to the linoleum floors and an onyx cross with a tiny gold Jesus. Last year she threw a bunch of condoms on a desk and said, "If you gotta do it, use these," before telling us all about her son Marcus who got cut from the Baltimore Ravens in training camp and was going to medical school. I loved her stories because Marcus, like Kurt Cobain and Krist Novoselic, made it out of Aberdeen alive.

I tune out and tap my pen in time to "Heart Shaped Box," studying Allison's face when she's not looking. She spends the entire time doodling. The room slowly fills with the chemical tang of Sharpie.

After an hour of Don droning variations on a theme, I really don't mind. A few bags of chips and some warm Coke go a long way for a girl like me. I'm free to study

Allison for any tell-tale signs of latent lesbianism (none) and speculate about her glamorous life in San Francisco. I can see her on a skateboard racing the Rice-A-Roni streetcar, which is really the only thing I know about San Francisco. One of the dorks is sizing her up through his Buddy Holly glasses. Maybe he's her type.

I hope not.

I keep waiting for Don to get specific, to pray away the gay but it never really happens. Perhaps, before I saw Allison, I might have even given it a shot. Being straight would make my life a hell of a lot simpler. But any doubts I had about my sexuality were wiped out at 4:23 p.m. today. I checked my watch the moment Allison walked in the door. At that moment, I fell in love.

There's no going back.

PAUL

Taylor is freaking out. I'd just walked in the door from soccer when her mom called and told me to get on over there as fast as I could. Taylor had been attacked. Those were her words. Before I could ask any details, she hung up. I raced over, driving like a maniac; worried that some pervert had dragged her into the bushes or some meth head roughed her up, taken her purse. I didn't even knock, just walked right into their marble entryway, right into the Great Shampoo Bottle Incident.

We live in a town where people get crushed by trees or mangled by machinery every day. Meth labs burst into flames. My mom works in a lumberyard where some guy loses a finger once a month. The whole shampoo bottle thing just strikes me as melodramatic.

Her mom is on the phone with the police, insisting that she needs to file report. "Don't you make light of this young man. It was a heavy shampoo bottle. My daughter has a cut on her face!"

"How did this get started?" I ask Taylor, who is at the kitchen table milking this for all it's worth. Last year she sprained her ankle in soccer. Her friends met her at her car, helping her inside like an Egyptian queen. They brought a pillow to the lunchroom so she could rest her foot.

The cut in question is more like a scratch. It's pretty long, from the edge of her eye down to her chin but it's not deep. Her father shook my hand on his way out when I arrived. "Good man. Good man!" he said before heading for the school like a man on a mission. They're treating this like Nikki slashed her face with a switchblade.

"We were talking about prom queen!" Taylor wails.

"You were talking about Fran."

"Yes! Of course. She's the *entire* problem and Nikki is on her side." She says this as though it's obvious and she should not be wasting her time spelling it out.

"Well, they are best friends."

"Of course they are. They're both homicidal lunatics!"

"Let me talk to your supervisor!" Taylor's mom screams. A moment later a wine cork pops in the kitchen.

I shake my head. "I wouldn't go that far."

Taylor's eyes shoot open. "Paul! Whose side on your on anyway?! Do you want that girl to ruin *our* prom?"

Taylor's mom covers the phone with her hand. "No one is ruining prom sweetheart. Not while I am PTSA president." She raises her eyebrows at me, with a *fix this!* look.

I pat Taylor's arm but she snatches it away. There is no winning with this family. "Of course not. I'm just glad you're alright."

"You don't even care about this, do you?"

"I came over here, didn't I?" For a brief moment I think about telling her that my dad has reached out. That he's coming to town and wants to see me. That I'm torn up and the worst thing is, my mom wants it. Which is even more confusing.

"Because my mom called you."

I can't help but sigh. "Taylor, please. Think about it. How else would I have known?"

"Paul—if you really care about someone you find out about things. That is the way relationships work. Anyway, you haven't even bothered to ask me to prom."

"We're going to prom Taylor. We've been dating for two years."

She sticks her lower lip out. "You haven't asked me with flowers and a cute sign in front of the whole school."

"Is that what you want?"

She's in full pout mode with her lashes fluttering and her lips sticking out. Taylor has great lips. Full, lush and unfortunately made for pouting. "Not if I have to ask for it."

"I'm confused. You just did ask for it."

"Well, make it a surprise."

"Okay."

"And wait until my skin is healed."

"Alright."

"And make sure it's during first period lunch and let

me know so I can wear something extra cute. There's a pair of fringe booties I'm gonna get. They'd look so totally cute with my Guess fades and my white peasant shirt. I should go tanning first, right?"

"I thought you wanted it to be a surprise."

"God Paul. Do I have to do *everything* for you?"

Here's the silver lining of a girl like Taylor: there's no room in this relationship for my problems. Ever.

CHAPTER THREE

"Thank you for the tragedy. I need it for my art."
Kurt Cobain

NIKKI

"You threw a shampoo bottle at her?" Fran yells as soon as the car doors are shut. We're in the parking lot in my mom's car.

I left the soccer field in a hurry after an awkward lecture from my coach who is deeply disappointed, surprised, and a whole lot of other totally boring clichés. I wasn't allowed to practice and thought Fran would be happy to see me early. But instead of chatting, she rushed ahead of me through the school parking lot in a total snit. "It was freaking shampoo. Not a grenade. Why are you so pissed?"

"Because—you idiot—you just handed her more ammunition. Poor little Taylor is being attacked. Poor little Taylor was beat up in the locker room."

"Oh my God! It's a scratch."

"That's not what she's telling everyone. She's making it look like you're beating her up because she's running against me."

I hit the steering wheel, accidentally honking the horn, which makes me jump. "That lying skank."

"Anyway, I don't care. I'm telling Mr. P. that I'm dropping out."

My heart beats really fast. "No, no, no you can't. Geez Fran, if you drop out she wins. What's fun about that?"

"I'm not putting myself up for all kinds of humiliation just because you want to get back at Taylor."

"That's not why I am doing it! Okay, well, yes, that is why I am doing it but it's so much more!" *I want this for Fran. Right? This isn't just one big distraction from the real problem: my future.*

She twists in her seat until she's staring right at me. "Okay then, tell me. Why is it so important to you that I run for prom queen?"

"Okay, for the sake of argument let's just say that I do totally love a fight. But you're a good cause. A great one. Why should the Taylors of the world always run the show?"

She shakes her head. "They *hate* me. And you don't have a clue what that feels like. You're the soccer star from the right kind of home with the right kind of clothes and parents with jobs and you're just like perfect. People like me don't want to be noticed. People like me want to blend into the background."

"Would you stop saying people like me?" I snap, irritated that she's making a line and putting us on either side of it. We have always been on the same side. Always.

The only difference now is that I'm going to college and she isn't.

"You don't lose at anything Nik. You don't have a clue what it feels like. It sucks. And that is what will happen. Taylor will win and I will have subjected myself to all kinds of hatred."

I pull my knees up against my chest squeezing them up against the steering wheel, trying to control my temper. If she only knew what I've lost. But I can't tell her. If I admit it, it's real. I'll have to tell my parents. "I hate this. I hate seeing you not fight. And you know what sucks the most?"

Our breath fogs up the car. "No. I guess I don't."

"You're not even trying. You're just totally giving up."

"I'm trying to just make it through these last few weeks."

Yes, I do love a cause and I'll always want to join the underdog but this is more. I lean in so she can see my eyes because I'm on fire. "I totally see it Fran. The way they look at you and talk about you and I want to like, punch them in the face. And maybe you don't give a flying mouse fart about being freaking prom queen but think about the next girl and the girl after that. Think about that one gay girl who actually does want to be prom queen. But it's never been done before. What about her?"

She's quiet for a long moment, watching a huge murder of crows blackening the sky through a hole in the fogged windshield. Their shadows disappear into a stand of cottonwood trees near the river. "Yeah but here's the thing Nik; nothing I do is going to make people see me any differently."

"That doesn't mean you freaking give up!"

Be honest with yourself Nikki. Some of this is a distraction.

FRAN

Tuesday night, I slip into my chair in the basement of the South Aberdeen Baptist Church while Don passes out the chips. "Nice to see you Frances!" he says, with an enthusiasm that desperately needs dialing back.

I sit, selecting the last remaining crumbled bag of undesirable pickle-flavored chips. Mike is seated, looking surprisingly chipper, although undeniably stoned. I waited until the last possible moment in the parking lot for Allison until Don knocked on the window. When I crouched down there he was, motioning for me to enter the church dungeon. Seconds later there is the thud, thud, thud of those amazing Frye boots. Allison appears. She gives me a look and slides into her chair. A fresh pack of colored Sharpies emerges from her backpack. She uncaps each one and smells it which is so weird and cool at the same time. Like a ritual.

While Allison doodles all over her jeans I actually begin listening to Don the Drone. Instead of repeatedly doodling Allison + Fran on my folder, I command my ears to take in Don's helpful suggestions to distract oneself from being bad. We need to get involved in sports. Like that's going to happen. Extracurricular activities? Yes, yearbook counts. That's a point in my favor.

When the skinny guy next to me eagerly asks if a Princess Diana scrapbook counts, Don shakes his head. "No."

The kid launches into an explanation of how Princess

Diana is an important historical figure, "plus, she like gave birth to the future king of England so-"

Don talks over him. "Thank you Emery but no."

Emery is pissed, indulging in a hissy fit of eye rolling and lip pursing, examining his black nail polish with his fingers fanned out as if to remind himself that yes, he's oh so fabulous. I write a note, crumple it up and throw it at Allison. She traps it under her hand, reading it under the table. DO YOU THINK HE'S GAY?

She grins while reading it, immediately scribbling something back in Sharpie. She throws it as Don digs his meaty fingers into his tiny potato chip bag.

PRINCESS DIANA OBSESSION AND PAINTED NAILS? NO WAY.

YOU'RE RIGHT. ISN'T HE THE QUARTERBACK?

I snicker and write, HE PLAYS FOR A DIFFERENT TEAM and toss it.

YOU'RE FUNNY. My face heats up when I read her writing. I'll save this note forever.

YOU'RE A BREATH OF FRESH AIR. After I toss it, I'm filled with cringing regret. *God, was that too much? Would a straight girl write that? Do I even want to sound like a straight girl or just totally play all my cards?*

Everyone else in class watches the balls of paper fly across the table with great amusement except for poor Emery, who I sense really wants to learn how not to be gay.

Allison writes: IS IT OKAY TO SAY THAT I HATE ABERDEEN?

OH MY GOD WE ARE ON THE SAME TEAM.

I THINK DON IS GAY.

That is the note that Don catches.

⁓

There is a little office behind the meeting hall in the basement of the church. It has a bulletin board covered with information about the food bank, divorce counseling services and a white board with so many events it gives me a headache. Allison and I perch on matching folding chairs the color of Doublemint gum facing Don, who slouches at a battered desk. His chubby fingers are laced together. It feels good to be in trouble with Allison.

Could this qualify as a first date?

"Now Allison I have talked to your parents and I know how deeply concerned they are about your life choices." He lets this sink in while I wonder what, exactly those choices are. Allison's got this *I don't give a shit* look. "Your attitude in this class," he shakes the note at us, "Is of concern, to say the least."

"I don't really think you're gay," I blurt out with immediately regret. It was bad enough writing it but saying it aloud compounds the damage.

Don turns fifteen shades of progressively deeper pink until he's nearly purple. "I'm not!" He thunders before repeating it again in a milder tone. "But the passing of the note was a slap in the face."

No, I think. This is about calling him gay.

"We're sorry," Allison says, looking at me and I nod, feeling thrilled that we're in this together.

"I should hope so. But I know how these things go." He smiles. "I was a teenager once too."

39

I seriously doubt that.

"And I know that authority is there to ridicule and mock." He undoes his clasped hands and refolds them again. "But what we do in that room could seriously impact your life."

Seriously doubt that too.

"It could help take you off the destructive path you've been traveling and bring you closer to the light of the Lord." I keep waiting for him to tell me that God hates fags and lesbians. That we're all going to hell in the same designer handbag, listening to our gay music and eating our gay food. That the second coming is nigh and the first thing Jesus is going to do is ship all the homosexuals to Australia.

But he doesn't. Don is starting to surprise me, which is really nice.

He gives a standard lecture that is a slap on the hand and actually pretty decent, given that we basically called him a fag. He's so nice I begin to wonder if he really is gay. What if he has this whole secret life and was forced to teach this class by his ball-breaking church lady wife who he dreads having sex with and musters through by imagining John Stamos shirtless?

Totally plausible.

Totally funny.

And if being gay doesn't get me sent to hell, thoughts like these will.

After the meeting, I have a plan to ask Allison why her parents sent her to this class (a roundabout way of asking "are you gay?") but as soon as we step out of the room we bump into Allison's mother who, up close, looks like

Japanese Barbie. An annoyed Japanese Barbie. She's far too well dressed for Aberdeen in a silk shirt with a floppy bow and pearl earrings.

"What is going on?" She gives me a hostile once-over while addressing her daughter. Allison opens her mouth but Don steps out of the office.

"We had a misunderstanding but it's been all cleared up. I really enjoy having Allison with us. I think you're learning things too, aren't you Allison?" He says this without sarcasm.

Allison gives me a guilty look as she nods her head. "Yeah, I am."

But we both know what she's learning.

It has nothing to do with Jesus.

At Thursday night's meeting, I walk into the room at the same time as Mike, who says "hi."

When I asked him what he's doing here, I expect him to say something about getting busted for pot by his parents, but he says. "A girl."

I keep staring and he shrugs. "She's churchy and I'm not." I don't say anything so he adds, "I thought this would help."

I nod like it makes sense.

Allison comes in late, sliding into the chair next to me, smelling of lavender dryer sheets, which I love. My pulse rises. I'm so thrilled at her proximity, I can't breathe. Like that moment at the top of the roller coaster where everything stops. Everything could be heaven or flaming hell but when she's near, it doesn't really matter. Don is already deep into a story about some kid who survived an overdose by taking Jesus' hand in the ER.

When he sees Allison, he stops talking and frowns. "You can't sit next to Fran."

"I won't talk, I promise," she says.

Don shakes his head. "Please move."

She takes the only free chair, next to the Buddy Holly guy. He gives her an eager grin, displaying his braces. She ignores him, unpacking her Sharpies. Soon the whole room is pungent with Sharpies. There's a whole world unfurling from her pen and I'm missing it.

After we hear about Jesus' rescue operation in the ER, which includes follow up visitation whenever the kid felt like shooting up or popping a pill, we get our chips and soda. I keep thinking how weird Don's story was, since Jesus randomly showed up in the kid's bedroom. What if he was naked or worse, masturbating? How awkward would that be in front of the son of God? How do you explain that one to the son of God?

All my energy is consumed with watching Allison without anyone, including Allison, knowing. Being nonchalant is much harder than it looks. I'm convinced that she's ignoring me until the girl next to me presses a note into my hand under the table, pungent with acrid ink.

IS IT TRUE THAT YOU ARE RUNNING FOR PROM?

Allison gazes at me from under her bangs with a sly grin.

Is she flirting? Would I know what flirting looked like if it hit me over the head? Not a clue. What I do know is that she seems impressed. The audacity of a total outsider running for prom appeals to her in a way that plain old Fran might not. Should I? For a second it feels like I'm standing at the edge of a cliff. To jump or not to jump— that is the question. It would make Nikki happy too.

My hands are shaking so badly I can't write back. I nod YES, thinking I'm insane. *I'm only doing this to impress Allison.* If I can't even write the word YES then maybe running for prom queen is not a good idea. *I don't want to be the poster girl for gay rights. I don't want the attention. Lightning rods only get hit.*

A few moments later another note is thrust into my hand.

ARE YOU CRAZY?

I glance across the table at those almond eyes. She's frowning so I can't tell if she thinks it's a good idea or not. Don has turned around and is facing the class so I study him for a moment, pretending to pay attention. His lips move but I have no idea what he's saying. He looks at me so I nod. When he's finally looking away, I mouth YES I'M CRAZY.

Allison laughs.

Just like that I'm running for prom queen.

CHAPTER FOUR

"I'm not like them, but I can pretend.
The day is done and I'm havin' fun. I think I'm dumb.
Maybe just happy."
"Dumb," Nirvana

PAUL

'm sitting at the kitchen table trying to do my home-work but I can't stop thinking about what Taylor told me at lunch. It's been running through my brain like a song. We were sitting at our usual table with her friends and Derek and Lane when she leaned in and whispered, "Don't tell anyone but my mom has called an emergency PTSA meeting." My stomach went queasy. I asked what it was about even though I already knew. "Blocking that loser from running from prom queen."

"She's not a loser," I'd muttered defensively. She's just poor. In some ways she's more normal than Taylor.

Taylor stared at me with her I'll-rip-you-apart-if-you-disagree-with-me look, one that I have seen on her mother's face a lot lately. Last night at their house when I'd tried to point out that maybe it wasn't such a huge deal to let Fran run for prom queen they both went after me like sharks. If sharks had screechy high voices and said things like "as if," and "I can't believe you can even go there!" One minute they're both tittering about prom dresses and hairstyles and the next they're on the attack. No wonder Taylor's dad has that hunted look.

I just think it's a free country. Or I did think that until I heard about Mrs. Davis' newest power move. I know how it's going to go. She's going to go up there dressed in some fancy- pants outfit, flashing her diamonds and expensive teeth. All the other parents are going to think she knows what she's talking about because she's rich. She knows exactly how to intimidate the hell out of them. And Fran, who has no one to defend her, will get railroaded.

Ever since lunch it's been gnawing away at my gut. This doesn't seem fair. Maybe it's because Fran and I used to see each other in grade school, barely awake in the damp pre-dawn eating free breakfast, choking down the watery eggs and grey greasy sausage. It was actually bearable until that moment when the bell rang and we filed out into the hallway as the other kids streamed in the front door. Some of them would snicker and call us the poor kids, freeloaders and worse. There's something about eating powered eggs from a huge vat labeled US Government Property that makes you realize that your life started out pretty crappy. She deserves a fair shake even if it is for something as dumb as prom queen.

Then I heard in the lunchroom that the Rotary Club was kicking in a five-thousand-dollar scholarship for the prom queen. That changed everything.

My books are spread out on the kitchen table but I'm staring at the phone when Mom comes in wearing her bathrobe. "Have you called your dad?"

I shake my head and she says I'd better get on the phone. I think of a hundred good reasons not to call but just say okay. I don't understand what she thinks I could possibly gain from seeing him. Maybe he's sober now but whatever. He can't go back in time. She ruffles my hair with a frown that means she knows something is wrong but she isn't going to say anything. "Come say goodnight before you go to bed."

Finally, I pick up the phone and dial a number I'd never called before. She picks up after two rings. "Hi, it's Paul," I say.

NIKKI

Paul called. Paul called. Paul freaking called. I'm singing this in my head like a musical. Rainbows and flowers are sprouting and I'm pretty sure I could actually tap dance if I wanted to. If I looked outside all the squirrels in the neighborhood are probably doing a conga line on the fence because, once more, for the record, Paul totally called.

Me.

Paul picked up the phone and called. Me. Even though it wasn't to say he'd dumped Taylor on her ass because he'd finally realized she's an idiotic twit who doesn't know how to dodge shampoo bottles and that he'd finally realized he was deeply, passionately in love with me and would I please, please, pretty please go to prom with him? Okay, so it wasn't the dream but still, he was thinking about me. Or maybe he was thinking about Fran. Whatever. In spite of his moronic infatuation with Taylor, he still has a kernel of decency buried inside. He is totally on our side.

Shit. Fran.

I pick up the phone and dial her number. "I'm picking you up in ten minutes." Slam. There is no time to explain.

As soon as she climbs into my car, I'm zooming down her street, hardly pausing for her to shut the door. "Hello, I almost fell out the door. What is going on?"

I roll down the window, which is jammed, swerving slightly onto someone's lawn. "It's crunch time. There's an emergency PTSA meeting tonight about prom. Taylor's mom got everyone all riled up by saying if they allow you to run for prom it's like corrupting American ideals or some total BS like that."

Fran goes pasty white. Or maybe grey. Anyway, she's changing colors and not for the good. "And we're going there why?"

I'm driving Speedy Gonzales style because Paul left it until the last minute to warn me. And if there's one thing I know how to do it's to make sure my voice is totally heard. If Taylor's mom thinks we're taking this one sitting down, she's got another thing freaking coming. Welcome to Planet Nikki. "Because we need to know what they're saying. It's like getting intelligence from enemy sources. Basically, we're spying." And possibly saying something but there's no reason to worry Fran with this minor little detail. No sense risking her jumping from a moving car.

"I don't care what they are saying."

"Honey," I wave my hands between us, "This, this thing we have, this best friend thing—it requires that you listen to me. It also requires you to tell me if that Allison chick is gay." Fran's face flushes beet red. Over the last two days she's casually mentioned Allison's name a kajillion times. Somewhere along the way she's forgotten that we share these little details with each other. These little details are important. They're like best friend things.

I have that rush I get when I know I'm up against something. If Fran hates the idea of charging into a gym packed with potentially hostile strangers, I kind of totally love it. "I knew it. I just knew it. You've got it bad. God this is exciting. First the prom queen thing and now a genuine love story. She is so freaking cool I can't stand it. She's like an Asian James Dean or something. That leather jacket she wears all the time looks vintage. She's like the coolest girl in school. I'm kind of jealous. Is that okay to say? I mean all I've got is a pathetic crush on Paul who follows Taylor around like a freaking lap dog and you're crushing on this gorgeous, available creature." I sound like I'm on speed. Every moment on this crusade is another moment I don't spend telling Mom and Dad but oh well. I'm a teenager.

She looks really uncomfortable. "This isn't happening."

"This is so happening. Isn't it exciting?"

"I'm not ready for this."

"Oh don't be a bitch. Is she, or isn't she? It's one syllable, either way. Dish."

She sighs miserably. "I don't know."

"If I was gay, I'd so be into her. That whole San Francisco Eurasian thing is so hot." I blow through a stop sign. Fran looks back at it wistfully. Good thing my dad is an attorney although he says he's totally done taking care of my tickets.

She glares at me. "Oh, that's incredibly helpful, thank you. If you were theoretically gay, you'd be theoretically into her."

"Theoretically." I swerve around an annoyingly slow old lady, which gets her walking much faster. Really, I'm performing a freaking community service.

"Did you not see the blind woman?" Fran asks.

I nod, looking over my driving glasses, which are sloped down my nose which makes the road a fuzzy blur. "She's totally faking it. That whole white cane is just for sympathy."

"I cannot believe that you are the daughter of a nurse."

"I know, right? Between the two of us we balance out the world. Florence Nightingale has a devil child. Ying and like, yang, right?"

"You're insane," Fran says.

What she doesn't know is that this is just the beginning.

I pull the Volvo into the school parking lot, knocking over a garbage can that rolls into another car, making my own parking space because well, I color outside the lines. The vice-principal and I have had some creative differences over what constitutes a parking spot. I get the feeling she's totally counting the days until I graduate. That makes two of us.

Fran takes a few deep breaths after I turn off the car. "I still don't get why we're here." In Fran speak this means *I'm not getting out of this car.* Which is fine. This is what I do.

I spin the keys around my finger. "Fran, you cannot let a bunch of narrow-minded bigots run around saying things behind your back."

She juts out her lower jaw. "I totally can."

"No, you can't." I gather my purse from the backseat. "Look, I know I'm more outgoing and you're the like, sarcastic sidekick but here's the thing. Oh screw it. Get out of the car."

"Look Nik, I'm not setting myself up just because you're a fighter. I'm just-"

I pause in my application of Dr. Pepper Lip Smacker. I'm tired of this game, the one where she lets people railroad over her in the name of trying to fit in. What's so freaking great about trying to fit in? Most people are losers. The hell with fitting in. "Pathetic? A pansy? Wimpy?"

"No."

"Apathetic? Regressive? Lame? Frail?"

"Would you just stop it with the SAT vocab? This is scary for me. You're the one who loves causes and debating stuff. You grew up in a family where Roe versus Wade was discussed over dinner. We watched The Price is Right."

I shake my head. This is so totally happening. "No. Screw that. I will not feel sorry for you. You are ten times better than anyone in that gym. You're funny and smart and exactly what a prom queen should be. Now you get your ass out of this car and come with me because we are going to stand up for you. Not because I have some genetic flaw that requires me to argue but because it's the right thing."

She looks a little shell-shocked, as if she can't quite

believe what I'm saying. She wipes a tear. "That's not your only genetic flaw."

I hug her before I start bawling. "Fucking A." I sniffle a bit as I kiss her cheek. "You really suck."

It is raining lightly as we climb the stairs to the gym. The windows are propped open. Someone is talking into the loudspeaker system but I can't make out the words. At the wide double front door Fran pauses as if she's going to sprint home. I give her a look of encouragement which seems to settle her.

She takes a deep, shaky breath. "Crud. We're really doing this aren't we?"

I push open the heavy gym door and grab her arm, pulling her in. "Totally carpe, like fucking diem."

FRAN

The auditorium is pungent with wet wool and BO lingering from wrestling practice. It is packed with parents, most of them just off work at the mill or the garage or grocery story. There are a couple of people in business suits and expensive haircuts. Mrs. Davis, Taylor's mom, is on stage orating like First Lady Hillary. She has the same glossy prettiness as her daughter, with an identical upturned nose (store bought). Her daintiness has a steel rod running through it.

"If we let this girl continue to stay in the race for prom queen we're saying it's okay to be deviant. We're saying ignore the Bible and every American family value we hold sacred." People applaud. Mrs. Davis beams happily. Her baby blue eyes flicker as she flirts with the entire auditorium. It's easy to see where Taylor gets her superiority complex. Mrs. Davis is the kind of person who is convinced that she knows what's best and will stop at nothing to get it. As the applause dies down, she lifts her chin at Principal P. in triumph. He taps his watch. She speeds up.

"And if she wins? Let's face it; kids can get some crazy ideas in their heads. Can you just see two girls on this stage holding hands?" There is murmur of protest. "These kids might be teenagers but believe you me they still take their cues from adults. They look to us for guidance." She pats her chest. "It's our God-given obligation—no, our moral duty to provide it."

Mrs. Harter, my yearbook advisor, sits on the stage beside Mr. P. studying me, looking disturbed. She shakes her head very slowly, warning me. Mrs. Harter has always been very supportive, telling me that I'm a talented photographer, checking out equipment for way longer than she's supposed to. I know she feels protective and I should listen to her.

My cheeks are on fire. My ears buzz with nerves. Each word hammers me further into the ground. What do these people think I am going to do? Infect their children? It is surreal, as if I've just walked into an episode of *The Twilight Zone*. This can't be happening. All these people can't be here to talk about me. I spent four years trying not to be noticed and now this? It's fascinating and horrifying, like a five-car collision. Except it's my life.

"Let's go," I beg. Nikki is riveted, her body vibrating with energy and purpose. I have to get out but can't leave her. She'll never forgive me.

Mrs. Davis clears her throat. "If the administration continues to ignore our demands, I'm raising funds for an alternate prom: the real prom. We're not going to allow our kids to have the best night of their lives ruined."

There is a lot of applause. Mr. P. moves towards the podium. She rushes to finish. "I'll be accepting donations after this. Just leave your phone number if you'd like to be on the committee. Thank you."

When she steps away from the microphone Mr. P. scans the audience, frowning, waiting for the applause to die down. He does this at assemblies, rocking on his heels until we're quiet.

Nikki whispers, "I didn't know being gay was like, un-American."

I don't even bother to whisper. "I did."

When everyone is quiet Mr. P. clears his throat, trying to get the tired parents to meet his eyes. "I understand that there are some people who are uncomfortable. We have a fairly homogenous student body at Aberdeen High School and it's difficult for some to accept students who are different. But isn't that part of what we want our students to learn? Don't we want them to be inclusive, open-minded people who don't fear those who are different?"

"Homogenous, not homosexual!" Someone yells.

There is nervous laughter. Do half these people understand what homogenous means? Maybe the dairy farmers do but your average mill worker or lumberman or meth addict dropout wouldn't. Mr. P. doesn't know who he's talking to. These are Dwayne's people. The only minorities they like are professional athletes. Aberdeen is a place where it's important to have someone to look down upon.

Nobody has to explain this to me. My mom calls Mr.

and Mrs. Garcia, who gave me a job and food when I was hungry, the wetbacks or spics.

"I encourage you not to divide our student body and turn prom into a political statement of intolerance. I cannot in good conscience prevent anyone from running for prom queen. This is a contest run by the students, for the students. She was legitimately nominated by her fellow classmates by popular vote."

"As a joke!" a man yells.

Mr. P. grimaces. "The girl in question is a stellar student, the editor of the yearbook and a very nice young woman. I'm not going to stop her from doing something any girl has a right to do."

"Even if she's a queer?" A woman holding a baby hollers.

I wish I were dead. My whole body goes completely numb. Nikki puts her arm around me and squeezes but it doesn't make me feel better.

Mr. P. finds the heckler, directing his anger towards her. "The prom stays the way it is. I hope you can find it in your hearts to encourage your children to respect-fully attend. Thank you and good night." Mr. P. is striding offstage when the worst possible thing happens.

Nikki takes her arm off me, waving at the stage. "Wait a minute!" She yells. "Don't we get a chance to like, say something?"

If I wished for death before, now I wish for cremation. Ashes buried for centuries.

Mr. P. returns to the mike, searching for Nikki, who is now, to my horror, waving both hands. "Yes Nikki?"

"We want a chance to talk," she shouts.

"No, we don't. We don't," I hiss urgently. "We really, really don't."

Nikki grabs my wrist, dragging me forward. "This is your chance to freaking speak up."

"I don't want to speak up. I don't want to go up there." *Shit. Shit. Shit.*

Nikki squeezes my wrist so hard it is painful. "Get up there with me and I will do all the talking."

I'm not ready to have this argument in front of all these people. Also, the top of my head is numb and I can't think straight. Whenever I've been the center of attention, I've always had this out of body experience, like I'm watching the whole thing from a safe distance, observing myself stammering or losing my place or staring at the floor like an idiot. I can feel it happening as Nikki drags me toward the stage.

We're causing a scene. *Double shit.* These morons probably think we're having some kind of lovers' quarrel. Rather than fight Nikki, I follow her up to the stage on my barely functioning legs. It's like watching a movie of my own life while concentrating very hard on not vomiting. But Nikki is so confident and strong as she takes the stage, it's infectious. Just as I'm beginning to think I can actually do this, we turn to face the seething, anxious crowd. Holy shit there are a lot of people. A lot of angry people. Every single one of them thinks I've caused the problem.

These people hate me.

I represent everything they fear.

I'm the enemy.

Nikki leans into the microphone. "Hi, I think some of you know me. I'm Nikki Hollister. I play forward on the soccer team and this is my best friend Fran Worthy. She's running for prom queen for the same reasons Taylor Davis is running. Because it's totally an honor and also, the Rotary scholarship will mean that Fran can go to college. I know that you think Fran is, like really different from your kids but actually she's not. She didn't want to get the school involved in a controversy. She didn't even like want to run for prom queen. But now that she's been given the opportunity, I think we have a chance to show the school and the world what kind of community we have." She pauses to scan the crowd for friendly faces. There aren't any. "Fran totally deserves this."

If I don't explode into a bazillion pieces right now. She nods at me. "I hope that you'll set a good example for your kids by supporting my friend Fran." A wave of relief washes over me.

Finally, it is over. We can leave.

But Nikki keeps talking. "Fran, why don't you like, say something?"

She pulls the microphone out of the stand, thrusting it into my hand. A million things run through my head, flashing before me like an end-of-life montage but mostly it's blind panic, a hundred bats flying in my face. The parents go weirdly quiet, studying me as if I'm road kill. As I watch the faces in the front rows, ranging from a man in dirty mechanic overalls to a woman in a Seattle Mariners cap, my brain coughs up one question. "What would Kurt Cobain do?" Some people might ask what Jesus would do but when I am nervous, I think about Kurt Cobain. He went to this same high school and somehow made it through each day when he was openly despised, spit upon, and called a fag for his long hair and art-loving ways.

I open my mouth and say something unbelievable. Something that will change my life forever. "Tell your kids that I'm going to get Nirvana to play prom. That's why they should vote for me. Thank you."

Just like that I've promised to get Nirvana to play at our prom.

CHAPTER FIVE

"What else could I say? Everyone is gay."
"All Apologies," Nirvana.

FRAN

Why oh why oh why did I shoot off my stupid mouth? The moment I climb on the bus a horde of mosquito-like freshman quiz me on how I'm going to get Nirvana to come to prom, pestering me with stupid questions like, "Why not Guns N' Roses?" "Why not Megadeth?" One sophomore says his mom gets her hair done by Kurt Cobain's aunt. "She said her nephew is a huge star and no way would he ever play prom and you're just lying to get attention."

As we're piling off the bus a senior named Lilly grabs my arms. "You're in my prayers Fran. God loves everyone, even the gays."

I rub my eye, wondering what to say. "Well, thanks?"

She shakes her head. "You're still going to hell."

The minute I'm off the bus, a gum chomping band

geek named Darren rushes up. "My mom said your mom was friends with Kurt Cobain's mom and Nirvana is going to play at prom. Is that true?"

"Yes."

"You're deluded man." He keeps up with me as we climb the front stairs and enter the school. "Thanks to you my girlfriend won't go to the school prom. You're really screwing this up for everyone. And for what? Think about it. You're being really selfish."

And he's one of the nice ones.

Mike stops by my locker. "Dude, we need to talk about the Nirvana thing because I have an idea."

Mike is trying to be nice but I'm not in the mood for whatever weird idea he's come up with. "Thanks. Can we talk later?" He nods as I rush off.

Taylor's minions have plastered posters all over the school for the alternate prom: DON'T BE FOOLED. THE REAL PROM AND THE REAL PROM QUEEN ARE RIGHT HERE. A sparkly pink arrow points to Taylor Davis' senior picture, outlined in puff paint. Her features are a symphony of symmetry topped by shiny blonde you only get from a pricey salon. If Darwin is right—being Prom Queen is her destiny. Why, exactly, am I doing this?

Although I'd arrived early to school, I am late to World History because PC follows me from my locker, spewing venom under his breath. His voice is bass low, slicing through the cacophony of chatting, laughing kids, worming its way into my brain. "Hey baby," and "I got what you need," are interlaced with threats about what will happen to me if I don't drop the prom queen nomination. We're surrounded by kids between classes and yet nobody notices. He's just a guy walking to class, talking to the girl in front of him. Anger pulses out of his every pore. My eyes stay locked ahead, focusing on making it to the nearest girls' bathroom where I lock myself into a stall, dully listening to two girls argue about prom.

"I'm making Eddie take me. I told him, prom is at school. It's like traditional and shit. I'm like a very traditional girl."

"And you think having a queer prom queen is traditional?"

"Oh give it up Chareese. She's not gonna win. So who cares?"

"I do."

Seconds before class starts, I hurry across the hall.

When I enter, the whole class looks up, erupting in whispers. Mrs. Bennett, who sometimes forgets her hearing aids, is writing key terms for the upcoming test on the chalkboard.

Carl Feiton hisses, "There's Kurt Cobain's best friend!"

Waylon Neer adds, "Maybe she should be named prom king! You can't bring a girl, you know that, right? There will be a fucking riot if you do."

Even the quiet Asian kid who never talks is giggling. "Homosexual prom queen! So funny! It's a joke, right?"

Second period is English. Mr. Conway leaves a kid in charge so he can get a cup of coffee from the teachers' lounge. Someone throws a wad of paper at my head. "Hey lesbo, when you talk to Kurt Cobain, tell him he sucks!"

Lisa Ng stops applying her lipstick. "Nathan, knock that shit off." She turns to me. "But seriously, this blows. People have to choose between proms which kinda sucks."

"The other prom was not my idea," I snap.

Lisa nods at me. "Shhhhht. Come here." I lean my head in nearly choking on her heavy perfume. "Just like tell me. 'Cause I like Nirvana and I'm not gonna miss it if they come but my friends all wanna go to the other one which is supposed to be all fancy 'cause it's like at a hotel and shit. So, you gotta just tell me alright?"

"Tell you what?"

She rolls her eyes. "Nirvana girl! Are they gonna be there or not?"

Mr. Conway comes back into class with a bagel in his mouth and cup of coffee clutched in his meaty paw. "Okay people, after reading your papers I want a truthful answer. No penalties just truth. How many of you read *The Bell Jar* and how many of you read Cliffs Notes? One finger for the book, two fingers for good old Cliffs Notes."

Lisa raises two fingers, her heavily stenciled eyebrows raised, magenta lips pursed.

I raise one finger and swallow hard. "Yeah, absolutely. They'll be here."

After fourth period, I rush out of class, ducking down a hallway to avoid PC. I round the corner at a brisk clip and collide into Allison who is lugging a cello.

She grabs the bulky case, protecting it from a fall. My binder skids onto the floor, hits a wall and pops open. Papers fly everywhere. Normally I would dive to the ground and gather every paper in one messy heap. Instead I just stand there like a huge dork, trying not to cry. I'm ready to lose it. To fall on the ground, bawling like a three-year-old. I thought my old life at school was bad. This is hell.

"Hey, I'll help you." Allison's kind voice is a lifeline.

She leans her cello case toward Monica, another Asian senior I know from grade school. Monica holds the case, frowning with disapproval as Allison joins me on the ground.

"Thanks." We quietly sweep up papers with our hands.

When I look at her, Allison gives me a little half grin, which is like being injected with sunshine. The flat green-grey walls are lit by rainbows. The worn linoleum becomes a field full of fragrant, softly swaying flowers. My hands itch to reach out, take her hand and hold her, dancing to music only we can hear.

"Allison, um," says Monica awkwardly, tapping her watch while balancing the cello.

Allison waves back at her without looking. "It's okay. Just put it on the ground off to the side. I'll be a little late. It's fine. You go ahead."

Monica lays down the case. "It's not that. She's, um well—" She lowers her voice. "You know—the prom queen thing? She's uh, *that* girl."

Allison ducks her head so Monica can't see her rolling her eyes. "I'll see you at symphony, okay?"

Monica remains rooted to the spot, sure that her friend isn't getting it. "Do you even know what I'm talking about?" She gives a stiff, strained smile. She's not the kind of girl that will trash me to my face.

Allison has opened my binder. She's absorbed in reading the lyrics to "Breed" that I've scribbled in Sharpie:

"Get away, away, away from your home." She gives another nod without looking up. "Yeah, I do need a ride after school. Thanks. See ya."

Monica shrugs. "Your funeral." She lowers the cello roughly onto the ground and stomps off.

The bell rings. A few stragglers run into class. We're alone in the hallway.

Allison hands me a bunch of papers. "They're not in order but you can figure it out later. At least that's everything."

We both glance around the empty hallway. Overlooking us is a banner for THE REAL PROM. "I think you just committed social suicide," I say.

"I'm not worried about it. Monica is a twit."

When I finally stand on shaky legs, I clutch my binder to my chest. My heart thuds against the black vinyl.

Allison cocks her head. "You okay?"

I shake my head. "I told the entire school that I could get Nirvana to play at prom just so they'd go to the prom at school. Now I actually have to produce them."

Allison bites her lip, lifting her cello case with ridiculous ease. "That's so awesome. You're not backing down. That's so cool."

I'm cool? Allison thinks I'm cool? "Yeah."

Now all I have to do is produce the world's most popular band. Hazel, who I've gotten to know pretty well from yearbook, talked to Kurt's aunt, who very nicely shot her down. No, she wouldn't talk to him. He's exhausted and the entire family just wants him left alone. No one will talk to him. Then, as a gesture of goodwill, she offered

Hazel a twenty percent discount on hair products. Hazel felt compelled to buy us all shampoo.

The next day we're in yearbook working on our final projects. Hazel is cropping her photos. I'm cleaning up and Mike, who has been thumbing through *The Stranger*, turns the page and points at a page excitedly. "Check it out! A Nirvana concert. It's next week! It's a sign." He holds up the article which features a concert poster. "This is what I was talking about. A concert. Now I've found one." He reads from the article, "A show to Raise Awareness About Rape in Bosnia-Herzegovina. Friday April 9th, 7 pm, The Cow Palace. There are a bunch of other bands. It's going to be epic. And you can talk to Kurt Cobain."

"Where's the Cow Palace?" I ask.

"Near San Francisco," Mike says. "It's a straight shot down I-5 which is about eight hundred miles. Without traffic and a couple of stops we could do it in under thirteen hours, easy. We skip that Friday, leave killer early, drive all day, get there, scope out some munchies, go to the concert and drive all night back, zombie style. We slide on home by mid-day. I can get my brother's car. We can split the gas. Done." You'd think this was all for Hazel because he's addressing her.

"What do we tell our parents?" Hazel asks. I'm surprised she wants anything to do with this. She's from a pretty religious family.

"Nothing, Hazel. We're gonna tell them nothing," I say.

"If we don't come from home school they're gonna wonder where we are."

"Which is why we're going to lie."

Hazel is quiet for a moment "I've never lied to my parents before."

Mike assembles his face into a mask. "Me neither." We all start laughing, except Mike, who looks annoyed. "What?"

CHAPTER SIX

"Hey! Wait! I got a new complaint."
"Heart-Shaped Box," Nirvana

FRAN

The idea pops into my head, glowing like neon. Invite Allison. It makes me smile through the dripping rain as I walk to Teen Life, picking my way around puddles.

When I arrive at the church the only empty spot sucks: near Don the Drone. I eat crushed chips, trying to ring out the hair dripping down my back. My wet flannel shirt smells like dog. Since we don't own a dog, this means I've forgotten to wash my Goodwill find. Nice.

Very Prom Queen-ish.

Allison is, as usual, fresh from an Herbal Essence commercial, even if she does smell like Sharpie and boredom. If boredom has a smell, it lives in church basements everywhere. She doodles without listening, clearly on another planet. Mike is grinning at me like we have a secret, which we do. Who knew that a guy who spends much of his time in a chemically altered state could mastermind a road trip?

Don hands out notebooks with a cartoon figure of a teenaged Jesus with a soul patch on the cover. He's with Mary, in a blue bathrobe, in front of a VW bug. In an even stranger twist, Mary holds the car keys. "These are your journals to keep. In them record every kind of impure desire. Record them and ask yourself why you are having these carnal thoughts."

I don't know if it's Mary holding car keys or "carnal thoughts" that makes me laugh. It gets Allison's attention. Meanwhile Mike has opened his and already filled up an entire page.

Don purses his lip. "Fran? Would you like the share the joke?"

I shake my head. "No, sorry." Last year I found the journal I kept in fourth grade. The cover had a sparkly kitten and a tiny silver lock, a birthday gift from Nikki. Inside it said: Mrs. Weiderman is so pretty and nice. She shaves all the hair off her legs becuz she is a runner. I want to tuch her legs. That is so wierd. Wat is rong with me?

Ah yes, fourth grade. The year I crushed on my teacher.

Allison goes back to doodling. The electric heater intermittently glows orange, then shuts off with a click. Does she look like the kind of girl who would run off to a Nirvana concert two states away with a bunch of semi-strangers?

No.

"Mmmm-hm, okay then, where was I?" Don says. "Analyzing these craven, youthful desires for sex or drugs or homosexuality will help you see that they aren't real. They are tantalizing mirages because they promise fleeting pleasure but what will they actually bring you? I'll tell you right now. They'll bring you nothing but pain, sadness, and distance from the love of the Lord. Once you see these temptations for what they really are; bumps on the road to salvation, you can overcome them with strong will and true faith in the Lord Jesus Christ. It is simply a matter of re-framing your desires. When you desire another person of the same sex, this isn't true passion or love, it's false. It's instant gratification that leads down the road to perdition. It might make you feel good for the moment, but it will not slake your thirst for love and goodness. It will not bring you closer to the Lord. It's called sin. Don't call it anything else because right now, right here, you are waging a battle for your soul. The draw of homosexuality is the devil placing his bid. He craves your soul and you have a life altering choice before you. Move towards the Lord or into the dark, muddy path of sin. Your choice is very clear."

Apparently, it's not that clear because a hundred years later he's still rambling on. Half of us have dozed off. Time moves like sticky tar.

When the class is over I grab a tiny pocket Bible on my way out, taking the stairs two at a time. In the parking lot, it is dumping rain. I'd forgotten my wet jacket over my chair. I search the dark parking lot. No Allison.

"What were you laughing about?" I spin around and there she is, hunched under the church roof under a black umbrella festooned with lime green Mr. Yuck logos.

"My fourth-grade journal." She waves me over. This is a sign. I'm going to ask her.

"What about it?" She offers a corner of her umbrella. Street light shines through the fabric, spotting both our faces Mr. Yuck green.

I am careful not to get too close but close enough to realize that Allison's eyes are hazel, shot through with grey and amber, like marble. Another thing I know about her. "Uh, well... just stupid kid stuff."

She grins, a green reflected polka dot on her cheek. "I read my journal last summer. I spent fifth and sixth grade complaining how horrible my parents were for not getting me a dog. Yeah. We lived in an apartment on the 6th floor. I was quite the drama queen. I called them 'relentlessly cruel and horrid.' I had this whole plan about how I was going to bribe some homeless person to give me their dog and hide it in our apartment. It was going to live under my bed and I'd re-name it Spunky. Poor little dog, living under a bed with a dumb name like that."

"That's funny. Did you ever get one?" *Wrong question. Ask her. Ask her you big chicken.*

"My little sister did, finally, when we moved here. It was my parents' big selling point on Aberdeen. If you move to this place where it rains like, all the time, you get a dog. The funny thing is I still like my imaginary dog better. Spunky, the under-the-bed dog. He lived on leftovers and drank coffee. That's another thing. I loved coffee in fifth grade. I thought it made me cool so I decided the dog should drink coffee too."

"Sounds like a cool dog."

"Imaginary dogs are the best." She sighs. "I think I'm going to record Don's voice for when I can't sleep at night. He's the King of Boring."

"He's got the Nyquil of voices. I mean, even when he's

saying we're going to hell, it sounds restful, like oh well, we're going to Canada. Hell sounds as scary as Canada. So, I might actually like it."

She grins. "I think we're going to be okay. I'm pretty sure Don can't personally send us to Hell."

When her mom's Lexus splashes through the parking lot puddles, I panic. Instead of the concert invitation I blurt, "Hey, do you want to hang out some time?" *Great, I might as well ask her for a play date.*

She tucks her hair behind her ear, raising an eyebrow. "You mean in a mutually supportive un-gay kind of way?" *Is she telling me something?* Her mom pulls up. "We live in Montesano. So, it's kind of a drive but-" Allison folds her umbrella, opening the car door.

"I'm going to California," I gasp like an asthmatic moron. "For a Nirvana concert. To see if they'll play at prom."

She rolls down her window. "What? When?"

Her mom leans over Allison, giving me a pointed clinical appraisement from head to toe. "Mom, this is Fran. Fran, my mom."

Although I'm terrified, I mumble hello. Mrs. Kondo nods curtly and says something to Allison in Japanese as she leans back into her seat. I flush, relieved it's dark. "April 9th. It's a Friday."

"That's so cool. I want to hear more but I've got—" Her mom drives off so fast gravel spits from her tires. They disappear down the street into the driving rain. *What the hell did her mom say about me?* This is the question that I obsessively turn over in my head as I walk home, coming up with everything from "That's the ugliest girl I've ever seen in my life" to "If you ever talk to her again, I'll kick you out of the house." The only thing that's clear is that her mom despised me upon site.

Luckily, there's one more Teen Life meeting before the concert. Unluckily, it's raining again and I've missed the bus.

NIKKI

That night it's there on the fridge like a warrant: Legacy Luncheon for Incoming Dawgs and their Alum Parents. It's the same date as the Nirvana concert. The invite matches half the blankets and knickknacks in our house. My parents met at University of Washington. They bleed purple and gold. It wasn't so much discussed that I would apply to UW as assumed. What they don't know is that I applied to UW only. Also, I didn't get in.

I pretended the letter was an acceptance and hid it.

I can't tell them.

I took the rejection letter saying that while my application was very impressive and blah, blah blah. I lit it on fire. And cried. And freaked out. And ate enough Ben and Jerry's Chunky Monkey that I nearly barfed before wrapping myself in a UW blanket before throwing it out the window (and retrieving it again.) I did all these things but I didn't do the one thing that always makes me feel better. I didn't tell Fran.

The weekend my parents plan on getting together with all their friends with smarter kids to celebrate another generation of Husky freshman, I'm running away.

CHAPTER SEVEN

"Teenage angst has paid off well. Now I'm bored and old."
"Serve the Servant," Nirvana

FRAN

'm so distracted on Tuesday that I forget my normal detour around PC's locker. Sure enough, his gravelly voice is in my ear within moments. "Listen lesbo you fucking drop the prom queen thing or things will get crazy. I promise you that." I am so mad at myself for going the wrong way that I spin around and just glare at him. His beady eyes pop, waiting for me to talk.

"What?!" PC yells.

I take a deep breath, leaning my face into his. His breath smells like a brewery with a side dish of Slim Jim. "Leave. Me. The. Hell. Alone."

"You know what you need?" He grabs his crotch as if doing some heavy lifting.

Something in me snaps. "I know, right? You're

absolutely right. It's so hard to meet a nice girl when everyone hates you. Isn't that right PC?"

His eyes go wild like he's seconds from bashing in my skull but there are too many people around. Instead he snorts back and hocks a dripping brown loogie at me, hitting my shirt. I almost barf at the sight of it dripping down my nubby flannel. "This is your last warning. Drop out."

He keeps waiting for me to cry.

I don't. At least not while he's looking. As soon as I round the corner I duck into the girl's bathroom, leaning against the cool tile trying to stop my heart from thumping. He scares me so badly, I have to think of something else. Allison. If I can get Allison to come with me to California everything will be okay.

I wash my face in the sink, studying my reflection in the mirror as I wipe my skin with a rough brown paper towel. Tired eyes. Surprisingly decent hair.

Allison is my lucky charm. If I can just talk to her, everything will work out fine.

But that's a big if.

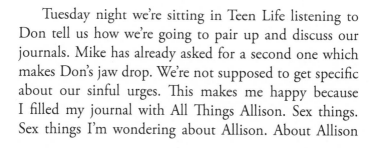

Tuesday night we're sitting in Teen Life listening to Don tell us how we're going to pair up and discuss our journals. Mike has already asked for a second one which makes Don's jaw drop. We're not supposed to get specific about our sinful urges. This makes me happy because I filled my journal with All Things Allison. Sex things. Sex things I'm wondering about Allison. About Allison and me. About the whole lesbian sex thing and how it will actually work. As far as I know there isn't a book or website called How to Be a Modern Lesbian but if there was, I'd be all over it.

Because I have a lot of questions and many of them have gone into the journal. Instead of making me recognize that this is a false, craven urge that's dipping me into Hell's almighty fire, it's helped me realize that if Allison is gay, I'm going to read the journal to her some day and see if she wants to try some of this stuff. To see if she's thought of doing any of these things with another girl. Because if she has; then maybe I'm not losing my mind.

Again, that's a big if.

When it is time to pair up, I nearly sprint across the room to reach her, which makes Allison giggle. She turns away from the dork with the Buddy Holly glasses, waiting for her to turn around and acknowledge that's he's there, as tall as her armpit, no doubt drooling to read her the juicy details of his fantasy life. But she waits for me. *Is she gay or just hates trendy glasses? Is there some secret lesbian sign that I don't know about?*

We sit next to each other at the table. Mike is already on page three with eyeliner girl although he keeps saying, "Can't read that." "Or that. Or that."

"Do you want to go first?" Allison asks.

"No. You go."

She opens her notebook and theatrically clears her throat with an impish grin. She's drawn on her journal with Sharpie. The Virgin Mary wears red lipstick and a mini-dress. Gold hoops sprout from her long, tousled hair. Jesus sports a pair of board shorts and a tank top exposing a hairy chest. Mary has a cartoon bubble coming out of her mouth that says, "I don't care if you are the son of God, you still have to do the dishes."

"Dear diary," Allison begins with a smirk, "Today I thought about telling my mom to fuck off nine hundred times. And that was before breakfast. My family lives in a totalitarian regime where Mom decides what we eat, what we wear, and what we're going to do with the rest of our lives. My dad and the dog thrive in this environment. My sister and I are like orcas in captivity." She goes on.

Twice I nearly fall off the chair trying to suppress laughter.

For a few minutes, while Don is near, Allison makes up stuff, pretending to read. "So, I thought about all those kids who smoke pot and make out in the woods behind the school and thought, no, they are the real losers. What if they get pregnant? Who is going to help all those little stoned babies? What will happen to those girls once they've had their babies and the boys want to keep getting stoned and riding their bikes to 7-Eleven for Pringles instead of becoming responsible members of society?"

While she reads, we both keep glancing nervously at Don, waiting for him to yell at Allison but he eats it up, patting both of us on the back.

After he leaves, we stare at each other a long moment before cracking up.

"Who is going to help all those little stoned babies?" I shake my head.

"How could he not get that?"

"Maybe he's just sick of us."

Allison blows out her cheeks, fluffing her bangs. "I'm sick of this class."

I take a deep breath. I'm on a high dive here, with my knees clattering from fear. Before I can over-think it, I'm asking her. "Allison, you should come with us to the Nirvana concert."

"You mean the one in California?" she asks, incredulous.

I plow over her skepticism with details, filling her in on the concert, the trip and mostly how amazing it's going to be. How we're ditching that Friday, leaving before school. We'll arrive an hour before the concert starts and leave immediately afterwards, driving all night to reach home that day.

This all floods out while Don circles the room. Although I know she's listening, we're both keeping a close eye on him.

As I talk, I get totally ramped, getting more and more excited because, hey, it's pretty much the biggest thing that's ever happened in my life. Because it's traveling, which I have never done (unless you count trips to Seattle to visit my aunt, which I don't), because it's Nirvana (Nirvana!) and because if Allison comes with me, it's going to change my life.

"I don't think I've ever seen anyone so excited about anything. You're like an astronaut talking about going to the moon."

"I can't help it. It's Nirvana." *Nirvana!*

"Yeah well, it's kind of adorable."

What? The top of my head almost shoots off but I manage to keep it together. Before Don reaches us, I quickly whisper the last part, "Mike thinks I can somehow sneak through security and get Nirvana to play at prom. I know it's totally insane but I've got to give it a shot, right?"

Allison grins and anything seems possible. "Doesn't hurt to ask." She lifts her hair off her neck, stretching. "I would love to go to a concert. This is kind of embarrassing but I've never been to a rock concert. My mom wouldn't let me."

"I've never been to one either."

Don strolls past but he lingers because Allison and I are clearly having a moment, aligning like planets. I'm about ready to climb out of my skin with excitement. I blab something just to keep him off track. "I think 'Just say No' says it all. No to everything. Even food."

Allison nods, her eyes still locked on mine. "And pot smoking, right? No thank you for me, I need my brain cells."

Don studies me with concern so I add, "And being a lesbian is like being brain damaged really, so I should not drink or smoke anything. Not that I am a lesbian because that's wrong."

Allison shakes her head as she grasps my shoulders. "Don't even say that word. You're not."

I nod. "You're right. Thank you, Allison." I squeeze her shoulder. What would it be like to run my hand down her long silky arm, perhaps bumping into one of her breasts? "Thank you."

There is a faint hint of a smile on her lips. I no longer know what the hell is going on. An MTV vision of Allison in nothing but Frye boots and a leather jacket flashes in my head. I'm going crazy.

"Good work girls, keep it up." Don walks off.

Allison's smile fades. "What were we talking about?"

Somehow my brain rights itself. "How you've never been to a rock concert."

She frowns. "No. My whole life was about playing third cello in the San Francisco Youth Symphony." She bites her lip. "And Math Olympiad. Asian cliché, right?"

I shake my head. "No." She nudges me with her hand and I can't wipe the ridiculous smile off my face. "Okay, kind of. More than two AP classes and you win some kind of Asian stereotype award. A gold-plated graphing calculator."

She frowns. "God, I am."

"There's nothing wrong with being smart."

Allison ties her hair back with a band from her wrist. "Okay, true confessions: I'm in every AP class offered. I can program tons of code and dissect a frog in my sleep. Also, I won the science fair at my last school."

"And you're going to be pre-med."

"Wow. Am I really that much of a dork?"

I shake my head, thinking she's amazing.

We take a break while Don drifts past. When he leaves, I plunge back in. "Have you ever listened to Nirvana?"

"I'm not dead. I even watch MTV." Her head hangs forward, obscuring her eyes with dark hair. "When they let me." She looks up. "So where are you going next year?"

Nowhere. "Community college. In Seattle." Apparently I can major in lying. It works.

"Cool. Do you have to pick a major?"

"Photography." *Ask now. Ask now. Ask*—"So do you want to come to the concert?"

Allison laughs. "Nirvana in San Francisco? For real?" I am milliseconds from tears. She pats me on the arm. "Sorry. It's just really, really a long shot for me. Finals. You know."

"I know. I know that. But the question is, do you even want to come?" She narrows her eyes, studying me closely. Right as she opens her mouth, Don claps his hands, telling us to join the group for a closing prayer. She gives me a regretful look and grabs her backpack, sitting directly across the long table. I keep attempting eye contact but she doesn't look up.

This time, when I close my eyes, I pray instead of faking it. *Please, please God, I know I haven't been super good at keeping in touch. But please, please, please let Allison say yes. I could really use a break here.*

I'm not sure if God grants prayers like this but I don't care. A long time ago I decided that God listens because if he didn't I'd be dead by now.

CHAPTER EIGHT

(Sixteen Days before Prom)
"With the lights out, it's less dangerous.
Here we are now, entertain us. I feel stupid
and contagious. Here we are now, entertain us."
"Smells Like Teen Spirit," Nirvana

PAUL

This Nirvana thing has gotten out of hand. By lunchtime the whole school is in a frenzy, arguing about who is lying and who is telling the truth. To make matters worse Mike is a one man press conference, skipping class to spout fountains of bullshit during all three lunches about how Fran called Kurt Cobain during a recording session in Los Angeles. Rumors swirl thick and heavy; it's all anyone talks about.

Taylor is going ballistic. She's practically crying at her locker between fourth and fifth period. "You have to stop her. She's got tickets to some Nirvana concert. She's talking to Kurt Cobain. I can't handle this. Do something Paul."

God I hate this. I feel completely helpless and if I'm honest, torn between thinking that Taylor is dead wrong and sympathizing with her because well, she's miserable. On top of it all my dad is arriving this Friday. "What do you want me to do?"

She grits her pearly teeth. "Find out if Nirvana is actually coming or if they're all just lying."

"What makes you think they'll tell me the truth?"

Her blue eyes flash with anger. "Why are you dragging your feet Paul? Do you want to help me or not?"

She slams her locker and hurries away down the hall. As usual there are about six guys watching her.

During first lunch, I looked into the lunchroom. Mike was blathering through mouthfuls of Twinkie to a crowd of jocks who normally wouldn't be caught dead talking to a stoner. "Yeah man, she did. She got the number from Kurt's cousin Daisy. He was high so he got Courtney Love on the phone to write down the details." As he spoke, Mike waved the uneaten Twinkie for emphasis.

Between each lunch period Mike smoked more weed. The details of his story shifted with each joint but it hardly mattered. People were so excited they chattered like monkeys, gobbling lies like potato chips.

Finally, I locate Nikki at her locker, clustered with three other senior girls. "Prom will be a night people will be talking about for like, years. Decades." She pauses for emphasis, continuing in a whisper, "That's all I can say." She winks. "Crowd control."

"Oh come on Nikki! I swear to God we won't tell anyone," Donna Piccardi says.

Nikki grins, eating it up. "And ruin all the fun?"

The bell rings and the girls drift off to class. Nikki slams her locker and realizes I haven't left. "What?"

She's so annoyed she kind of scares me. "Never mind. I got to get to class."

"Paul, do you think I'm going to give you, like, insider information? You are totally sleeping with the enemy."

Holy crap. She read my mind. It surprises me so much that I blurt out the truth. "No I'm not," I snap, before turning the other way.

***

During second lunch Taylor's friends are selling tickets to "real prom" at both doors to the lunchroom. Their sign is decorated with American flags and photos ripped from magazine of boys in tuxes and girls in gowns holding hands. Painted in big curly letters: "A Traditional Prom." Every couple in the picture is white.

I stop by the table to inform Taylor that I haven't found out anything yet. She's thrilled because they've sold over fifty tickets.

I point to the sign, jingling the change in my pocket, a nervous habit that drives her crazy. "You're kind of turning this into a political thing. It's prom, Taylor. It's supposed to be fun."

"Hold the phone mister. Am I the trouble maker?" Taylor snaps. Kayla and Mandy give each other a look.

I have to laugh. "You tell me." Whoops, I'll pay for that later.

Taylor's mouth hangs open in shock before she sees Fran and points. "There's your little friend. Go talk to her."

"You know what, I will."

I catch up to Fran in the hallway. When she hears me, she spins around like she's afraid of something but relaxes when she sees it's me. "Did Taylor send you?"

It makes me feel completely whipped. "Please tell me you're not letting Mike drive you to California."

"You know what Paul? I have taken just enough crap from everyone today. Yes, we're going to California. Yes, Mike is coming. And Paul, we're going to get Nirvana to play prom. So, tell your girlfriend to watch her back."

She walks out of the lunchroom, tossing her uneaten lunch, tray and all into the garbage. I'm left wondering how, exactly, I ended up the enemy.

When I drive up to my house there is an unfamiliar car parked in the driveway. I drive past just in case it belongs to my dad.

Friday morning, I pick up the phone.

"Heya sport, it's Dad."

I hang up.

I cannot be around that guy.

FRAN

The next day, Friday, with only fifteen days left until prom, I am rushing down a long empty hall, late to my least favorite class, PE. If I time it just right, I can undress without a snickering audience in the locker room.

Ellyn Oaksmith

I'd almost reached the gym door when I felt a solid kick on the back of my leg. My knee buckles and I go down, managing to break my fall with my hand. Confused, I glance around and recognize the torn black Converse from the many times it's tripped me. It's PC. Oh no. This is not happening. Focus. I have to focus if I'm going to survive.

Quickly scrambling to my feet, I face him, heart thumping wildly, my mouth dry. He is wearing a Nine Inch Nails t-shirt. How random. My mouth is chalky with fear but I try to talk, hoping it will distract him from his usual mission. "You like NIN?"

He isn't buying it. "You're all lying, aren't you? That Nirvana concert fucking sold out days ago. There's no way you could have gotten tickets."

Paige Carlyle. That is his name. Everyone gave him so much crap about it in Jr. High. He's gone by PC since 9th grade. That's probably the reason he spends so much time in the weight room bulking up. Aberdeen is the wrong place to name a boy Paige. His lizard eyes flick over me, glancing at my breasts. If he knew that I had tickets in my pocket, they'd be gone. "Yes. I'm lying."

"If you were lying you wouldn't fucking tell me." He keeps clenching his fists like he wants to hit me.

I raise my hands. "I can't win here PC. What do you want?"

"You know what I want, don't you?"

Bile floods my stomach, making nauseous. Yes, I know what he wants. It's what he's been working towards since day one.

An angry sneer splits his face as he pushes me with both hands. I fall backwards into a row of double lockers, my head slamming into a lock. It bites into my scalp with a burning sting. The back half of my head is on fire. My vision goes grey, like a television losing reception. Somehow, I manage to stay upright, twisting my butt against the lower locker, which is cool and solid. My head buzzes. I lower my head, trying to faint. If I lose consciousness this won't be real.

Crouching against the lockers for support, I wait for my vision to clear by concentrating on the ground. There are four white speckles and a piece of hardened gum merging into some kind of shape. A shark fin? A sail?

He bends down towards me, breathing in my face. "This is your last chance, bitch. Drop out or you'll be sorry."

***

The next Tuesday, Allison and I stare at one another across the room during Teen Life. Rain splashes against the window. My head throbs although it quit bleeding on Friday after I cleaned it up in the locker room and pressed it with paper towels. Friday, I kept thinking I should talk to the school nurse, Mrs. Hoffstead but she's kind of scary. She has a long, hairy wart on her chin and a brisk, efficient by-the-books manner. She'd report my injury and make me tell her how it happened. I've lived in the flats long enough to know what happens with bullies. PC would deny everything. It's my word against someone who as far as I know has no history of violence. Even though I suspect Mr. P. would believe me it wouldn't do any good. PC would back off long enough to make me think he had moved on to someone else. Then things would get worse.

I can manage him. It's hard to admit that an idiot like PC has become my worst nightmare. Especially to someone like Nikki who never takes shit from anyone. She would fight back like a freaking ninja warrior. How is it that I've become this person who lets a moron like PC hurt me? I should be able to steer clear of him or get him to back off. So, I keep quiet. It's the easier choice.

On Tuesday, right before Teen Life Class I sit on the bathroom sink and try to check the cut but it's impossible. The best I can do is carefully fold my hair into a low bun and hide it but even that hurts. Three Ibuprofen haven't dulled the pain. The sight of Don the Drone swilling potato chips makes me nauseous. What if I have a concussion? All I know about head injuries is that they are varying degrees of bad and I shouldn't sleep all day, which is exactly what I want to do. I still have to pack. Should I even go? A Nirvana concert is the last place to seek urgent medical attention.

With everything racing through my aching head, the last thing I want to do is worry about asking Allison to the concert. She's been avoiding me all class.

Don is reading from the Bible as I mentally rehearse asking Allison to come to the concert. "'My eyes stay open through the watches of the night that I may meditate on your promises.' (Psalm 119:148) Hmmmmmm," he says, holding his wobbly chin. "Food for thought." He giggles. "Not junk food either."

Don waits for someone to laugh but everyone is either staring off into space or doodling. Allison is scribbling with a purple Sharpie. So, he asks us to meditate on the last two days of our lives, telling us to close our eyes as he slowly reads his favorite passage for meditation. "Watch your thoughts; they become words. Watch your words; they become actions. Watch your actions; they become habits. Watch your habits; they become character. Watch your character; it becomes your destiny."

As soon as my eyes close, I see PC's sneering face. How am I supposed to focus on God when I am worried for my own safety? Kurt Cobain understands this dilemma although he's a long way from Godly in most people's opinion. My head aches so much I can barely concentrate on Don's discussion of destiny. How we are molding our futures with each small or big decision. It's funny he's chosen this particular message on the eve of my big trip, which has been paved with one whopping lie about Nirvana after another. When will I learn to keep my stupid mouth shut?

When I sneak a look at Allison, she is looking up from her doodling, staring at me but she closes her eyes so fast there isn't a hint of what she is thinking. I take out a piece of paper and write down in Sharpie: Friday Morning, 6:00 AM, McDonald's Parking Lot on Wishkah. I have a ticket for you. We'll be back Saturday morning.

I ball up the note, wait for Don to look the other direction and throw it. Just before it hits her on the chest, I shut my eyes.

CHAPTER NINE

"I'd rather be hated for who I am,
than loved for who I am not."
Kurt Cobain

NIKKI

How on earth could we have counted on Mike? He's twenty minutes late. We huddle in a pool of light in the McDonald's parking lot as I keep encouraging Fran, trying to keep her spirits up by dramatically recounting the message I'd left at the school last night, pretending to be her mom, calling her in sick. Of course I ham it up but Fran's not listening. I am a whirling dervish of energy trying to ignore the biggest lie of my life: that I'm in Seattle and will meet my parents at the Husky lunch. I'd rather have them drive to Seattle and wonder why I'm not there than be honest. I am a horrible person and an even worse daughter.

I'm scum.

The bacteria that you find on scum.

Fran's pinched face is turned towards the road. "He's flaked out."

"You're so fatalistic."

"I can't believe we trusted this whole trip to Mike. I wouldn't trust Mike to get lunch, let alone show up on time."

Hazel lopes up to us, bouncing on her Doc Martens, her curls tied up in a ponytail. "Hey, my parents are actually kind of chasing me so let's go inside."

I throw up my arms, exasperated. "I freaking knew it. It's that whole Christian passive aggressive thing where you hate lying so you do it really badly so you'll totally get caught." *Not like me. I take it to new levels.*

Hazel's eyes flash. "I don't do that."

Fran rolls her eyes. "Remember in third grade when you said an angel from heaven gave us the candy bars we shoplifted from the minimart?"

"What did you tell your parents?" I demand.

"That I joined a knitting club." Hazel won't meet my eyes.

"Seriously?" I say. "An early morning knitting club?"

"It's better than the angel thing," Fran says. Hazel shoots her a grateful look but I don't care. She's totally screwing everything up. I cannot be here when my parents get back.

We push into the bright restaurant, joining the lines of semi-zombie workers waiting for boiling hot coffee and a handful of grease.

Hazel un-wraps a stick of gum, keeping a wary eye on the parking lot as she chomps. "If my parents show up, I'm hitting the bathroom, okay? Come get me when they're gone."

A middle-aged construction worker stares at us, shaking his head. Hazel giggles at him behind his back as Mike shuffles in the door.

"My brother changed his mind," he mumbles, staring at the tiled floor.

"What do you mean?" I shout. These freaking people. I mean seriously, they're totally driving me insane.

"I mean he just changed his mind. He's mad at me for stealing some of his pot so he doesn't want me driving his car."

"Did you steal the pot?" Fran asks.

All three of us glare at Mike, who shrugs miserably, patting his backpack. "I told him I'd pay him back. I needed the money."

"You freaking idiot!" I mutter, stepping away to get some perspective. It doesn't help. All I can see is my parents' confused look.

"He's such a douche. I told him about the concert and he just said tough shit."

A half an hour later we are at a booth littered with cups and wrappers. The more coffee we drink, the worse the situation feels. Mike is arguing with Hazel about hitch-hiking. He is trying to explain how he can single-handedly protect us all from rapists, axe murderers, and every creep on the road with his spindly, underfed, over-sexed body.

When this argument founders on our good sense, he brightens with a new thought. "There are four of us. If we take a ride from one person there is no way they can physically overpower or outrun us. Look, even if we're not strong we can outrun any fat old pervert in a heartbeat! We're teenagers!"

I scoff, "Dude, your lungs are freaking trashed from years of smoking your brother's pot."

"Exactly!" A deep voice booms from behind the condiments. Hazel's dad is six-foot- three and can easily bench press Mike. He wears a neon-striped safety vest stretched over a barrel chest. His mustache needs its own zip code. Hazel slides down her seat until her chin is level with the yellow table top.

Her dad crooks his finger at her while addressing Mike. "Listen numb nuts. Don't talk these girls into anything. Hazel, now!"

After Hazel leaves we're silent until Mike holds out his hand. "Fuck it. Give me the tickets, I'll hitchhike there, sell the other three tickets and be back by tomorrow morning."

"In a body bag," I snap, chewing a thin red straw. I have a stack of them from the dispenser. Hopefully they'll stop me from punching someone.

"Aww, it doesn't matter." Mike sighs.

"I'm so sick of this, I'm going home." Fran digs out her tickets with tears in her eyes. This cannot be happening. Our whole plan cannot fall apart before we even leave town. I'm so not staying here. I'm wracking my brain for a solution when I spot Paul at the food counter in his varsity jacket anxiously scanning the restaurant.

He spots us and rushes over. "Hey! I'm so glad I'm not too late." He addresses everyone but his eyes lock on me. I try to hold onto my anger and not melt. *He's Taylor's boyfriend. He's so not yours.* "Don't do this. I doubt you'll even make it in that piece of crap car but if you do that concert is going to be out of control." He points at Mike. "No offense dude but you and these girls are going to get your asses kicked in the parking lot before you get inside. Hell's Angels go there, okay, so why don't you-"

"I don't care," Mike says.

Slapping the tickets on the table, Fran hoists her duffel. "We don't have a car. Mike's brother changed his mind. Hazel's dad is going to report all of us to Principal P." She turns to me. "I cannot do this prom thing and be brave or pretend that this whole road trip is going to end up as anything other than a huge fiasco. Look at us. We can't even get out of the parking lot."

She's trying hard not to cry but her voice quavers. "Yesterday someone, well—I've had it. I'm done." We all sit in stunned silence while Fran rushes out of the restaurant.

PAUL

Fran didn't need to say she was beat. I couldn't put into words how I knew but growing up with it, I just knew. She had that look. Everyone thinks that meth and unemployment are the scourge of Aberdeen but a whole lot of women come to work with bruises and flimsy excuses and no one says a thing. My goal is to find out who hit her and go beat the ever-loving crap out of them. I know there's plenty of grey area in life and I shouldn't think with my fists but when it comes to hitting a girl, I'm not going to sit back. No way. I don't know a whole lot about Fran but she hasn't had an easy life and she sure as hell isn't having an easy senior year. She doesn't deserve this. Nobody does.

She's walking pretty fast so I break into a trot, grabbing her shoulder. "Whoa. Wait a minute, hang on. Who hit you?"

The sunrise is a bruised orange trying to push through the clouds. When she turns towards me, looking so sick of it all, it gets to me, the way she looks finished, done. "What difference does it make?"

I frown. "Who was it?"

Beads of rain glisten on her face. She tugs her flannel shirt tight around her chest. "Nobody you know. Anyway, it doesn't matter."

I look away, sure she's lying. I mean, Aberdeen is only so big. Across the parking lot Nikki's face is pressed against the McDonald's window, chewing her red straw, looking like she wants to bust out the door and take over. Thank God she doesn't. "Yes, it does Fran. It kind of matters a lot."

She shakes her head, wiping her nose with her sleeve. "I'm fine."

I clench my jaw and fists wanting nothing more than to just punch someone in the face. "Tell me."

She studies me, sizing me up. "I'm okay. Please don't tell them. I don't want anyone else to know, okay? Please?" She tries for a grin but it comes out twisted. "Wow. Super intense for six a.m., right?" She takes a deep breath. "I'm not going to tell you who he is but when he found out the concert was sold out, he wanted my tickets. And now we're stuck. He's going to show up here any minute in his truck and take our tickets."

I wipe my forehead, glancing up at the golden arches.

"Are you one of those conspiracy theorists? Watch a lot of detective shows?"

"Fine, don't believe me." She hurries across the parking lot.

"That's not what I meant." It was stupid to joke. Before she reaches the other side, I'm in front of her. "Stop."

"No." She darts around me. "Don't you have to report for duty with Taylor or something? Does she know you're talking to me?"

"Listen to me."

She yells over her shoulder. "No!" and takes off down the road with her duffel hoisted on her shoulder.

I yell but the noise of the morning traffic buries the sound. I keep repeating it louder until she finally hears me. "I said I'll take you!" The funny thing is, some part of me already knew that this was the plan. My dad had been calling every day, telling me about his new life, his new commitment to sobriety and how he wants to make amends. Part of his steps or something. Whatever. Leaving town is the perfect solution. He'll be gone by the time I get back. Problem solved.

She drops her bag, walking back. "What did you say?"

"I said I'll take you." It's the perfect solution.

"All the way to California? Are you serious?"

I look back at Mike and Nikki leaning against the McDonald's window, watching us. Even though this is a neat little solution, skipping town, there are some red flags. Technically, I'm stealing my mom's car. She will crucify me, not to mention my coach when I miss the game tonight. Also, I am helping the girl running for prom queen against my girlfriend. Still, I'd rather deal with all of it when I get back than have to look at my dad's face for one second.

FRAN

"We're going to be totally late," Nikki says, shoving her bag into the back of the Taurus station wagon before going to pick up our food order from inside the McDonald's. In a town full of battered, ugly cars, the Taurus is a standout. It has the low profile and dull sheen of a dead shark.

"This has to be the un-coolest car on the planet," Mike says, eagerly displaying the dozens of homemade bongs he's carrying, turning to block Paul's view. They're made out of empty Tic Tac containers.

"You can always walk to the concert," says Paul.

"No thank you. Did I tell you how grateful I am? This may be the ugliest car in the entire world but I am totally jam packed with gratitude for rescuing our asses." While he talks, Mike runs his hands over the bongs like he's Vanna White, displaying a prize.

"Nice," I tell Mike. He's very proud of the mini-bongs, lined up like tiny treats in his old Star Trek lunch box.

He's stashing them under the seat when Nikki rushes up with warm bags of food, shoving one at Mike as they both fight to gain entry into the front seat.

"Oh no you don't!" argues Mike as he and Nikki push and shove for position, scrambling to get in.

Nikki's butt is almost settled into the seat when Mike grabs her by the sweatshirt and hauls her out, howling. "That's not fair! I called it."

"Dudes in the front, girls in the back!" Mike says.

"You sexist pig!" Nikki screams, attracting unwanted attention from people in the parking lot.

I'm in the backseat, growing anxious that we haven't left yet. Last night Dwayne came home late, wobbly on payday booze. I'd left the door open as I packed. *Hey rug muncher, you finally running away?* He'd thrown a wad of crumpled one dollar bills. *Here's my fucking contribution.* What he didn't know was that one of them was a hundred dollar bill.

Paul twists back, resting his elbow on the tattered front seat. "I told you we should never have had kids."

"Huge mistake." Nikki's on Mike's back, pulling his hood over his eyes as he spins around, trying to get her off his back by backing into another car.

"Hey, is there room for one more?"

Allison is in the narrow space between cars wearing a jean jacket. She's slightly out of breath as she nervously tucks her hair behind an ear. One slender arm is wrapped around her cello. Speckles of rain glisten on her dark hair. My window won't roll down so I just nod. Yes. Hell yes.

Torrents of rain unleash from the sky. Nikki squeals and jumps off Mike's back, making a dash for the car. Paul jumps out to help Allison stash the cello in the trunk. Dumping rain is a lousy way to start out on a road trip but suddenly I don't care. Suddenly nothing matters. Allison is here.

We're on the outskirts of town on the evergreen-lined Olympic highway heading east. The car stinks of wet wool as the squawking windshield wipers do their best to keep up. Mike moves the strut of the cello which pokes over the backseat between him and Allison at eye level. She tries to adjust it so it's closer to her. "Yeah, I'm sorry about the cello. If I left it at home my mom would know something was up."

Mike leans into the fogged window. "Yeah, no big deal."

"We can change places if you want," Allison offers.

"I'm fine," Mike says, clearly not happy.

Nikki twists in her seat, her voice pitched high and fake friendly. "So, this is a shocking new development. What made you decide to join us?"

Allison raises her eyebrows. "Um, well, because Fran invited me."

Nikki gives me a look, fluffing her wet hair. "Okaaaaay. Nice of you to tell me that Fran."

"I didn't think she'd come." Why is Nikki acting so weird? She's been even more jittery than usual, checking her watch like crazy.

Nikki tilts her head. "Why not?"

Allison flushes. "I had a physics final for one thing."

"You could make it up," Nikki says.

"Yeah well, my mom isn't too big on skipping school."

"So how'd you convince her?"

Allison looks out the window. "I didn't."

Nikki's eyes widen. "So, your mom like, has no idea where you are?"

"She thinks I'm at a friend's house."

"Hope she buys it," Nikki says, twisting to the front. "Because if she doesn't, we could all be in totally deep shit."

CHAPTER TEN

*"Drugs are a waste of time. They destroy your
memory and your self-respect..."*
Kurt Cobain

NIKKI

I wish I were totally the kind of person who was happy for my best friend to have her crush along for the ride but I'm just not. Allison is pretty, if you like that whole wispy, hair-hanging-in-her-face kind of thing. Showing up for this trip at the last minute completely changed the vibe. Paul, Mike, Fran and I have known each other since, like kindergarten. Yes, Mike is a pothead now but I knew him when he used to bring potato bugs to school and drop them down kids' shirts. Allison, while undoubtedly cool, has shifted the focus. The minute she showed up it's like Fran swallowed a flashlight. It's freaking disgusting.

Yes, jealousy could be a factor. I've gone from best friend to like, persona nongrata ever since Allison showed up—*with her cello.* I mean, who takes a freaking cello to a Nirvana concert?

The vibe has gone from a group of friends to a weird double date with a stoner thrown in for good measure. Paul keeps turning the radio station to all these horrid Mariah Carey ballads, getting all misty. "Taylor loves Mariah Carrey!" he says for about the fifteenth time as if anyone in the car gives a crap.

"Of course she does. They're both self-absorbed divas who spend a lot of time kissing mirrors." I look at my watch for like the fiftieth time. My parents are now on their way to Seattle. Will they say anything to their friends or slink away when they find out I'm not on the incoming freshman class list?

"Knock it off Nikki," Paul says. When he frowns he gets this adorable look. He's so all American, Ralph freaking Lauren handsome that he can't really look totally mad. It's like he's pretending to be angry or something.

"Knock what off?"

"Stop talking about Taylor. She's my girlfriend."

"That you totally left back in Aberdeen," I quite justly point out.

"I couldn't very well bring her."

"What are you going to tell her?" If I could let it go, I would. But I can't. I need to be fixated on something else other than my poor parents who are about to find out that their daughter is a total loser and big fat liar.

Paul shakes his head. "Nothing. Which is exactly what you're going to tell her. You got it?" He looks into the rearview mirror. "That goes for everyone."

"I'm pretty sure that's a relationship don't," Mike says from the backseat.

"Like I'm going to take relationship advice from you?" Paul says into the rearview mirror.

Mike shrugs. "Hey, I read Cosmopolitan magazine. Helen Gurley Brown knows what she's talking about."

Paul smiles. "Right. That makes you an authority."

"Become the man she wants you to be - Helen Gurley Brown." He does air quotes, which is totally funny.

As rolling green farms turn into the suburbs of Vancouver, Washington and we pass over the flat grey-green Columbia River into Oregon, I keep sneaking glances at Paul. Even though I know it's childish, I pretend we're boyfriend and girlfriend on our way to a concert. It works until he opens his mouth.

"I told Taylor I was sick. Do you think she'll believe that? She has two finals today. I hope she doesn't worry too much about me."

"Trust me, she totally won't," I snap. I keep punching the station buttons searching for a decent song but apparently all they listen to in Oregon is freaking Mariah Carey, who I liked until I found out Taylor *looooooves* her.

Paul's knuckles tighten on the wheel. "Why are you always so negative about her?"

I take a deep breath, gazing out at the silvery Portland skyscrapers across the river. They're nestled at the foot of lush green hills. Gosh, where to freaking begin? First of all, she's a stone-cold bitch. Secondly, she's gunning for my best friend and third of all Paul, wake up and smell the cat food, I'm like right here. I've always been. "Have you seen her on a soccer field?"

He gives me a long stare before turning his attention back to the road. "You don't really know her."

Oh, trust me, I do. "My shins also know her pretty freaking well."

"She's competitive. She has drive. What's wrong with that?"

I lift my leg across Paul's lap, pointing downwards, which happens to be his crotch. Maybe I did it on purpose. Maybe not. "You see that?" His neck flushes. "That is a scar I'll always have compliments of Taylor."

"That's soccer Nik. You know that," he says. "Stuff happens."

I want to ask him if one of his forwards is a smack-talking, ball-hogging diva who trips him at practice and trash talks him in the locker room. But oh no, he wouldn't believe his precious Taylor could be so nasty. He warns me not to change the station as he taps his fingers to yet another Mariah Carey song, "Dream Lover."

Mike lets off a fart and smiles in his sleep. In the rearview mirror, I see Fran duck under the cello and whispers to Allison, "Paradise, right?"

For some reason, their chumminess totally pisses me off. I get out the map, rattling it loudly, wanting to take charge of this trip because it will make me feel better. "Ashland. The place with the Shakespeare festival. That's the halfway point. We'll stop there."

Paul shakes his head in time to the song. "We'll stop when we need gas."

"Hazel totally marked the halfway point and I think-"

Paul shakes his head, singing softly, "Dream lover come rescue me. Take me up, take me down. Take me anywhere you want to baby now. I need you so desperately. Won't you please come around? 'Cause I wanna share forever with you baby."

"We're going to a rock concert. You know that right?" Mike mutters with his eyes closed.

Paul raises a bird to the backseat. "Shut up Mike. It's a good song."

I chew on another McDonald's red straw. "Hazel's pretty good at planning. If we knew we were stopping in Medford, we could totally plan our car naps. What do you think Fran?"

Fran shrugs. "Sure, whatever."

Sure, whatever? This is her freaking trip. Is Fran dropping me? Our first road trip and I'm being dumped?

Paul rolls down his window a little, breathing in the air. Mike shivers in his striped Baja hoodie. "Dude, roll that sucker up. *Es muy frio.*" He rubs his arms. "I only packed the one drug rug."

"I'm trying to stay awake," says Paul.

"That's reassuring," Allison mutters, which is annoying. Oh wait, everything she says is annoying.

"I already slept. I'll drive after we get gas." Mike is suddenly awake, bumping into the cello, wiping a crust of drool off his chin.

"Please let him. He'll have to put on his shoes." Allison holds her nose.

Paul nods as the song finishes. "Okay." He punches the buttons again, searching for another Mariah song. Nirvana comes on, "Smells like Teen Spirit." Mike and I scream the lyrics at the top of our lungs. Fran is involved in some stupid conversation with Allison.

"Come on Fran!" I scream. "It's Nirvana!"

"Oh my God." Paul shakes his head like a grumpy old man.

"You don't even like Nirvana, do you?" I shout, waving my arms.

Paul stretches one arm over the backseat, yelling at Mike. "Dude, give me the tickets to put in the glove box so we don't lose them."

"What?" Paul lowers the radio volume, repeating the question. Mike doesn't respond. The look on his face makes my stomach churn. "Hey, did you hear me?"

Mike has turned dead white. He knocks his forehead again the cello. Allison blocks him so he's hitting her open palm. "Shit."

I stop mid-chew on my straw, peering over the back seat. "Mike?"

"Fuck. Fuck. Fuck. Fuck." Mike whispers in horror.

"Where are the freaking tickets?" I ask.

———

We're in a truck stop outside of Salem, Oregon, in the burning heat. Heat shimmers off the blacktop. Diesel mingles with the deep fryer stink wafting from the truck stop cafe. Semi-trucks grind in and out of the adjoining parking lot. I'm nervous about getting kicked out of this Trucks Only area but Paul had to stop. As soon as we pulled off the freeway Mike and I have been at each other's throats, unable to stop. I'm so mad I could explode. I cannot go back to Aberdeen.

"I didn't throw them away. You left them on the table!" I scream. "I was cleaning up after you!"

"You threw them away!" Mike howls.

"You had like, one thing to do Mike. One freaking thing and you totally screwed it up!"

"It's not my fault!" Mike throws his arms up.

"Hell yes, it is! You totally ruined everything!" Sweat runs down my face. Fran isn't happy but I can't help it.

A white Oregon state police car with a black badge on the door glides up the blacktop. I grab Fran's arm, marching her towards the cafe. Allison points out the policeman to Mike and Paul. The three of them jump in the car, telling us they'll park around back.

"Be careful," Paul yells at us.

As we walk inside the cafe, there are tears in Fran's eyes which makes everything worse. I look at my watch. My parents have just reached Seattle.

FRAN

The truck stop is half empty, pungent with diesel and cooking oil. We take a window booth overlooking the gas pumps and I-5, ordering Cokes from a bored waitress. We're silent, frayed to the point of snapping. Mike's head rests on the table, buried in his crossed arms. Nikki chews on her renewed supply of tiny red straws. When the waitress returns no one looks up. Allison politely explains that we're not hungry.

"How do you know?" Nikki snaps. When the waitress raises her eyebrows, she says, "Just the Coke."

The waitress snaps her order pad shut, shuffles off. Allison glares at Nikki. We're all annoyed and likely thinking the same thing. Turning around, going home, giving up. Forks clink on plates at nearby tables. Heat blasts from the opening door as truckers come and go.

"I'm going to make a phone call." I'm lying to get away from the mess. This day is freaking ruined, not to mention this trip.

"Me too." Allison bangs her knees on the table in her eagerness to get up.

"I should call Taylor," Paul says but just sits there, doodling in the condensation on his Coke glass. Nikki slouches beside Paul. She glares at Mike who whispers, "Fuck, fuck, fuckity, fuck..."

"Watch your language!" Paul commands.

"Shit, shit, shit, shit..." Mike sighs.

Allison trails me to the silver bank of phones between the men's (labeled roosters) and women's (hens). A steady stream of truckers in Wranglers, cowboy boots and Deere baseball hats hit the john. They nod, give us appraising looks.

"Totally not the ideal place for a convo." Allison leans against the grimy red-tiled hallway to let people pass.

We're beside a chipped pale blue condom-dispenser affixed to the wall. "They think we're hookers so possibly not."

She pushes the hair out of her eyes with a grin. "But I have a question."

Nikki waves as she parks herself at a phone, feeding in a hand full of quarters. I move closer, feeling Allison's breath on my cheek. "Can't we do this outside?" She's going to suggest we give up, go home, fold. If she does,

I'll hate her for losing faith even though it's been running through my mind.

"How old were you when you came out?" She keeps an eye on Nikki.

Okay. "I didn't."

Her eyebrows arch. "What?"

The state policeman strolls past in his blue Smokey the Bear hat, which he tips, eying Nikki suspiciously. "It's kind of a long story."

"I love long stories."

"In dirty hallways at truck stops?"

"Adds to the story. We'll always remember this exact spot."

I inhale for strength, sucking in Lysol and stale grease. I can't think of a worse place for an intimate conversation. "The summer between junior and senior high Nikki talked me into joining her rec soccer team. Her mom paid for everything and drove me."

"That was nice."

Nikki is so involved in her conversation that I don't worry about her listening. "Well, yeah, except it made me feel like a charity case, which I totally was but anyway, one day the coach was late and Taylor-"

Allison raises one dark eyebrow. "Whom we loathe and despise?"

"Whom we abhor and detest." I love this little game. "She immediately morphs into this drill sergeant making us all stretch while forcing us to play 'Who's your crush?' I'm totally bored and watching this really graceful girl across the field. She reminds me of Mia Hamm and Mia Hamm is my hero. And Taylor, who is already this alpha queen bee and super scary shouts 'Who's your crush?' I don't even think about it. I say 'her,' meaning the girl kicking the soccer ball because I have no idea what I'm saying. I'm daydreaming out loud about this girl who reminds me of this famous soccer player. Nikki tries to cover for me but this girl named Shelby says, 'She can't have a crush on a girl, can she?' and then all these girls go dead silent. They're all staring at me like I'm some kind of alien. Trina Carter says 'Oh my God, she's a lesbian.' And they back up. They take a few steps back like it's contagious. Someone tells the coach who tells me that I'm making the other girls uncomfortable and I might want to stay home until things die down for a while. I tell Nikki's mom that I quit because my ankles hurt. And that fall, when I show up at high school, I'm suddenly that lesbian. Nikki ate lunch with me every day. Then we met Hazel and Mike."

"Did you ever try to cover it up?"

I shrugged. "I didn't even know what a lesbian was. I just liked girls. Always did."

"She knew?" Allison nods at Nikki, who has turned her back to us.

As we talk, our foreheads almost touch. She smells like clean cotton and lemony shampoo. "She did. One time in 6th grade her dad took us camping. We were fishing off the dock and I asked her if she ever thought about kissing a girl. She said no, did I? We had this hilarious discussion about the difference between kissing girls and boys until her dad came down to the dock and said the hot dogs were ready. If it weren't for her I doubt Hazel or Mike or anyone else would have had to courage to talk to me. I had a crush on her for a while. I never said anything but-"

The police officer strolls past, finger-combing his

mustache. "Say—aren't you girls supposed to be in school?"

Allison straightens up, brushes the hair off her forehead. "We're on our way to a state band competition in Ashland."

He takes off his hat, wiping sweat from his reddened forehead. "That right?"

Allison grins and nods vigorously. "Yep. Have a nice day."

He takes a few steps. "What instrument do you play?" He's looking at me.

"Guitar."

The officer scowls. Allison says, "It's a new thing. The guitar section. Very popular. You've never heard of it?"

He doesn't believe her. "No. There is no such thing and there never will be. Good day ladies."

"Oh my God! Guitar, really?" Allison hip checks me.

"Haven't you seen the all guitar band?" I mimic strumming and marching down the hallway into the restaurant. "Now I have a question for you."

Nikki rushes up behind us, wrapping her arms around our shoulders, hopping up and down. "I did it. I did it. I just totally freaking did it."

She ruined the last few seconds I had with Allison. "What?" I say somewhat sulkily.

"Come here." She drags us to our table, slapping a credit card on the table. "I stole this!"

"Shhhhhhh." Paul nods his head at the police officer reading the newspaper at the counter.

Nikki glances over, whispering. "From my dad. He says never to travel without like, serious emergency cash."

Paul slaps his forehead. "So, you stole his credit card?"

Allison whispers in my ear. "Did this just turn into a crime spree?"

"And," Nikki says with the pride of a math teacher explaining a tough theorem, "I called Ticketmaster and got us new tickets."

"Genius!" Mike says. "Did it work?"

Nikki slides into her seat, un-wrapping another straw and chewing. "Not at first. The woman was all—it's sold out and you like, lost the tickets but I purchased them on this card-"

"Did! It! Work!?" Mike pounds on the table. The police officer glances at us over his bifocals. Nikki offers a one karat smile and princess wave. He nods pleasantly.

"Yes." She sighs. "We have to go to Will Call. And show ID." She waves a piece of paper. "She gave me the ticket numbers."

Paul throws money down before anyone has time to check their watch. "I'll drive."

Mike digs into his pocket, unearthing two pretzels and a pack of orange Zig-Zag rolling papers. "How fast can that piece of shit Taurus go?"

Allison and I count the money piled on the table. As he pushes out the door Paul argues with Mike. "No tickets. We are not speeding."

As we head out into the suffocating heat, Mike says, "If we don't speed, we might miss Nirvana."

That's when reality smacks me in the face. I'm headed to a Nirvana concert. To possibly even talk to Kurt Cobain. If we get there in time, which is the thought in my head when I hear the thump, thump, thump of a flat tire.

CHAPTER ELEVEN

What else should I be? All apologies.
"All Apologies," Nirvana

NIKKI

Allison is stoned and Fran is totally pissed. When we stopped for a flat tire Allison snuck off with Mike, who introduced her to the delights of mini bongs. They remind me of my Aunt Tina and Uncle Bud at the Fourth of July picnic where he always drinks way too much beer and she sulks. It's quite shitty of me but I'm kinda loving it. Looking at the two of them in the backseat, Allison with the glazed red eyes and slack jaw like she's been slapped with a dead fish and Fran, all sour and tart, I realize that I want Fran back. Of course, I want her to be in love but not with Allison. Which I realize is pretty freaking crappy of me. I can't help it. I have my own life crisis which will probably cause more long-term damage than Fran's.

And yet.

Bam.

Maybe I have it in for Allison.

Maybe as in yes.

For one thing Allison is cooler than everyone in our entire school which just isn't fair. The way she wears her jeans, all ripped and low slung and that drop-dead leather jacket, not to mention those killer Frye boots. Her whole look just makes me feel like such a hick. The fact that she's dead gorgeous in a GAP model multi-ethnic way is just not fair. She makes me feel like freaking mall trash.

I bet this is the first time she's ever smoked weed in her whole nerdy life. She's like one of those sheltered kids that hits camp and goes freaking insane. It's highly entertaining. They keep having conversations that totally crack me up which is difficult because I'm driving and apparently also giving Paul, who rides shot gun, a total nervous breakdown. The guy is like, visibly sweating.

"What are all those cows doing there?" Allison asks as she gazes out the window.

"Being cows," Fran snaps back.

"Weird," Allison says.

"No, it's not weird. What's weird is you smoking dope."

"It's a free country," Allison says. She ponders this profound statement. "You know, it really is. We're lucky to live here."

Fran sighs. "With the cows."

Allison studies Fran. "Don't you think we're lucky to be living with the cows? Cows are nice, aren't they?"

"I don't know. I don't know anything about cows," Fran snaps.

I glance at Fran in the rearview mirror. She rolls her eyes. The shared moment at the expense of Allison gives me a bloom of happiness. I know it's wrong but so what? I'm never going to have another best friend like Fran who's known all my secrets since I was old enough to have them. Okay maybe not this latest one but I'll get around to it. I'll be damned if I'm going to lose Fran to some stoned Eurasian chick with great freaking, like everything.

As I've slid into the anti-Allison camp (population: 1) I've become a teensy bit obsessed at how Allison is reacting to Fran, studying her for signs that she's interested. If she's actually going to reciprocate Fran's infatuation, then I might try to be nicer because then there's no point, right? I keep looking for her to gaze at Fran or point out some perfectly stupid roadside attraction just to get her attention or casually brush up against Fran because they are sitting side by side. The sexual tension is crawling over the car but I get the feeling it's only coming from Fran. And instead of tension it's just frustration.

If Allison is one of these girls that feeds on having people infatuated with them, toying with them like cats playing with a half-dead mouse, then I'm probably going to kill Allison. Or at least maim her for life.

I keep obsessively glancing at them in the rearview mirror as Mike and Allison pass a bag of Coronets across Fran's lap, giggling like hyenas as they pretend to play the little bugle shaped snacks like horns.

"Okay, what's this one?" Mike pretends to play a melody.

"Oooooh ooooh! I know! I know!" Allison raises her hand, hitting it on the roof overhead, then laughing and shaking her hand. "That hurt."

"For crying out loud, would you look at the road!" Paul hisses at me because, well, I have drifted a bit into another lane.

"Don't worry, I've totally got this," I snap back, correcting the situation.

"You're going to kill us, you know that right?" Paul says, slapping his hand over his eyes.

I tell Paul to hush, thinking that death would solve the whole college problem. How can he not be interested in the backseat dynamic? It's like a freaking soap opera. He's too busy mooning over Taylor to even know I'm alive, which also pisses me off so I might as well have some fun.

"Here, I'll play it again." Mike sticks the horn-shaped snack to his lips.

"Stars and Stripes!" Allison yells.

"You just screamed in my ear," Fran grouses.

"You didn't let me finish!" Mike offers Fran another joint. "Smoke this. It helps hearing too."

Fran shakes her head, irritated.

"Okay, my turn!" Allison yells in Fran's ear and begins her own song, despite Mike's continued objections.

Paul keeps barking "hey" and "watch out" because, well, I am interpreting the white lines very freely but that's why those bumps are on the highway, right? When I point this out, he rolls his eyes in a very demeaning way and asks me if I was taught to drive by an eighty-year-old blind woman.

"Do you like, wake up every morning, look in the mirror and say 'Hello Mr. Perfect?' I snap.

A little muscle in his jaw jumps. "Do you wake up every morning and say 'I think I'm going to kill someone?'"

"As a matter of fact, that's exactly what I said today. But I didn't know it was going to be you."

"What is your problem?" *Where to freaking begin?*

I glance in the backseat at Fran and Allison, who are bickering over the Great Coronet Incident and decide that I have to talk to someone. I learned a trick from my parents a long time ago which is that if you roll down the windows in the backseat, just a little, the road noise prevents the people in the backseat from hearing anything said in the front. Once I've made up some bullshit story about why Mike and Allison need to roll down their windows, I tell Paul everything that's bothering me about Fran and Allison.

And here's the shocker: he's really freaking nice about it.

Maybe I could tell him how I totally tanked my life.

I glance into the rearview mirror at Fran, increasingly miserable as Allison and Mike toss Raisinets into each other's mouths. Most of the time they miss, bouncing off Fran's head.

Although I'm feeling smug about the whole situation, I have to admit, there is nothing lonelier than being stuck between two stoned people. I'm sure Fran envisioned having long, heartfelt discussions with Allison instead of being pelted by junk food. Feeling slightly guilty because I'm enjoying her pain, I decide to distract her. "You're going to smuggle your camera into the concert, right?"

She perks right up. "Of course. I doubt I'll ever make

it backstage but I want to be able to take pictures of them from the auditorium."

Allison talks through a mouthful of Coronets, waving a finger. "Oh no, no, no. This is so happening. You're talking to Kurt Cobain. I skipped a physics exam for this. The question isn't if you're seeing him, it's what are you going to say when you do?"

We pass a truck loaded with produce as Fran shakes her head. "I'll say 'hi Kurt' and then barf on my shoes because I'm so nervous."

I keep looking at her in the rearview mirror, which makes Paul even more anxious about my driving, especially because we've just started to climb a mountain pass. To our left is a barrier heading off a cliff. To the right is a wall of stone. But like, whatever. I'm about ready to say something when Allison butts in. "Think of him as a regular guy from Aberdeen."

Fran shakes her head. "Who sells millions of records and will go down as one of the greatest songwriters and musicians of his generation."

"You know he poops, right?" asks Mike as he blows on the window, drawing naked women, making fingertip nipples with his pinkie.

Allison smiles. "Keep it simple. Something like: I know you're really busy but I was voted for prom queen and just because I am gay a lot of people are boycotting prom."

I get excited and talk over Allison. "And If Nirvana played, it would be a huge deal and everyone would come."

Allison, looking pissy and annoyed, jumps back in.

"Your wife won't mind because I might be young and hot but I'm seriously gay."

"That just about sums it all up," Mike says. "Young, hot and seriously gay."

"Seriously gay?" Fran frowns.

"Seriously lesbian doesn't have the same ring," Mike points out. "Lesbian sounds like someone who could totally kick your ass."

"A lesbian could totally kick *your* ass," Paul points out before turning to Fran. "Never mind what you're going to say. How are you going to get backstage?

"There's going to be lots of scary dudes with arms as big as my body. What do they call them?" Mike says.

"Security?" Allison says.

Mike nods. "Right. Security. And they'll be out to get you."

"You're high," Fran says.

Mike's eyes go all wide, which is funny. "Oh my God, I am. So anyway, here's the set up. Pretend this is the stage and the security guys will be like, right here," he points to his lap. "And you'll be here," he points to the window of the car. And Kurt Cobain will be like," he looks perplexed. "Okay, just pretend that the window is a stage." He stares at Fran.

"What?" She says.

"Is the window a stage?" he asks. "Is that believable?"

"Can we talk about this when you're not high?" Fran asks.

"Do you have two years?" Paul says.

Mike points a finger Paul. "I'll deal with you later."

"He totally brought up a good point. What about security?" I ask.

Fran frowns. "I don't know."

We've nearly reached the top of the pass but the single southbound lane is blocked by a huge freaking cattle truck that creeps like a caterpillar. I floor the gas hoping to pass him but the Taurus won't move any faster. "How about if we provide a distraction and you run past security?"

"What kind of distraction?" Fran asks, looking dubious.

"You could pull up your shirt," Mike suggests.

I laugh. "You could pull down your pants."

"Oh no. That would cause a stampede. Women would be fighting each other to get to me." Mike puffs out his chest and makes a muscle with his arms.

"Or to get away," Fran mutters.

Paul shakes his head. This is the right moment to see if I can pass the stupid cattle truck. Turning the wheel, I take a tiny dip into the oncoming traffic. What happens next is a little bit like a horror movie. Or a traffic school video. Or—well, whatever it is, it's really not, like good. As a matter of fact it's pretty epically bad and my jokes about killing someone are going to come true unless I pull my shit together totally fast. Oh my God. There is a car directly in front of us, headed our way. In a second we'll collide at 60 miles an hour. The driver's eyes widen in terror. The scariest thing is that we're so close I can see his freaking eyes. We're that close and getting closer super-fast. He has nowhere to go but totally over the side of an embankment. This barely registers as my arms automatically jerk us back into our own lane. The driver pounds on his horn as I veer quickly to the right.

Everyone in the car is dead quiet except for our heart beats. That must be my pulse, pounding in my head. Holy mother of freaking God that was like, close.

Paul leans his head between his knees, panting. "Oh my God," he whispers.

"Holy shit!" Fran croaks.

"What happened? Why is everyone freaking out?" Mike asks.

"Nikki maybe you should give someone else a turn to drive," Allison says, panting heavily in fear.

"Why? I'm totally in control here." *What a bunch of freaking babies.*

I still have to face my parents.

PAUL

At the next rest stop in some tiny little burg I jump from the car and dash into the bathroom. I hover over the grimy toilet thinking I'm going to heave up my guts. I've just had an out of body experience courtesy of the psychopath in the seat next to me. Nikki is the absolute worst driver in the universe. First of all, who decides to pass a huge semi on a two-lane mountain pass? We were within a split second of a highway fatality and she looks at us like we're all a bunch of idiots for screaming. If she hadn't reacted instantaneously, jerking the wheel to the right, we'd all be dead. The worst part is that she sees nothing wrong with her behavior. She acts like we're paranoid just because we don't want to be splattered across the interstate.

The weird thing is that, except for the time she nearly killed me, I actually enjoy hanging out with her. Before the near death experience, we were having this intense conversation about Allison and Fran. Nikki brought up all these interesting things about friendship and love that I'd never thought about before. She's protective of Fran but in a really good way even though right now she's trying not to be jealous of Allison. Which I do think is a little weird but girl friendships are something I don't really understand. Nikki's so smart and fun to talk to. On and off the soccer field she's passionate and intense. She's someone I could actually, possibly, talk to about my dad.

I could never say this to Taylor but Nikki is the star forward of the soccer team. Of course, Taylor sees herself as the best but Nikki is a large-scale planner who sees the field instinctively and has a genuine shot at making the team at UW. Taylor's cut out for sorority life and hunting rich boys. Nikki will become an activist or run some weird little company that makes something nobody knows they need until she opens her mouth and starts talking. That is, if she doesn't end up smeared all over a highway.

I'm washing my face in the men's room when I overhear Fran fighting with Nikki in the girls' bathroom. The bathroom situation is weird, with the dividing wall between the men's and women's bathrooms not reaching the ceiling leaving an eight-inch gap. Whoever designed the building had some serious issues. Even though I know I'm not supposed to eavesdrop, I can't help it. Mike comes out of the stall and we stand there in the dingy bathroom listening, studying the graffiti telling us who is a whore, who sells drugs, and who to call for, oddly, a really bad time.

Allison is in the mini-mart so of course, the other two girls are talking about her.

"How can you say I'm ignoring you? You were in the front seat trying to get us killed!" Fran says.

"Oh my God. Can you just like, let it go? I knew exactly what I was doing. You are all a bunch of freaking drama queens," Nikki says. "I was just checking to see if could pass and I couldn't. End of story. Stop making into this into some huge dramatic story that you can spread all over school."

"Oh, right because that's so me," Fran spits out.

"You're not exactly acting like yourself you know," says Nikki.

The hand blower comes on and I can't make out what they're saying.

"We shouldn't be doing this," I point out to Mike, who shrugs, saying, "Yeah but whatever."

Neither of us makes a move.

"I'm sick of you pushing me around, telling me what to do!" It's Fran, yelling now.

"Someone has to freaking tell you what to do. If it weren't for me you'd be moping around school with your whole poor me attitude. Did it ever occur to you that other people might have problems too?" Nikki shouts.

"No. It didn't. Because you stopped talking to me!" Fran shouts.

"This is awesome," Mike whispers.

I kind of hate myself because I sort of agree. What is Nikki's problem?

"You stopped listening. The second Allison showed up

I was white noise. And now that she's here you're being a complete and total bitch."

Mike and I stare at one another in shock.

"Whoa," Mike whispers. "Harsh."

I nod in agreement. I have that prickly feeling I get when I'm doing something I know I shouldn't be doing. Like taking the Taurus and skipping out on my team and coach just because I just don't want to face my dad. And yes, this bathroom is pretty disgusting and smells like urine mixed with Pine-Sol and gas but I'm not leaving Mike in here. Whatever this is we're in it together, which is really strange. At school, our paths do not intersect. I'm an athlete and he's a stoner. I sit with Taylor at lunch while he's getting stoned in the PE bathrooms, blowing smoke into the vent, skipping 5th to get munchies at 7-Eleven. Yet here we are in some random southern Oregon truck stop eavesdropping on two girls from home.

"Screw you Nikki. You know what this is? You're jealous."

"Oh right! You think I want to be, like prom queen? Are you out of your freaking mind? Why in the hell would I want that?"

"Oh no. *That* is not what I meant. You don't want to be prom queen, you want to be Taylor."

What? How in the hell does Taylor figure in this whole bizarre scenario?

There is a long silence during which Mike points out that we'd better split if we don't want them to know that we've been eavesdropping.

"Well at least Paul isn't like, getting stoned and throwing food at me," Nikki says.

"Quit criticizing Allison!"

Mike drags me out of the bathroom into the simmering heat. I can't help looking back at the bathroom wondering why in the hell Nikki would want to be Taylor. They are on complete and total opposites sides of the girl ecosystem. It's like a racehorse wanting to be a fish.

As Mike and I stroll out onto the blacktop, trying to look casual, it occurs to me that until Taylor's name came up a few moments ago, I hadn't thought about her once since we left Washington State.

FRAN

Miles ago, as Allison wondered aloud about how exactly cows falls in love, I fell asleep. When I open my eyes, I have to squint to bring Mt. Shasta into view. It hangs like a Japanese floating print in the sky. We pass a sign with the map of Oregon thanking us for visiting. My head throbs so I fumble for my purse, dig out three more Ibuprofen and gulp them down with bottled water, turning my head to hide from Allison. Maybe they'll quiet the high buzzing and dull ache in my brain. Allison's head rests light on the cello poking over the seat. The next sign is a peacock blue sign with three orange poppies welcoming us to California: Siskiyou County line.

"Can we stop?" I ask Nikki even though we haven't spoken for miles.

"No!" Mike and Paul snap like twin cranks. This rabid non-stopping must be a genetic trait for furthering the species. Sightseers got stomped by mastodons.

Nikki whips the car into the roadside gravel, parking

in front of the sign. A dusty stand of Ponderosa pine slopes away from the freeway.

"We don't have time," says Paul, jerking violently forwards. "This is a terrible place to stop we could get-"

Nikki hops out of the car, sprints to the sign, posing like Vanna White turning letters. Paul turns to me but I've already loaded my new camera with fresh film. The sharp chemical smell ignites a spark of happiness. I'd never even held a camera until I took photography freshman year. The first time I held a lens up to my eye it's like the whole world made sense. I'm outside before Paul can argue. Allison follows me, stretching like a cat. Something dusty and green, maybe sage, mingles with the tang of tar and hot asphalt.

Paul rolls his window down, yelling at me as I squint through the lens, focusing. "We don't have time for this!"

Nikki tilts her head, beckoning with a crooked finger. "Hop out people. Fran's never even been out of like, Washington State. One freaking picture." She waves her hands. "Both of you! *Vamanos!*"

Allison turns to me. A warm pine-scented wind blows our hair. "You've never been out of state?"

"It's not a bad thing," Nikki snaps. "She's totally got loads of time to travel."

Allison shakes her head. "I never said it was a bad thing."

Nikki rolls her eyes. "Right."

Mike gives in, exiting the car with his hair mashed in a hundred different directions. "Nice effing camera lady."

Nikki swipes the neon orange crust of Cheeto dust from Mike's cheek. With a groan, Paul slams the car door, pointing at the sun. "I'm telling you guys, look at the sun. It's two o'clock. We still have 338 miles. That's over five hours of driving ahead of us. We're going to be late for the concert."

"Only a freaking Boy Scout would know that stuff," Nikki says with a smirk. "Are you like an Eagle Scout?"

"Maybe." He shades his eyes with his hand. "Don't look at the sun."

Allison stands back, unsure if she belongs in the photo. My hair blows around the lens making it tough to focus. Nikki stretches, admiring the view of Mt. Shasta off in the distance and the craggy hills covered in pines, subtly shifting until she's beside Paul. Mike beckons to Allison, throwing an arm around her.

This is the picture I snap: both girls bookend the boys. Paul points at the sun, squinting as he throws a casual arm around Nikki and Mike. Nikki grins, thrilled to have his arm hooked over her shoulder, unworried, for the moment, about whatever is eating at her. Allison is to the far right, under Mike's arm, looking directly at me behind her wire-rimmed Lenin sunglasses. Mike gazes sleepily over his sunglasses, loose-limbed with sloppy elegance. Click.

God I love that sound and the feeling of capturing a fleeting moment.

"Thanks you guys!" I clip on the lens cap.

Nikki makes a move for the car keys but Paul tosses them to me. "Your turn."

"What?" I hold the keys like a dead mouse. A tingle of fear and excitement creeps up my spine. How can I get Allison to sit next to me?

"You don't drive?" Paul asks.

Nikki bumps me with her hip, trying a little too hard to be buddy buddy. "She totally does. I taught her."

"That's not very reassuring but okay. You girls sit in the front," Paul says, talking to Allison and me. "Mike and I will sit in the back and tell you how to do everything better."

"Well thank God. Otherwise we couldn't find our way out of a paper bag," Nikki says as she beats out Allison with a mad dash to the car. She slides into the front seat making a not so subtle joke out of it with her clownish steps.

Allison joins me a few feet from the car. "Well, that just happened. She's acting really weird. Very possessive."

"We had a huge fight in the bathroom."

"I'm sorry I'm causing problems for you."

I study her over the top of my sunglasses. "Don't be. That's Nikki's problem. She's actually jealous. She has a thing for Paul. More than a thing. An obsession really."

"Well that's rough."

"Yeah. So go easy on her."

"So, you're happy I showed up?"

I burst out. "Are you kidding me? Totally."

She tilts her head. "Because you were acting kind of irritated."

"Noooooo." *I wasn't irritated I was furious that you were stoned.* But I'm not going to say that because I don't want to ruin the moment. "I want you here more than I want to see Nirvana."

She lowers her sunglasses to gaze at me. "Wow." I can't

tell if it's "Wow, I'm happy" or "Wow, you're freaking me out." Are all relationships a mix of bliss and paranoia, birthday cake and poison? We have one of those long moments where the world disappears. I want to kiss her more than I want to breathe.

She removes her sunglasses and throws an arm out to encompass the arid red hills, peppered with scrubby pines, flowering bushes and bursts of spindly orange poppies. "Well, welcome to sunny California, where meeting a rock star can actually happen."

The question is will it happen to me?

NIKKI

I got the front seat. Uh huh. Yes, it was a dick move but I don't freaking care. I just felt so excluded while they stood there off in their own little world, making zero effort to include me. They huddled in a very relationshippy way, all serious and dealing with issues. For a while there, not that I was obsessively looking, they were glaring at each other like they were mad. Maybe Fran is seeing that Little Miss Sophisticated is just a normal slob who drags her cello on road trips, gets stoned and thinks she can talk to cows. I hope so because Fran and I seriously need to have some fun. If Paul weren't so freaking judgy I would totally be getting stoned. I bet it would make me an even better driver.

My immediate worry is Fran's driving skills. What neither of us mentioned is that it's been two years since those driving lessons. Paul would totally lose his shit if he knew that Fran like, never drives. This car is such a piece of junk who really cares, right? Nor do we mention that Fran stopped driving after she accidentally reversed into a huge truck in a parking lot. The guy was a hunter with a dead deer strapped to the top, with glassy eyes that seemed to be staring right at us. It was horrible. I had to do all the talking because Fran took one look at the poor deer and started crying. Luckily the guy mistook her sadness for remorse. Anyway, she's not nearly as good as I am.

I've decided to make the most of the rift between Fran and Allison by being patient, which is not normally my strong suit. I don't say a thing while she takes for freaking ever to adjust the mirrors. Rome was conquered faster than this. Seriously. I am dying. To my credit, no one can tell.

"Okay, almost ready." Fran is as dead serious as a NASA pilot. I know she's freaking out so I give her my best Girl scout smile. "No problem. Take your time."

Mike and Paul exchange a look of male bonding and raised eyebrows. It says yes, girls take freaking forever at pretty much everything. Since my new attitude doesn't include them, I flip them off. Mike pretends to catch the gesture and throw it back, which I have to admit is kind of funny. Mike is like 80% asshole and 20% sweet. Compared to most guys his age, it's like, a pretty decent ratio. Bonus points: he never talks about college.

"How often do you drive?" Paul asks, getting suspicious.

"All the time. Constantly. She drives a ton." I answer before Fran has time to nervously blurt out the truth.

Allison gives me a weird look which I counter with a gigantic, beaming smile. She fake grins back creating this continuous ebb and flow of dishonesty which suits me fine. Unlike most people, I love playing games. I always win. She might be wildly attractive but I've known Fran since our tetherball days.

"Watch out for the semis," Mike says as another one rumbles past.

"Thanks Mike," Allison smirks, "I bet her plan was to hit one."

"Don't assume the engine has guts," Paul says. "It has four very old, tired cylinders."

"I thought you were kidding about the male cliché stuff," I say.

"Well," Paul leans over the front seat, "You did teach her how to drive."

Ha freaking ha. I have this flash forward of living at home next year, begging to borrow the car, working some shitty job. How bad is it that in my mind it was okay for Fran but not for me?

Fran waits for a break in traffic, pushing down the gas pedal until it hits the floorboards. A semi appears out of nowhere, thundering in the next lane. Mt. Shasta floats ahead while she gains speed. A big smile spreads across her face. I'm so happy for her. She deserves this trip. Not only that, she deserves it to be perfect.

I turn on the radio and punch the buttons until miraculously, I find "Come As You Are."

All five of us nod our heads to the beat, pushing the hair from our eyes as a fragrant green wind dances through the car. There's something magical about sitting in the front seat with my best friend on a road trip listening to her favorite band. When she first discovered Nirvana freshman year she came over to my house and totally made me listen to Bleach twenty times in a row. I'd never seen her so obsessed. Something in their music spoke to her in a way that I'll never understand. Mom said it's because Fran desperately needed a place to escape. Nirvana came around at the right time. So, I shut up and let her play as much Nirvana as I could possibly take. Then, like now, I'm happy for her. I roll down the window, let the wind whip my hair. For a moment we're all rock stars, singing along, chasing love and adventure and most of all, chasing Nirvana.

Before we reach Redding, Fran pulls into a rest stop off the highway. While Allison buys a Snapple from a vending machine, Fran and I stay in the car. She drums her fingers on the steering wheel. The silence is totally awkward.

"Allison is nice," I say.

Fran rolls her eyes. "You hate her." The car rocks as a semi pulls into the rest stop behind us.

I shrug. "I don't know her."

She levels her eyes at me. "Stop it."

I twist my lips, trying to hold back the truth. "I'm not a fan."

"Then why did you just say she was nice?"

"Because I am trying to freaking mend fences."

She rolls her eyes. "By lying? What is your problem anyway?"

Where to begin? The top of the heap is that little thing called my future. Because I was so cocky about getting into UW I lied and said I'd applied to four other places.

The second problem is Paul, who is legally blind to my many charms. He prefers his women tiny and mean with bleached teeth that could light up a stadium. Also, my best friend is fawning over a girl who is difficult and who is ruining our once in a lifetime road trip. Finally, if my dad finds out that I borrowed his credit card he's going to go ballistic and totally send out a hit team to help the sniper he hired when he checked my dorm assignment at UW. He's probably issuing instructions right now on how to scatter the body parts. "My problem is that you aren't having enough fun."

"And you're going to fix that how?"

"I'm going to fix things with you and Allison."

Fran's lip goes up into what might be a snarl. "The girl you hate?"

"Hate is a very strong word. If you want to get involved with an emotionally manipulative person who sends you mixed signals to feed her own ego, she's your girl."

"Wow. You got all this from spending three hours in a car with her?"

"I can read people. You should know that about me. Remember when I said Mrs. Crespy was going through a divorce?"

"That has nothing to do with-"

At that moment, we both notice the shadow of someone standing by the open back window. Holy mother of God, it's Allison. The shit storm of problems just turned into a category 5 freaking hurricane. My heart thumps out of my chest. How much did she hear? At what point did she creep up on this oh so private conversation? While she climbs into the backseat I try to catch Fran's eye but she won't look at me. Her hand is clasped over her eye, her forehead resting on the steering wheel.

"Great Nik. Way to go," Fran mutters.

"I didn't like, mean it. I wasn't-"

"Oh just shut up." She turns back to glance back at Allison, who meets her gaze with fury before slamming the door shut so hard the car shakes.

"You two didn't waste any time slicing and dicing, did you?" Her voice could cut steel.

I have to admire how she's handling this. The girl has balls. "Um, I'm sorry." It sounds much lamer coming out that it did in my head.

Allison gives me a tight, angry grin. "Fuck you and the horse you rode in on."

What? What happened to little Miss AP? "Very mature," I snap, despite myself.

Allison thumps her chest. "Look, Fran invited me on this trip. So, you'd better learn to make the best of it because I'm not going anywhere."

"I said I'm sorry," jumps out of my mouth.

Allison rolls her eyes. "You really don't know when to shut up do you?"

My head snaps back, blinking. This happens to me— never. Nobody stands up to me, ever. "I deserved that."

Allison nods. "Back the hell off."

Fran is smirking which pisses me off but I still scramble for a way to make this okay. "Would you like to sit in the front?"

Paul and Mike climb into the backseat. "I would

rather pour molten lava into my eyes than sit with either one of you."

So much for mending fences.

Mike lights up as if he's just entered a party. "Holy shit. What did I miss?"

PAUL

I'm not exactly up on what happened during the last stop but Mike is the only one talking. Except it's not really talking. It's more like a filibuster. He rambles on and on and on about whatever pops into his hollow head. His brain is a nuclear dump site of pop trivia, celebrity gossip and arcane random junk thrown in because, well, God knows why. The guy just blabs. I thought people were supposed to get silent and paranoid when they smoked weed. Not Mike.

I now know that Prince employs a full-time tailor, that there is a monkey small enough to fit in a tea cup, that corpses, when left in the ground can host over seven billion microbes that assist in decomposition. I know details about the Secret Service that I have to admit are kind of interesting, like how they have emergency plans for when the president decides to pop into 7-Eleven for a Slurpee or go skeet shooting. I keep waiting for Nikki to make a crack about how he's planning an assassination attempt but she's staring out the window as if we left her puppy at the last gas station.

Nikki must have done something wrong because finally she turns around to talk to Allison is a surprisingly somber way. "That was impressive, you know? The way you like, stuck up for yourself."

"Screw you," Allison snaps. Mike's eyes go super wide as he does a double take at his seat mate. "I'm not done being mad at you."

"Will you tell me when you're done?"

Allison just sighs. Fran glances in the rear-view mirror but Allison won't look at her. "Give it a rest Nik."

Nikki rolls her eyes. "What? I barely said anything."

Allison snorts. "Hmmmm. I'm emotionally manipulative to build my own ego?"

"I didn't mean it like *that.*"

I have to laugh. Nikki has a mouth on her but she's all heart. "Go ahead, I'm waiting to see how you're going to get out of this one."

Nikki squirms in her seat, panicked. "Oh my God!" She moans. "When are we freaking going to get there?"

CHAPTER TWELVE

"If my eyes could show my soul, everyone
would cry when they saw me smile."
Kurt Cobain

FRAN

I miss High Allison because at least she talked to me. Miles roll past and her silence smothers me. I don't know much about relationships but I'm pretty sure they can't hinge on one person always being stoned. I take a deep breath. There's never going to be the perfect moment so I might as well go for it. I touch her arm. "Hey, are you okay?"

She turns to me with resigned, sad eyes. "My mom stopped by Monica's house to drop off my contact solution and ran into Monica's grandma."

"Oh no."

"Oh yes." She glances around the car at everyone who is pretending not to listen. Paul might be faking sleep but probably not because he's snoring away in the front seat, which he chose to keep a close eye on Nikki's driving.

They're all deathly still, trying to eavesdrop over the rattle of the car.

"Yeah, so the grandma didn't know anything about me sleeping over. I'm sure they were both freaking out, flapping their arms and chattering away in Japanese about the lousy, ungrateful Nisei."

"I'm sorry." *Nisei? Do they make cars?*

"Wait, it gets worse. My mom jumps on her broom, heads over to school, yanks Monica out of class and gives her the third degree. Monica was no doubt thrilled I was in trouble and blabbed everything to the entire school. Now my dad is trying to talk Mom out of flying down to San Francisco and bringing me home. She has major control issues."

I know she won't want to hear this but what the hell. "Or just maybe she loves you."

She shakes a finger. "You know that time we were talking in the church parking lot and she drove off? She wanted to know why I was talking to you."

"What did you tell her?"

"That you were having gay urges and I was trying to talk you out of them."

"Gay urges?" I don't know whether to laugh or cry. So, I laugh.

"It's not funny. She wants to know where I am every second of the day. I end up saying the stupidest stuff just so she'll leave me alone. I cannot breathe in that house."

I lower my sunglasses, peering over them like a TV shrink. "Young lady, explain to me these gay urges. Are you having these urges yourself?"

"No!" She looks around frantically as though the gay

police will jump out and arrest her. "Why can't she just let me go for twenty-four measly hours?"

"Because you'll join a gay cult and eat gay food and smoke gay dope. Oh wait, you already did that."

Mike snickers, then claps a hand over his mouth, pointing out the window. "Funny cow."

Allison glares at the back of Mike's head before turning to me. "You're not taking this seriously."

"You're right. Do you really think your mother is going to waste hundreds of dollars just to get you back to Aberdeen a half day sooner or maybe even later?" I have no idea how much plane tickets cost but I know they're not cheap.

She grabs a bag of candy, un-wrapping a watermelon Laffy Taffy. Her teeth turn bright pink. "You have no idea. She is Asian, she is tiny and she is her own weather system. When it comes to wrecking my life, money is no object."

As expansive suburbia gives way to the outskirts of Oakland, Mike digs in his jeans, handing each of us two elegantly rolled white joints with a flourish. Allison takes hers without question, sniffing it like a seasoned pothead, which freaks me out. "We'll smoke one in the parking lot and one in the arena."

Paul leans over the seat to hand his back. "No thanks dude. We're gonna need our heads clear for this scene."

"Dude, have you ever been to a concert?" asks Mike.

"Yes." Paul crossed his arms, defensive.

"What kind?"

Paul frowns, muttering. "Beloved Son."

"Christian rock concerts do not count."

"They can get pretty wild," Paul counters.

Mike lights up his joint and also, Allison's, which pisses me off. She won't look at me.

"Some dude speaking in tongues is not the same thing. I'm talking girls showing their tits and people puking," says Mike.

"I'll take the first thing," Allison laughs. There is a shocked swiveling of heads. She exhales. "What? You'd all agree, right? Boobs are better than puke."

I'm dying to ask her if this is her coming out party or if she's going to flirt and tease until I'm a sad little pile of ashes. I read once that gay men have their ears pierced on the left-hand side. What do lesbians do?

Paul studies Nikki, checking her reaction to the gift.

"What?"

"Nothing," Paul says. "I just-"

"Just like, what?"

He sighs. "I'm not going to go into all the 'Just Say No' details but-"

"But you're freaking dying to!"

He shakes his head, frustrated. "Never mind."

She smoothes her hands on her bare legs, a gesture he follows with appreciation, finding it hard to focus. "I'm sorry. Go ahead."

He shakes his head as though to clear it. "Did you just say you were sorry?" She glares. "Okay, I just think that since we're athletes, we have to be held to different standards."

Mike, holding in smoke, releases it into the front seat. "Fucking A, you totally do."

Paul grimaces. "Thank you Mike."

Allison grins. "Advise from the peanut gallery."

"And the football team like, blowing chunks every weekend after a kegger?" Nikki asks.

Paul nods again, paying attention to the road. "Yeah, yeah, I know. But maybe the football team isn't the best resource for life lessons. Anyway, you don't smoke, do you?"

"Um, no," she lies. I know she's tried it. She regretfully hands hers back to Mike, shoving another red straw between her teeth. "Thank you for the kind offer."

I pocket both mine, wondering if smoking pot will help my headache. "Thank you."

Nikki gnaws on her straw, unfolding a map. She shows Paul the best route to the Cow Palace through San Francisco following I-5 until it turns into I-80. Somewhere along the way she has to find highway101. I gaze out the window at a cluster of oak trees on a parched brown hill, wondering what Allison thinks of me and tallying all the possible signs of her being gay. The best sign would be if she just kissed me but then again when is she supposed to do that in a car full of people? My second biggest worry is how, exactly, I'm supposed to get past security to talk to Kurt Cobain.

A few miles down the road I put a hand on Allison's arm. "Don't worry about your mom. She'll calm down."

Without looking, she withdraws her arm. "No, she

won't." I shrivel like a worm. What I am learning about relationships is enough to make me long for the days when a crush was someone you hit on the playground. Is she mad about the mother situation? Is she mad at all? Does she want to stab me with a plastic fork leftover from that disgusting microwave burrito thing she bought? Does being in love mean asking yourself a series of gut-wrenching questions to which there will never be an answer?

A half hour later we're deep in Oakland on the freeway in front of the flashing red and blue lights of a California highway patrolman. Everyone in the car is in complete panic mode.

"Hide the fucking weed!" Mike screams.

CHAPTER THIRTEEN

"It's better to burn out than fade away."
Kurt Cobain

PAUL

"There isn't any place to pull over," Nikki says in wide-eyed panic, glancing at the flashing lights in the rearview mirror.

My full ride athletic scholarship to UW flashes before my eyes. "This piece of paper is worth more than I make in five years," my mom had said, waving the official offer like it was magical, which, honestly, it kind of was. Two weeks ago, I went to a signing ceremony at Hec Edmundson Pavilion where we received a lecture on the responsibilities and privileges of college athletes. "No flunking, no late night keggers, no drugs, no underage girls. Don't think you won't be one of those kids who gets their scholarship yanked. It happens all the damn time."

My dad'd be the first to tell me that lack of a fancy degree didn't hurt him none.

This can't happen.

Normally I am that guy who stays calm while everyone else freaks out. Normally I'm not a guy driving a car that may very well have been reported stolen, loaded with God knows how much weed. For all I know Mike could have a duffel bag full of the stuff courtesy of his brother the dealer, whose customers are at least half the high school. If I opened my mouth now, I'd scream like a girl. Luckily Nikki is the one who squeals, coughing as the red straw she's gnawing slips down her throat. She's right. This stretch of highway was made for half as many cars. A freeway project with trucks and construction equipment jams up an entire closed lane. Nikki is a terrible driver to begin with, let alone with a motorcycle CHP flashing his lights.

I lean over, taking the straw from her mouth. "It's okay. Just turn on the turn indicator to let him know you're exiting. He'll follow."

Nikki's hands shake so I bend forward. "It's okay Nik, we're fine."

She grabs another red straw from her pocket, shaking her head. "No, we're not. I stole my dad's credit card. How many lectures has he given me about honesty and integrity? Like a trillion or something. He's so pissed off we're probably all going to jail. I will never live this down. He'll lecture me until one of us freaking dies. He'll send me to juvie." She gasps as a more horrifying though occurs. "Or like community service. I'll have to wear one of those orange vests."

I don't know her dad but I've seen him around the soccer field. He doesn't seem like the vengeful type. He strikes me as the normal, upstanding kind of dad every kid wants.

"Great, now we're all going to jail. Maybe my mom will be here in time to bail me out." Allison sighs, sliding her two joints into her bra.

"Dude. We're not going to jail," Mike says in a monotone. I don't know how much weed he's smoked but I'm pretty sure it could fell a rhino.

"We're in a stolen car with a stolen credit card with a dude in a drug rug who smells like a walking bong." Allison gestures at Mike, who slowly lowers his sunglasses, exposing pinkish glazed slits.

"Be that as it may—exhibit A." Mike smoothes a hand over his freckled skin. "We're white." He repeats the gesture with the other arm. "Exhibit B. We're from the Washington coast. Ergo, we're very white."

"Speak for yourself asshole," Allison snaps.

Luckily everyone's too distracted to erupt into a racial conflagration. Nikki takes an exit onto Heggenberger road, which is packed with traffic. We end up in a left only lane with the police motorcycle lights still flashing, tailing us like a bad dream.

"There's a gas station," I say. "Go there," which is exactly where the cop is signaling with his leather gloved hand. The gas station and what I've seen of Oakland is pretty brutal. There are graffiti tags on the crumbling brick walls, garbage littering the street, bars on the windows of run-down businesses.

"I. Am. Like. So. Freaking. Dead." Nikki nearly digests the red straw.

Allison mutters in a mixture of Japanese and English.

"I'm going to be a fucking doctor," is the only thing that makes any sense to me.

"A doctor? No shit?" Mike says, lifting his bare foot. "Can you look at this thing on my toe? The nail is all funky." She slaps his foot down, giving him an evil glare.

My experience with hysterical girls is limited to Taylor and her constant feuds with her so-called friends but if I don't calm Nikki down the officer is going to notice her gnawing on a straw like it's a carrot and search our car. "Your dad wouldn't have the license number. He doesn't know whose car we took. That can't be it." We pull into the Chevron station.

"Are you not listening? That Monica chick is blabbing all over school. My dad is like, an attorney. His job is digging up shit on people and totally using it against them. We're fucked!"

"You swear too much." The minute it comes out of my mouth, I know it's a mistake.

She looks over at me with eyes so huge they are going to pop out of her head. "Fuck!"

"Okay. Okay. I get it. Not the time. We'll talk later." To avoid those freaky eyes, I dump the contents of the glove box onto the floor. It's a sad and embarrassing exhibit of my mom's life: unpaid parking tickets, second notice bills, a plastic rosary, a full box of mashed Kleenex, a cheap comb, some off brand granola bars, a badly laminated ancient Sears photo of me and my brother in matching overalls and finally, a wadded-up ball of paper that must be the vehicle registration.

Nikki's hands shake as the officer gets off his motorcycle. He approaches her window. He's so out of shape; he's got man boobs.

He takes off his mirrored shades. It's a woman with red hair, eyebrows and squinty blue eyes mashed into a white helmet. "Registration and license please."

Nikki hands over her license with trembling hands. I reach over her, handing the registration paper which I've done my best to smooth out. "This is my mother's car. Would you like to see my ID ma'am?" Nikki might think I'm too clean cut but this Eagle-Scouting, church-going, all American boy is so going to save her wise-cracking butt. Yes ma'am, no sir might not work every time but it doesn't hurt.

After the cop studies the paperwork, she bends over to get a good look. Mike, with his usual lack of, well, everything, gives her a ridiculous two-fingered mock salute, gazing at her over the top of his stupid white sunglasses he picked up at our last stop thinking he could pull off Kurt Cobain's look. But he just looks fried. Any moment he's going to slither off the seats.

"Hey there pretty lady!" Mike says. She gives him a long, withering look. Her uniform buttons glint as she pivots, walking back to her motorcycle to talk on her radio.

"Hey there pretty lady?" Fran sneers. "Did you think she was a hooker?"

Mike grimaces, clenching his fists. "Oh my God! She would make a hot hooker! So fine! Can't you just see it?"

"I can see us going to jail." Allison mutters from behind her hand, talking to Mike. "I really cannot believe how stupid you are. I've never seen anything like it."

"Thank you," Mike says. "One must do what one does well."

Nikki is about ready to launch into the back seat, muttering under her breath. "I am going to kill him. I am going to freaking kill him..."

I put my hand on Nikki's shoulder. "Hold that thought," I say before asking Mike in my calmest, hostage-situation voice, "What did you do with the weed?"

"Most of it's in my tighty whiteys." Mike giggles. "I sorta hope she takes a peek."

"Mine's in the seat crack-" Fran stops talking because the cop is approaching. What if she finds the box of mini-bongs? Why didn't I make Mike dump all that stuff? Oh wait, because I was pretending to be cool.

The cop leans down to peer at Nikki, whose face goes into rigor mortis. I willfully make myself calm as the cop says, "Do you kids know why I pulled you over?"

"N-n-n-n-no." Nikki's teeth chatter.

"You've got expired tabs."

Mike leans over from the backseat. "They're Washington tabs." He jerks his thumb at me. "His mom can pay them when we get back home, right?"

The officer nods. "Yes." She studies Nikki's shaking knees for too long. "Everything okay in here?"

Nikki nods. "Ye-ye-yes."

The officer glances at the girls in the back of the car. "You girls have anything you want to say to me?"

"Um, thank you?" Fran says.

The officer laughs. "Uh, you're still getting a ticket. I meant are you girls okay? Your friend here seems like she could use a break from driving."

Allison leans forward in her seat, flashing a pristine

smile. "Thanks, really. She's just one of those nervous types, you know?"

Nikki glares at Allison via the rear-view mirror.

The officer grins. "Oh I know the type." She slaps the roof of the car, making Nikki jump, which elicits a snort. "They've usually done something wrong." She writes in her little book. "Look kid, I'm going to write you a citation for expired tabs. You'll have to leave the vehicle until the tabs are paid up."

I reassure Nikki, hoping she won't haul off and punch Allison. "Don't worry I'll pay it." Then to the officer, "I don't understand. We're from Washington so how're we supposed to get home?"

The officer scribbles, walking around to copy the license plate. "Not my problem kid. Greyhound?"

"Hang on!" I'm about to get out of the car to talk to her but she says, "Whoa, whoa. Settle down now." I lean back in the passenger seat, bending over Nikki. "We just leave the car in Oakland to get stripped for parts or stolen?"

She shakes her head, ripping off the pink citation, handing it to Nikki. "You can't drive a car with expired tabs. That's the law."

I shake my head. "Yeah but we don't have another car. And we sure don't have the money for my mom to fly down here. Can't we just drive it home?"

The officer pulls on her shades. "You've got an awful lot of questions. Do you want me to impound this vehicle? That will keep it safe but your mom will have to pay the towing fee."

Mike pipes up from the back seat, pointing at Fran.

"Have you ever heard of the Make-A-Wish Foundation because this girl is dying and her very last wish is to see a Nirvana concert."

"Shut up man," I say, swiping at Mike's knee. I bend over Nikki. "Look, my mom lent us this car not knowing that the tabs were expired. She's a single mom raising two kids and she just doesn't have that kind of money."

"Then she shouldn't be lending out her car. Don't make me impound this car son."

"I'm not your son," I snap, immediately regretting it.

The glasses come off as she pokes her head into the window until I can see the beads of sweat on her nose. She studies us as if she's seen one too many idiot-stuffed automobiles today. "Okay, you follow me back to the station. I'm going ahead of you, right under that I-80 underpass. If your girlfriend gets back on that freeway, you're taking your chances with the law, *son*." She turns on her heels, mounts her motorcycle and starts it.

"What a total bitch," Nikki says, turning the ignition.

"I know, right?" Allison says.

"I was talking about you," Nikki snaps.

As we slowly follow the cop down the street Nikki gets to a stop light on Heggenberger road with a big green sign for I-80 into San Francisco. We're supposed to go north, which will take us back home. As Taylor points out regularly, I'm not a guy who reads people well unless we're on a soccer field. But this time the silence in the car reads crystal clear. Everyone wants to head south, towards the 101 into Daly City and the concert. We've been arguing about it nonstop. I don't want to get my mom's car impounded but I sure as hell don't want to go home and deal with my dad.

"If we get stopped the cop will ask for a toke," Mike says. "It's Californication man. People here smoke weed like we drink beer."

Californication? I'm not even going to ask. "We're underage. Do you know how many guys would love to see me get busted for pot so they can have my spot at UW?"

"Oh my God, you seriously think the whole world is connected and big brother has his eye on you?" Mike argues as the light changes.

Allison hunches down, studying the cop. "Why is she having us follow her instead of the other way around?"

No one answers.

This is a disaster.

"I really don't care. I'll go to another Nirvana concert," says Fran, who looks a little strange, pale and flushed at the same time.

Allison shakes her head.

"Go left!" Mike yells as Nikki follows the motorcycle through traffic under the freeway overpass.

"It's too late!" Nikki says. "We should just drive home."

Why do I always have to be the voice of reason? Why do jackasses have all the fun? "We should follow the officer."

"Left! Stop now! South bound!" Mike screams.

"Do it Nikki!" Allison shouts. Great, the only other AP nerd in the car is now officially AWOL.

The nice thing about heading south would be avoiding endless hours on a Greyhound bus spent wondering if my dad was still hanging around. And that's a best-case scenario. How do I tell my mom that her car is in California? She won't yell. She'll cry. God what if my dad used it to sneak back into her life with some lame thing about boys needing a man?

There are two lanes of traffic behind us. We block the middle lane leading straight and turning to the right to northbound I-80. "We're going to miss the concert if you don't head south!" screams Mike.

"I can't do this," Nikki says as we block all the congested traffic. The drivers furiously honk in a demented symphony that echoes under the freeway. A homeless man, his belongings piled high, puts both hands over his ears. Nikki won't budge. "I already stole my dad's credit card. I'm not making the call on this one. If this car gets, like impounded I will not-"

My head feels like it's going to explode. There's no accounting or thinking happening, just words. I cover my eyes. "Turn left."

Through my sweaty fingers, I see Nikki's face brighten. She glances behind her, sticking her head out the window, edging left into a solid lane of traffic. "Hell to the yes."

Mike hangs out the rear window, gesticulating wildly, convincing angry drivers to let us into their lanes. Nikki ignores the furious honking, slowly edging her way into the left turn lane. I can't watch as she plows directly in front of a Toyota that doesn't want to let us in, grazing the other car.

"My mom's car," I moan.

"It's fine," Nikki says breezily. "It'll blend into all the other dents, right?"

The driver, now behind us, lays on his horn, rolling down his window, screaming his head off in an unknown language.

"Dude, thank you!" Mike says, happily waving his fingers in dual peace signs. "We're going to a Nirvana concert!"

"Fuck you asshole!" screams another driver as Nikki cuts him off.

Mike ducks his head back into the car. "Man! People in Oakland are uptight."

The left turn light goes yellow just as we reach the front of the line. Nikki guns it, turning into oncoming traffic. The Taurus has nothing to give. A Krispy Kreme van barrels towards us, ready to plow into our side. We all scream hysterically as Nikki coolly drives.

"We're going to die!" hollers Mike. The van's engine is about ready to smash into my face as Mike wails, "Krispy fucking Kreme!"

Nikki must have a guardian angel somewhere because we should be dead. Through some combination of sheer luck and random near misses, we escape being hit. As we chug up the on-ramp onto the freeway no one seems to believe it. We're surrounded by cars, staring at the wide-open expanse of the Bay Bridge, spreading gracefully across the water in the pink sky. In seconds, we went from near death to stunning beauty. I'm not sure which one is making my heart jump around.

Oddly enough, I'm very happy to be next to my own personal would-be angel of death. Nikki makes one really foul-mouthed angel. I'm never sure what she's thinking but it's always interesting. Everything about her and this trip gets more complicated and dangerous by the second. The only thing that I'm one hundred percent sure of is that I'm no longer just running from my father. I'm now officially running from the law.

CHAPTER FOURTEEN

"I'm not gay, although I wish I were,
just to piss off all the homophobes."
Kurt Cobain

NIKKI

"You are not smoking pot in this car!" The smell of pot gets Paul's attention. It's weird because even though he's the one that made the call to head south, he's the most stressed out. It's really hard for him to do the wrong thing. I, on the other hand, seem to excel at it.

Mike holds the joint across the seat, speaking with a lungful of pot he's holding in. "Chillax. Take a hit."

Paul tries to grab it and throw it out the window but Mike yanks his arm back, exhaling, blowing the pot into Paul's face. "Ha! Ha!"

I try hard not to laugh as I exit onto the 101. Thank God we're almost there. "He doesn't freaking want to get stoned Mike, he's an athlete." I begin searching the radio stations for a good song.

"Have you ever smoked pot?" Paul asks.

I shove another straw into my mouth, realizing I don't care if Paul thinks it's a weird habit. It calms me down while I think about lying so I don't disappoint him. I keep punching the radio buttons. "Yes. A couple of times."

"A couple of times multiplied by ten," Mike says with another lungful. He giggles. "Times a thousand."

"Shut up Mike," I say.

"It's a gateway drug. Bet she's gonna score some China White at the concert."

"Shut up Mike," Paul says. Unlike Fran, Paul has a chip on his shoulder about being poor. Like one hit of pot will make him hit the streets, like his meth head dad.

"This is Mike, shutting up."

"Yeah like that's going to happen," Allison snorts.

A police siren wails in the distance. Everyone is quiet as the sound comes closer, rising over the traffic noise. No one says a word as cars move to the side to let the police pass. The police come up right behind us, lights flashing blue, red, blue, red, accelerating our heartbeats. I gnaw furiously on my straw like a freaking rabbit, glad that Paul is looking out the window, lost in his own thoughts. I wonder if he ever talks to his dad.

The police car pulls up directly behind us.

Mike moans. "That's a cop, right? Or is it a state patrol? What is the difference? We're going to jail. We're going to be locked up. We'll have to take fucking Greyhound! I get sick on buses!"

I'm in full panic mode, muttering, "What do I do what do I do what do I freaking do?"

After demanding that someone get Mike to shut up, Paul turns down the radio and takes over. "Indicate and move to the exit lane. Not left. Indicate right. We're getting off the freeway."

Miraculously, when I move over, the police car zooms past us down the highway. I'm already on the exit so we have to drive around a funky little neighborhood full of gingerbread houses as I search for the southbound freeway entrance.

As we crest onto the freeway, which is jam packed with cars, Fran says, "Turn it up."

"Smells like Teen Spirit," is on. Fran starts singing along quietly. Allison hums. After a few moments, Paul joins in, smiling at me, which gives me a jolt of what must be joy. Pretty soon we're all humming along, which is totally great and somehow appropriate for this exotic, Oz-like city.

The traffic lightens. We edge our way through the Mission District, although I can't see anything because the freeway is high on an overpass and it's growing dark. Palm trees poke up from the street like prehistoric flowers. We're all quiet, listening to the radio. It's like, peaceful.

"This one goes out to those lucky dogs in the Cow Palace where my man Jeffrey tells me The Breeders just took the stage for the Bosnian Rape Victim Benefit." The gravelly-voiced DJ talks in a low, hypnotic voice. "Next up, L7, Nirvana and Disposable Heroes of Hiphoprisy. Man, it's gonna be an epic thrill folks. I know it's not cool for a DJ to say he likes the obvious choice but here's mine."

"Heart-Shaped Box" fills the car with strumming bass licks. Kurt Cobain growls into the dusky night.

We sing along as the Taurus gamely rattles down the freeway. My butt is numb, I'm sick of driving. But I'm happy. Fran chatters on and on to Allison about the boring technical features of her new light pack and camera. I wonder if Allison understands that owning this camera is the biggest thing that's ever happened to Fran, although from the look on Fran's face, maybe it's now Allison. The car fills with white light as Fran pops off a few test shots. Paul glances in the rear-view mirror. Even though I'm sure he's going to tell Fran to knock it off, he doesn't. He's lost in thought or maybe just reading the signs so we don't miss our exit. Who freaking knows? I'm just enjoying the moment.

FRAN

Forty-five minutes later we're rattling into the parking lot of the Cow Palace as the sky fades into soft pewter. Mrs. Chesley, my English teacher, calls this the gloaming. A madhouse of bikes and pedestrians amble in front of our bug-spattered windshield, talking and laughing.

A band of pain spreads across the back of my lower head. Thinking about holding Allison's hand calms me down. I'm quivering with a potent mix of excitement and pain, hoping no one notices. Kurt Cobain is in that enormous half-dome air hanger of a building. He's inside. There.

The more people who crowd in front of our creeping car, the worse I feel. We're late for the biggest event in my life.

"I can't believe this piece of shit car made it!" Mike yawns, stretching a ripe, hairy pit in front of Allison.

"I can't believe I didn't kill you," Paul mutters as he scans the dusty lot for a parking spot.

"There's this thing called deodorant. Heard of it?"" Allison pushes Mike's arm downward, plugging her nose.

"Why yes I have. I just can't remember to put it on," Mike says, sniffing his pit. "Ripe and ready to pick." As he does this, he looks at me, doing a double take.

"Shit girl, you look like white on snow." This draws Allison's attention. "I mean you look super fine and everything, that's not what I'm saying at all. You just don't look so good. You know?"

"Are you okay?" Allison asks as if she already knows the answer.

I don't want to go backwards into everything that happened with PC. I want to throw myself into this night, this experience. Forward is everything. No looking back. I can taste the grit of Nirvana between my teeth, the way their music flows in my veins at home but more intense. Mike lights up a joint. Without a word, he hands it to me.

"That is the last thing you should be doing," Allison says. Which is exactly what I'm thinking but since she isn't offering any alternative and I'd do anything to get this hammering out of my brain, I take the joint.

I take a hit, avoiding Allison's glare. Paul is too busy helping Nikki find parking to give me a lecture. Miraculously I don't cough. Years of watching stoners in school bathrooms pays off with flawless toking technique. After two hits, the nausea lessens. The pain is numbed, not eliminated, floating somewhere off the coast.

It's easy imagining the parking lot filled with trailers and mooing cows for a rodeo. The Cow Palace is a giant half cylinder that looks like an airplane hangar. It could house a couple 747s being towed by elephants.

Nikki navigates the miles of paved parking lot. It's a madhouse of darting and weaving, tailgate boozing, and pot smoking. Bikes, motorcycles, cars and some weird half truck, half motorcycle machine that belongs in Road Warrior.

Allison's annoyance boils into fury. Before I can take part in a second joint, she snatches it from me. Mike shrugs regretfully, too intimidated by Allison to pass it back.

Paul has Nikki pull up to a parking spot blocked by a tattooed biker. The biker grimaces, exposing a gold tooth. We're driving around a second parking lot when a scrawny shirtless man darts in front of us waving a gun.

"Oh my God!" Nikki slams on the brakes.

The man slaps both hands on our car's hood, scowling into the window. It's not a gun. It's a long skinny silver bong.

Paul leans out of the window. "Excuse me sir, sorry to bother you but do you know where there's any parking spots?"

The man scowls a long time before answering. "There's some over there." He waves to the west before disappearing between the parked cars.

"We should listen to him," says Paul.

"Because he's fried out of his mind and lost?" Nikki asks.

"Because he's obviously been wandering around this place a long time and might know what he's talking about."

A few moments later, we find a parking spot. Nikki takes the straw out of her mouth. "The Boy Scout was right."

"Don't call me that," Paul snaps, jumping out of the car.

Climbing out of the car I catch the distant thrum of loud rock music. I take a deep gulp of the faintly pot-scented night air. The sky fades into indigo. The Cow Palace juts out of the quiet neighborhood like a sleeping giant.

Paul and Allison think we should go straight to the box office to see if we can get our lost tickets.

"I'll be there in a minute. I want to see if there's a way to sneak in backstage," I say.

"I'll go with you," Nikki says. "I love shit like this. We'll sneak past security, hide against the walls. We'll be like Encyclopedia Brown. Girls that bust up gender stereotyping and get rocks stars to play at our prom."

"Yeah, okay why don't you go with Paul?" I say, hoping she'll telepathically understand that I want to be with Allison.

"Oh." She's instantly deflated, looking hurt. "Right."

I feel guilty but not guilty enough to change my mind.

It's a long walk around the side of the Cow Palace. Mike joins us because Paul, (who should embrace his inner Boy Scout,) thought we should have a guy along, even if the guy is a half-baked nincompoop. As we walk, Allison points out that Paul has good intentions but needs education on the effects of marijuana. "It's like sending us with a potted plant for protection."

"I wanna be a blanana plant," Mike says amicably, "Blanana. Blanana." He waggles his sticky tongue. "Bla-Banana. There. I did it." He giggles.

Allison shrugs. "Case in point."

Behind the main theater are a series of smaller halls and a long, narrow fire lane packed with large trucks. There's scarcely a foot of space on either side of the trucks except for the loading docks in the middle. We stand at the entrance of the alley which is blocked by a metal bar posted with No Entrance. A security guard in the alley approaches us.

"You kids scram. The ticket booths are up front."

Mike steps forward, pointing at me. "She has to talk to Kurt Cobain."

The security guard, who has a chipped tooth and a short, sweaty Afro, laughs. "I bet she does."

"Dude, I could lie to you and tell you some made-up BS but what I'm going to tell you is better than that because it's the truth," Mike says.

"Don't waste your time. Anyone bothers those bands it's my job, hombre."

"Listen, you smoke weed?" Mike asks.

"Why you wanna ask me a question like that? I'm working here. Now beat it."

Mike motions for the security guard to follow him. "This girl has a great fucking story and I'm going to tell it to you because we are from the same place Kurt Cobain grew up. We're graduating from the same high school he did and we know a lot of the same people."

"I don't care if you know Shaquille O'Neill, you ain't getting down that alley."

Mike plows on with astounding animation given all the ganja. "This is the craziest story because you see this girl?" For some reason, he points at Allison. "She was nominated for prom queen and that made the parents at the school furious. They were so angry they demanded that the principal eliminate her from the race. Cut her down cold. Forbid her to run. You wanna know why?"

The security guard nods, immersed in the story.

"Because she's Asian." Allison nods in agreement.

"No shit? Where's Kurt Cobain from anyway? Up in Idaho where all those Neo Nazis racist motherfuckers live?"

"Close. Washington State. There are racists everywhere, you know?"

"Mmmm-hmmm," the security guard agrees, mopping his forehead. "True that. They breed like rabbits, ya know."

"So, you want to know what we're going to do?" As he talks Mike slowly rotates, getting the security guard to shift until they are both facing away from the alley. Behind his back, Mike motions for me to run. Allison nods, raises her eyebrows and gives me a thumbs up before pivoting to block the security guard's view down the alley.

Shit. In my head, I saw her coming with me.

I'm doing this alone.

If I stop to think, I'll freak out. Go. Go now. Taking

a deep breath, I duck under the metal bar and dash, hunching awkwardly until I slip into the shadows between the trucks and walls. It's a tight fit. Security lights slant down from above bisecting it into two: white artificial glow, where the roadies work and deep black shadows where the trucks are parked. My heart thumps crazily but surprisingly I'm not scared. Staying in the shadows I creep down the side of the building until I'm behind a truck, sniffing diesel and hot tar. The truck cab blocks my view of the men unloading.

Music from the opening band blasts out of the open bay doors where men shift huge silver boxes with dollies and pallet lifters. Over the buzz of the distant band is the hydraulic hum of machinery. The corrugated siding presses against my back as I try to stay invisible. The looming buildings take up all the sky except for a narrow strip. I wait for fear to arrive but I feel sharp, clear, and more alive than I've ever felt.

Directly across from me is the loading zone and backstage doors. If one of the roadies looks up into the shadows, they'll spot me. I have to take that chance and hope I can sneak inside while they're ferrying equipment. For now, I wait for an opening.

"Damn! That's the wrong fucking one, Harley." A roadie groans as he hoists a speaker the size of a Volkswagen with two other roadies. His gut spills over his rodeo belt and tight black jeans. A brown stream of tobacco squirts from his mouth onto the black tar road.

Harley, a skinny blonde dude with heavily tattooed pipe-cleaner arms holds one corner. "The tape on this one says Nirvana. Read it yourself dude."

Rodeo Belt staggers towards the loading bay. "It ain't

my job to check the bands but this ain't the right size. They're sharing those huge amps they already got set up. Nirvana's got their own soundboard. We'll unload this and you go find the right fucking soundboard."

"The soundboard is inside where you fucking told me to put it," Harley says. "What crawled up your butt this morning? A whole bunch of grouchies?"

Meaty fingers clutch my shoulder as a blast of halitosis hits me hard. "What do you think you're doing?" It's a middle-aged cop with a flushed, serious face. "This is a restricted area. No groupies."

"I'm um... I'm not a groupie."

"Then where's your backstage pass?"

"I don't have one." As we speak a white van pulls up. The doors slide open and the members of Nirvana climb out. Krist Novoselic first, followed by Dave Grohl, and then Kurt Cobain, who wears a blue cardigan, torn jeans and white sunglasses. He's smoking. Less than five feet from where we are standing. Kurt opens the back of van, taking out a battered guitar case with a few peeling stickers. He's so close I could take three steps and touch him. It's like a dream. The cop tightens his grip.

"I brought my own fucking guitar this time Harley!" Kurt yells at the roadie who grins as he flips off Kurt.

Kurt turns to Dave. "That's the thanks I get for not firing his ass? He flips me off."

Dave shrugs. "So, fire his ass. Just tell Arthur you want him out. Boom. Done."

"Naw, I like him. He sucks but I like him."

Dave shakes his head. "You're a shitty businessman, you know that?"

Kurt grins. "Good thing I can play a fucking guitar."

The band climbs the short flight of stairs single file to the loading dock towards the door marked Dressing Rooms, Talent. Seeing them slip away wakes me up. If I don't say something now I've lost my chance.

I twist my shoulder, breaking free of the cop's grip. "Hey!" I yell.

As the other two cross the loading dock, Dave Grohl, who is still on the stairs, glances back. The low sun hits his face full on, blinding him. He heads for the open door. I've got a fraction of a second to run.

As if he can read my mind the cop tugs my arm. "Come on kid, you don't belong here."

If I have to beg, I'll do it. "Please, please, please let me talk to them. I have to ask them something."

As the cop tilts his head, his face softens. "What 'ya gotta ask them?"

"If they'll play at my prom."

The cop pushes me in front of him. "I can answer that one for ya kid. The answer's no. Whatever it is, the answer is no. That's what they pay me for. To tell kids like you no. Now go on and enjoy the concert. And don't keep bothering the band, okay?"

I'm not crushed. I'm floating with happiness. Running down the alley, I join up with Allison and Mike, heading towards the entrance of the Cow Palace. "I could have touched Kurt Cobain. Well, not exactly. I was so close. He's really handsome."

"Was he smoking weed?" Mike asks.

I pause in the swarm of people. "Seriously, I meet Kurt Cobain and that's what you want to know?"

Mike nods. "That's what I want to know."

I shrug. "I don't know. I was trying to figure out how to talk to him with a huge cop hanging onto me. I could have. But I don't feel like I blew it. I mean, we could get in there after the concert. They have to leave, right?"

"You don't think every groupie in the world will be there?" Allison asks.

We scan the busy ticket booths looking for Paul and Nikki. Excited people stream into the cavernous building through multiple doors from which music booms, heavy on the bass.

I can't stop grinning. Seeing Kurt made anything possible. Anything. "So what? That's what we're here for right? If it was that easy on the first try who is to say I can't actually talk to him?" I argue.

A deep line appears between Allison's pretty eyes. "Me. After the concert they'll have twice the security. Hundreds of people are going to have the exact same idea!"

"What's wrong with you?" *Why isn't she happy for me?*

"What is pissing me off is that you are acting totally weird and you have dried blood on the back of your head and you're pretending like everything is fine, when obviously it isn't."

"I'm fine."

She blows her bangs out of her face. "You've been popping Ibuprofen like M&M's, you're very pale and you're acting weird."

"I'm not acting weird."

"You're smoking dope."

So are you Miss Perfect. "I'm a teenager at a rock concert. I'm pretty sure it's required."

"You're using it as a painkiller. I'm not stupid." She takes a deep breath, trying to calm herself. "Do you want to tell me what's going on?"

"Nothing."

"You're lying to me and it's bullshit."

If it were anybody but Allison, I'd walk away. "Every day that I think I can't make it one more day I think about how Kurt made it out of Aberdeen. He didn't give up. That is how I keep going." I point at the Cow Palace. "Kurt Cobain, Krist Novoselic and Dave Grohl are inside. And maybe this is wrong but because of the way he writes songs, I feel like Kurt Cobain is the one person I could talk to and he'd really understand everything. I know the chances are infinitesimally small that it would work."

"Miniscule." She grins.

"Minute."

"Subatomic."

"Oh, very nice," she says.

"But here's the thing Allison. What if I could do it?"

A smile lights her face. "We'd never forget it."

"Nobody would."

She grabs my hand. "Promise me that you'll get your head checked out after the concert."

I cross my heart with my fingers. "I promise."

Her face lights up and then she's hugging me, whispering in my ear. "Kurt Cobain isn't the only person who might understand."

She kisses me on the cheek. I don't know whether to laugh or cry.

When we finally locate Nikki, she's upset. We're in front of the arena with concert goers streaming into four open doors. "The tickets weren't there." Her eyes pool with tears.

"What the effety-eff-eff-eff?!" Mike sputters. "What happened?"

Paul pulls us to the side so we're out of the way. "They had no record of the tickets. This lady took Nikki's credit card and looked it up. There was nothing. We told them about her phone call and she said she didn't know what to do. There was no record of the ticket sale in the first place on the computer."

Nikki is crying and I feel like plopping on the ground or, better yet, lying down dead. Paul puts his arm around Nikki, telling her it's going to be okay, he'll figure something out.

"No, we won't," she snaps. "This whole trip is a disaster. We paid good money for those tickets and they ended up in the trash thanks to Mike." She has a crazed look on her face.

"Hey do not lay this shit on me. You trusted me. I wouldn't trust me," Mike says.

Mike is dancing to what must be The Disposable Heroes of Hiphoprisy because even in my crashing hysterical meltdown, I notice my life is falling apart to a completely awesome dance song, "The Language of Violence."

"Sweetheart, don't place your eggs in this fragile basket. I am only human. Would you like some weed?"

Mike asks Nikki who shrieks, "Oh my God we drove seven hundred and eight-four miles in one day! Can't you at least say you're sorry?"

Mike claps his fingers together as if he's carrying castanets. "Sorry. So-so-so-so-sorry. Don't wanna piss off the girl who is in love with someone else's boy-"

Nikki slips out from under Paul's arm, launching herself at Mike, knocking him onto the pavement.

"Nice friends," Allison says as Mike holds Nikki back with his hand and Paul tries to drag her off of him. She takes my hand, dragging me.

"Where are we going?" I ask.

"To fix this."

<hr>

"You're going to fix this and you're going to fix this now," Allison says to the clerk at the ticket booth.

The clerk is a washed out middle-aged woman with long stringy grey hair and an impatient manner. "Look, I already told those other kids if I don't have no record of the sale, I can't release any tickets. We are sold out."

Allison leans in, tapping on the Plexiglas. "Are you calling me a liar? We bought five tickets and that dumb ass," she points at Mike, who is on his feet, dancing away from Nikki's punches, "Left them at a McDonald's in Aberdeen, Washington. I'm not lying and I'm not going away until you give us five tickets." She splays her fingers on the glass. "Five."

A man with sleeves of tattoos waiting behind us pushes forward. "Just give 'em the tickets so we can get in."

"I ain't giving out free tickets," the clerk snaps. "You better run along now or I'll call the cops."

"Call them. We paid good money for those tickets and we deserve to see a concert," Allison insists.

Tattoo Man taps his finger on the Plexiglas. "You should have a transaction receipt linked to the sale with the credit card. But you didn't even bother to take her credit card, did you? Well I'll tell you what, either you give us those tickets or I'll jump back there and show you how to use your own damn computer."

The clerk's piggy eyes turn into slits. "I'd like to see you fit through the hole."

Tattoo Man moves so fast he's a blur. His arm slips into the booth, grabbing the clerk by the front of her shirt, twisting it until he's choking her. "Give these kids their fucking tickets and quit dicking around!"

The clerk's face flushes bright red, her eyes bulging. "You can't do this!" she squeals.

"The hell I can't. Five fucking tickets. Now!"

The woman accompanying Tattoo Man, resplendent in leather pants and a hot pink tank top with BITCH spelled out in rhinestones examines her long nails, bored. "Hank, I'm gonna go get some popcorn."

Hank, sweaty with the effort of holding the clerk, isn't happy. "Jesus Marnie. Can't you wait until we're inside? I'm just trying to get our fucking tickets."

"Oh alright." Marnie picks at her nail polish.

"Put the fucking phone down! Five tickets!" Hank yells into the Plexiglas.

The clerk finally realizes that Hank isn't going anywhere soon and security is nowhere in sight. She counts out five tickets. Hank releases his grip on her shirt to take them. "Here you go ladies. You and your friends enjoy!"

"Thank you," we both say. Allison takes the tickets, thanking him again. "We need to disappear fast," she whispers.

As we hurry over to our friends, the clerk is telling Hank that there's no way in hell she's going to give him his tickets.

CHAPTER FIFTEEN

"I'm so ugly but that's okay 'cause so are you."
"Lithium," Nirvana

PAUL

"Hon, you can't take in that camera," says a bespectacled guy in overalls, squinting as he pushes up his glasses. He taps the Canon strapped around Fran's torso. The four of us are at door three entering the arena. This guy feels like the last hurdle in a long, difficult race. I am the only person on this crazy trip with anything resembling a conscience, which totally sucks. When I had to drag Nikki off Mike, preventing yet another fight, I didn't know whether to smack her or kiss her. Not that I would ever hit a girl. But still.

"She's reporting for the school paper," Allison says.

"Where's her press pass?" Bespectacled guy demands.

"I forgot it." Fran lies way too naturally.

The guy crosses his fat arms. "See, that's the thing. If you were really press you wouldn't forget it 'cause it also gets you in free and that's one thing those cheap bastards won't do is pay for their own damn tickets. Sorry kid, you can't take it in."

Fran holds the camera against her stomach like it's the most expensive thing she's ever owned, which I'm sure it is. Nikki looks at me with that "do something" look Taylor constantly wears. Except on Nikki it isn't bitchy, it's kind of sexy. I'd love to do something if it would impress Nikki.

"She has to," I say, stepping forward with authority but the guy just shakes his head. "No she don't."

Mike grabs me by the arm, mouthing the words "Trust me!" and says loudly, "Here, I'll run it to the car. I'll be right back. Wait here."

Before Fran can argue, he's unsnapped her camera and slipped outside like a cat, disappearing into the twilight leaving us stranded.

"He would make an awesome thief," Nikki observes.

"I'm pretty sure that's what just happened," I point out. "He's going to sell it for more weed." Fran looks worried so I add, "Just kidding."

"Jesus Paul," Nikki says, giving me a dirty look. "It's her *camera*."

I cannot win. I try to be cool so she won't call me a Boy Scout and she sides with Fran. "I'm sure he'll lock the car."

"I'll stay here with Fran if you guys want to go in," Allison offers.

"I'll stay with Fran," Nikki insists.

"No, I will," Allison insists.

So, this is weird.

Fran squints like she has a massive headache. At some point, I'm going to have to tell Allison and Nikki about Fran being hit.

"Would everyone just shut up?" Fran snaps.

This is my moment. I have a choice: Boy Scout or.... the music is kind of awesome. I bob my head, feeling it in my knees, moving in a way I know is stupid and pathetic but hell, it's fun. I spontaneously grab Nikki's hand, swinging it in time to the beat. "This is the shut-up dance."

"I like the shut-up dance," Nikki says, staring at our hands.

I know she's freaked out. We've always been friends and I have a girlfriend but she's adorable. Oh shit. Is that what I'm thinking? Okay, time to stop thinking.

I lean over and whisper to Nikki. "Shhhhhhh. We have to shut up."

The music stops and I don't want to let Nikki's hand go. I hold it there and pretend to act like it's normal. Luckily Fran is distracted, worrying we're going to miss the moment Nirvana takes the stage. Allison's working to reassure her. What would be weirder? Holding her hand longer or just dropping it? Girls never have to think about stuff like this. They're just unconsciously adorable enough to mess with your head.

"Should we leave him?" I ask, dropping Nikki's hand with a shrug with hands gesture that hopefully makes it seem unrehearsed. "He's liable to just take off."

"You know how I feel about him," says Nikki, picking tiny pieces of gravel from her roughed-up elbow and flicking it.

"Until I saw you laying into Mike I thought Taylor was exaggerating when she said you attacked her," I say to Nikki. "Now I kind of believe her story."

Nikki's mouth curls into a snarl. "I threw a shampoo bottle."

"A shampoo bottle that cut her in the face." Okay, that came out wrong. I was trying to say that she's tough.

"It was a nick. You should have heard her talking about Fran. No one is going to talk about my best friend like that and get away with it. Especially not Taylor the twa-" Nikki stops herself.

"What?" I ask. I won't be good but I have to know.

"It's a mean nickname. Let it go," Fran says.

"Rhymes with shot," mutters Nikki. "For the record, I did not make it up."

I can feel my face flush and kick a cigarette butt. Last summer something happened with Taylor and Darren White when I was off working on my uncle's fishing boat. I never said anything but the way she crawled all over me, pretending she'd been so lonely without me was almost worth it. "Maybe we should leave a ticket for Mike."

"He's got my camera," Fran points out.

It's awkward, stopping mid-flow in a sea of people, trying to recover from that horrible conversation while we figure out what happens next. We need a plan except I'm all out of them. I just want to be that guy holding Nikki's hand. It's crazy but I feel like I could tell Nikki anything. Even about my dad.

I look at my watch. Five minutes to the main act. "How about if Nikki and I go in and get us some seats and you guys follow after Mike comes back?" *Two friends holding hands in a huge crowd is a good idea and not even close to cheating, right?*

I'm reaching for Nikki's hand when Mike appears without the camera, panting. Nikki hands our tickets to the bespectacled man, busy cracking his pudgy knuckles. "Alright-ee-o enjoy the concert!"

Mike walks backwards, giving the ticket taker a jovial salute as we're admitted into the Cow Palace. Surprisingly, I'm getting more excited by the second. The cavernous hall is muggy and reeks of pot, manure and popcorn laced with burnt sugar undertones. It's nothing like the Sacred Son concerts. Like cattle we push along a path lined with metal rods feeding us to the main entrance. Music throbs inside. When Nikki gets pushed into me, I make my move.

"Here," I say, holding out my hand. "Safety in numbers."

She gives me a grateful smile that cracks me wide open. "For safety."

Shit. Shit. Shit. She's beautiful. Why wasn't I paying attention?

We're studying the signs over the tunnel leading into the arena as Mike removes his jacket revealing a strap across his chest. He spins it around, proudly revealing Fran's camera. He unsnaps it from his body, offering it with a long, skinny arm. "One camera for the little lady!"

"Thank you. God, thank you!" Fran hugs the camera like a baby. "Oh my God this is awesome! I've got a fresh roll of ISO 400 film loaded and an experimental ISO 800 in the bag just to see what happens with the bright stage lights."

Mike shrugs. "English please."

She stands on her toes and gives him a kiss on the cheek.

Mike holds Fran's arm. "I just gotta say something." We're all ready to go but Fran motions for us to wait while Mike speaks. "I came up with the concert idea because I uh, thought it would get me in good with Hazel but now, I'm like, all in for you Fran. So, go get Nirvana man. You deserve it all. Totally."

She gives him a big hug and another kiss on the cheek.

Mike. Who knew?

I link arms with Nikki and lead us deeper into the arena. Although I can't see them, I'm pretty sure Allison and Fran are holding hands too. Mike trails behind like a big-eyed kid in a candy store, nodding his head to the music.

Someone must be looking out for us because the house lights come up when we walk into a fog of smoke, BO and hordes of people. We push through crowds that shift like water. The sheer magnitude of the interior is overwhelming. The size of the exterior should have prepared me but the solid mass of humanity jammed inside socks me in the gut. I hold onto Nikki's hand pulling her in my wake, glad that I'm holding her hand for multiple reasons. The floor is sticky with soda and beer. Mike loses a flip-flop and bends over to retrieve it from the forest of feet. A man with a mouthful of popcorn laughs. Kernels fly in my face, damp and oily.

"Thanks dude!" says Mike, dipping his hand into the

bucket of popcorn. Before the man can comment, we're weaving away, a human centipede. Although it's hot, a lot of people wear flannel shirts over tank tops, which I guess is a nod to grunge. Anyone from Aberdeen knows that Kurt didn't wear flannel shirts for a fashion statement. Everyone wears them. They're warm and the second-hand stores have loads because loggers and fishermen wear them. I bet Fran and Cobain shopped at the same place: Goodwill. Cobain said it's weird that people think Nirvana started grunge fashion. People were missing the point. Poverty was the point. That's one thing we've got plenty of in Aberdeen.

Not being the least bit cool, I don't recognize the music playing over the loudspeakers but the energy and buzz from the last group on stage, who I now know was L7, is palpable. Maybe they're just excited to hear Nirvana. Clusters of people share foamy plastic cups of beer, sloshing it on the floor as they pass. I lead us to the back of the arena, glancing behind me occasionally to watch the roadies setting up, barely visible in black against the huge white screen backdrops. The black speakers are the size of backyard sheds. My plan is to climb high enough up into the stands to find seating. Allison and Fran lag further behind so we stop to wait for them. Before they reach us, they lean in close enough to kiss, discussing something. Fran points at the stage.

Fran joins us, pointing back at Allison, who waves. "We're going to stay on the floor. I want to get as close to the stage as possible."

"Come with us," Nikki pleads. "It'll be more fun if we're all, like together."

Okay, so she doesn't want to be alone with me. "Let's find a place to sit and wander around if we want."

We're causing a logjam with streams of blocked people. "Come on man," they protest. "Get going. I'm trying to reach my girlfriend," says a goateed guy with a pierced lip.

"Go take some excellent pictures Franoid," says Mike, squeezing Fran on the shoulder. He turns to the angry goateed dude, immediately striking up a deal to sell him a mini-bong. "That's so cute!" goateed dude says, digging in his leather pants for five bucks. Nikki and I are pushed into the crowd before we can finish our conversation.

I yell something about meeting up at the car but it's no use. Nobody can hear me and Nikki, true to form, is laughing at me.

FRAN

"We can't reach the stage!" Allison shouts after a long push through walls of people.

"We have to!" I want to be near the stage more than I want to breathe. My head hurts and the smoky air isn't helping. I creep forward, using my camera, saying *excuse me* until it stops working. We've hit a solid mass of sticky people. A man with grey hair woven into stiff beaded braids drinks from a flask. His eyes are as blue as the glass beads. I'm pushed up against his chest although he's trying not to crowd me. It's impossible. I'm stuck.

"Tequila?" He offers the flask, decorated with roses and skulls. Allison ducks under an armpit, popping into view.

I pluck my t-shirt away from my sweaty skin. "No thank you. We're trying to get to the stage."

"Good luck honey. These folks are a peculiar creature known as uber-fans." He waves the flask over the head of the woman pressing into his chest. Her cigarette smoke floats in our faces. "They've been standing for hours to keep their spots. Interlopers will not be tolerated." He takes another sip. "You could yell fire and these folks wouldn't budge. I've seen it at Dead concerts. Very intense."

I lift my camera. "I'm a reporter."

He squints. "And I'm Gandalf sweetheart. If you were credentialed you'd be backstage talking about the rapes in Bosnia. That's what pisses me off. These kids don't care about the real reason for this concert, helping those poor Bosnian girls. They just want their MTV, their bread and circus." He waves smoke from his face. He wears several rings, one a heavy silver skull with onyx eyes.

Suddenly the absurdity of my situation hits me: I'm on the weirdest mission ever, pouring heart and soul into—what? A dream?

"You're right. I'm just a fan from Aberdeen trying to get Kurt and Krist to come home and play at my prom." Allison grins, encouraging me. "I'm gay so they nominated me for prom queen thinking I would never win." I point at the stage. "If they show up, there's a chance I could win."

Gandalf offers his flask. It burns going down my throat and I realize I'm parched. "Ha! Now I have heard damn near everything. There is nothing more poetic, nothing more tragically beautiful than a completely hopeless quest. You are the Don Quixote of your shitty little town. Sorry, your hometown. That wasn't very neighborly of me."

Allison leans in. "No, you're right. It is a shitty little town. But it's our shitty little town."

He jerks his thumb at Allison. "Sancho Panza here is a beauty. And you're both on this quest?" We nod. He raises his flask, howling. "Beautiful. Ab-so-lutely fuck-ing gor-geous." He wipes his mouth, pockets his flask and hollers into the crowd. "Make way for this kid! She's Kurt Cobain's cousin and she drove all the way from Aberdeen in the great state of Washington to surprise her long lost cuz. Come on people! Move aside!"

His booming voice is a foghorn. People turn, paying attention. Delighted, he slaps me on the back. "Good luck kids!" He repeats his orders, bellowing, "Make way!" until I am four people away from the front of the stage. I turn around to thank him but my view is blocked by all the people I've just passed.

Gandalf's lie makes its way through the crowd, parting the sea until I'm so close to the stage my nose is nearly pressed against it. We've overshot our mark and need to back up to see anything. A tiny girl in a wife beater tank climbs up on her boyfriend's broad shoulders. This allows me the space to slide in beside them. A security guard slips out of the shadows on stage. He points at the girl but talks to her boyfriend. "Dude, she's got to get off."

The girl points a finger at me. "She's Kurt Cobain's cousin. Tell Kurt his cousin's here." She bends over, tapping my shoulder. "Tell him your name honey."

The security guard gives me a flick of the eye before pointing at the tank top girl. "Off now. Or you're out."

She slips down, grabbing a friend's beer. "As soon as they're on stage, I'm right back up." She pokes her boyfriend's stomach. "You promised. I can't see for shit on the ground."

"Are you okay? Allison looks worried. "You look a little-"

The lights go out. No dimming, just whoosh, instantaneous black. Electricity pulses through the crowd as if we've all plunged down the same rollercoaster. It takes a moment to get oriented. People pull out lighters, waving them around crazily, buzzing with the thrill of anticipation. I triple check my camera to make sure it's loaded. It'll be tough to get a steady shot in such tight quarters. Whatever I shoot will be about the crowd too, their interaction with Nirvana. What happens off stage is far more important than I realized.

Tank tops girl yells. "Kurt, your cousin is here! Whoooooo! Cousin power! Right fucking on! She loves you and so do I!"

My ears burn as tank top girl's jealous boyfriend threatens to dump her on the ground.

"It's Kurt Fucking Cobain man," she argues. "I do love him!"

He drops her on the floor and the ensuing scuffle blends into the surge of noise when Dave Grohl slips out of the shadows, climbing over some speakers into the drum kit. I start shooting as he adjusts the height of the cymbals which is why I miss Krist Novoselic stepping onstage with his bass strapped to his torso. His hair is short and his round face has thinned out. His shirt is white, maybe blue. It's hard to tell because the stage lights reduce color to a desert monochrome. His black jeans seem powdery grey. For a moment, the two of them play with their instruments, glancing sideways at the crowd, flirting, getting the crowd stoked. Dave thumps at the drums, adjusting something near his foot.

When it seems like they're not expecting anything else, Kurt Cobain darts out of the shadows with his brown Fender Jaguar, a white t-shirt, ripped faded jeans and fuzzy blue cardigan, fresh off the back of some wizened old Aberdeen VA Hall duffer. Kurt's shoulder length blond hair falls into his face, glowing bright then fading as he steps in and out of the shadows. He's completely absorbed in his guitar and doesn't seem to notice that he's inches from a crowd of screaming people. As Krist plays a melody, Kurt tunes his guitar, dropping a rag onstage, going over to talk with Dave Grohl, who nods. Kurt returns to his side of the stage, crowded with speakers and two stomp boxes. He prowls restlessly, fiddling with something on the ground before going back to Krist.

It's hard not to keep snapping off shots. Every moment is precious, worth saving. Part of me wants to record every single image: Krist lit up by colored lights, faded to white, Dave behind the mountain of equipment, surrounded by drums and brass cymbals, his drumsticks white as bones. *Is that why their first album is called Bleach?* I force myself to put the camera down so I don't run out of film.

"You look so happy," says Allison.

My heart is ready to burst out of my skin. "I'm in heaven."

"Rape Me" is the first song Kurt plays but then he stops. His hair falls into his face as he adjusts his guitar as if nothing matters but getting it right. When he starts to sing something splits open in me. Happiness could be the right word. More likely it's complete joy. It's the same voice that's reached into my brain when I was hurt, scared, lonely, so many times. It's totally different from lying on my bed staring up at the posters. I'm surrounded by thousands of people who all know the words, who sway and dance and sing just below the electronic blast. Allison's hand finds mine. Never in my life have I felt so good. The song travels through my breastbone, my skull and my spine, reverberating throughout.

I'm so happy. I want to wrap my fist around this moment and squeeze it dry, pin it down, keep it forever. This is bliss, a word I could never understand.

This is it.

I know.

I'm lost in the moment as they play "School", "Breed", "Sliver" and "Come as You Are," which is when everyone really dances. It's impossible for me to take any pictures because we're moving as a group; pushing, pressing, twisting, shaking, and fusing with the song that's been stamped into our brains. Allison grins and waves her hands. Her dark hair drapes over her eyes. She raises both slim arms to push it off her forehead. Stage lights shine on her. She's so beautiful.

For a moment, the pain behind my eyes flashes into the colored lights pulsing onstage, passing into the back of my brain where I don't recognize it as pain. Now I know what Kurt Loder is talking about when he casually chats about concerts on MTV. This is why people drive hundreds of miles, pay big bucks to hear a favorite band. But this is more than my favorite band. This is Nirvana.

"Oh my God! This is amazing!" Allison hollers.

"Milk It" leads to "About a Girl." Sometimes the songs melt into one another or they hit a complete stop. I keep wondering if Kurt will talk, like he did on MTV. Between the sets he focuses on tuning, playing with the strings as though they've loosened. After "Blew" there is a long pause and I'm sure he's going to talk but Kurt keeps somberly adjusting his guitar, oblivious to the adoring crowds. During the songs Krist and Kurt bump up against one another, occasionally running back to say something to Dave Grohl. Maybe this is the only way to perform, to forget everything and hope that the audience is having as much fun as the band as they create rock history. Fun is the wrong word. They are simply in the moment; working together to create art. Making this night stand out from all the others before and after.

Kurt picks out the simple, enormously familiar opening to "All Apologies" to rising applause. Although my headache has returned with a stabbing vengeance, causing me to squint in the flashing lights, I'm struck by the melody's simplicity. A skinny black guy next to me starts humming along. It grows until the first three rows are humming. Krist joins in and then the drums and the humming turns to singing, although they're whispering as if they don't want to miss the real show: Kurt singing this song. My temples are squeezed so tightly it blocks out the light. My vision blurs at the edges and I stagger. The salty metallic taste of fear is on my tongue. I bend, trying to catch my breath.

"Don't barf on my shoes!" Someone yells over "Heart Shaped Box." *I love that song.*

"Are you okay?" Someone yells into my ear.

Is that Allison? "Do you need to get out?"

I wait for the buzz in my ears to dim although with the music, it's hard to tell when it's gone. "I'm ok."

Allison rubs my back. I lift my head because a huge howling surge of excitement fills the arena. Nirvana is playing "Negative Creep." I take a few snaps of Kurt, swaying with his guitar, striding across the stage. As he joins Krist I use up the rest of the roll. If I'm going to faint, I don't want to risk having my camera stolen. I zip it into the bag. I can't believe that after all it took to get here; I might have to leave while Nirvana is onstage.

Allison asks a skinny girl near us for her water but as it's passed along a stoned guy with a silver nose ring drops in the butt of a joint, giggling hysterically. Allison and I stare at the wormy joint in the water. She's saying something but all I hear is a dull buzz.

As the stage lights flash red, blue and purple, my vision blurs into a pinpoint. Everything goes black.

CHAPTER SIXTEEN

"Hey! Wait! I got a new complaint!"
"Heart Shaped Box," Nirvana

FRAN

Something wakes me up. I smell of dust and what must be Yuban, like they serve in my mom's bakery. When I open my eyes, I'm in a small dingy room lying on a lumpy old couch, wincing under a fluorescent haze. Nirvana is still playing "Negative Creep" somewhere in the distance which makes me sick with regret. My head is thick and heavy, filled with oozing warm tar. A film of cigarette smoke hangs from the ceiling, making me cough. A fat man squeezed into an office chair behind a banged-up metal desk hears me and smashes his cigarette into a plate of food. "There she is folks! Hey, here, drink this."

I uncap the bottle of water, sit up and drink. His security badge says Walt Walters: the most generic name in the history of names. As if compensating for his boring name, Walt sports a formidable long drooping mustache. He reminds me of a walrus.

Allison smiles in relief. She sits on a table near a grimy window facing a narrow hallway. "You're awake," she whispers.

"You're lucky your friend here got you to security. You were out cold." He squints, trying to bend over his huge belly. The buttons on his shirt threaten to pop. If they do, they'll take out my eyes. "You take any drugs?" I shake my head, trying to assemble my face into what I hope is a non-stoned, innocent look. "I'm supposed to radio the medics if you're one of them druggies." He bends over to study my pupils. His teeth are yellow and his breath reeks of salami. "You got some tiny pupils for a girl that says she don't do drugs."

"Don't drugs enlarge your pupils?" Allison asks.

"Depends," Walt says, searching his messy desk for something.

"Can I please have another bottle of water?" He hands me one without comment, lumbering back to his chair. It groans in protest.

"That there is called the crazy couch. I cannot tell you how many drugged out, drunk, mentally unstable, freaky shitheels landed on that sucker. We get all kinds. Even a few rodeo clowns. You ain't never seen anything sadder than a drunk clown that cannot stop crying. This one fella got dumped by his gal over the phone and was threatening to kill hisself unless I got her on the horn and tried to talk her into taking him back." He picks at his teeth. "By golly I did too."

I pretend to follow his story while trying to telepathically communicate with Allison. We need to get the hell out of here and finish the concert. Can we just walk out? I stall for time while my brain clears. "You got her back for him?"

He shakes his pillowy jowls. "No but I called her. Did my best. She probably had another fella what with him being on the road so much. Musicians too. They end up here weeping and carrying on. Usually about some woman. And money too. One of the Allman brothers ended up in here boo-hooing about bankruptcy. They had the bright idea of buying a 747. You wanna know why? Because Jefferson Starship had one. Don't know which Allman brother it was. They all looked the same. Them long-hair hippy types all blend together. I swear to God. You are sitting on a historic couch. Been there since the Beach Boys played back in 1976. Or was it the Eagles?" He hoists himself up, lights another cigarette and waddles over. I keep a close eye on him while I guzzle the last of the water.

As I swing my legs to the floor, Allison reaches behind her and produces my camera case. "Here's your camera," she says in a loud voice. Leaning in she whispers, "You can get backstage from here. I think."

"Thanks." A glimpse out one of the office windows confirms that we're somewhere in the administrative section of the Cow Palace. I turn to Walt, who's filling out paperwork. "I'm feeling better now. Thank you. We should go find our friends."

He shakes his head. "You got something wrong with your peepers kid. I'm calling the medics."

"I'm fine." I study the hallway again. This office must be off to the side of the arena.

"Really, she's okay," Allison says. Walt glares at her. "My dad's a doctor."

"Is that so? Well he ain't been working in this place for thirty-two years and he ain't here." He picks up a radio on his desk, talking into it like he's a cop. "Hey this is Walt in the security office. Yeah, I got a kid here that came in passed out. She needs looking over."

Is there really something going on with my eyes? Was the weed we smoked laced with something horrible? Or is it my head, which has ached since PC pushed me against the locker? The Walrus points his finger, trying to pin me in place.

I stand up, strapping on my camera. The music has stopped. It was a short set but it makes sense, with all the other bands involved. Nirvana rarely does encores. When they exit the stage, they are done. Allison's head tilts towards the hall as if she's thinking the same thing. The concert is over. We're backstage.

His eyes get big as he snorts. "You stay right here. I got a whole bunch of security guards with nothing to do but chase after you."

"We haven't done anything wrong," Allison says. "You can't lock someone up just for fainting." She takes a step towards the door.

The Walrus pushes himself out the chair with surprising speed and is at the door blocking it. If we had a chance to walk out, it's over now. "If I let you go and you're on drugs or holding, I'm liable."

"Look, I'm Asian. We don't do drugs. We don't hang out with people who do drugs. Don't you know that?"

"Maybe so but you're staying put until you get cleared." He crosses his arms.

Shit. We don't stand a chance against his tonnage. I stand up, clutching my camera. "Let us out."

"No way, no how. Now it ain't my job to search you but someone's gonna." He's stubborn and annoyingly smug.

A hot wave of panic hits. In my pocket are four or five joints from Mike. I'm going to end up in jail. I'm never going to talk to Kurt Cobain. Kurt, Dave, and Krist are getting ready to leave the Cow Palace right now. Their van is parked out back. They're loading their instruments into cases, getting ready to travel to a hotel, maybe in another city, headed to their next gig. If I'm going to see them in person it's got to be now.

"Let us out." I soften my voice. "Please?"

Allison scans the room, frowning. "We don't have much time," she mutters. "We have to do something." She turns to Walt. "Look, we didn't drive 800 miles to be locked up in your shitty little office. Get out of our way."

His jowls waggle as he shakes his head. "Aw, ain't that cute? The Siamese kitten's getting all fought up." He holds up his hands in mock fear. "What you going to do? Scratch me?"

Allison's face flushes with anger. She lifts the grey folding chair beside her. "You." She swings it above her head in one swift motion. "Are such-" She gives me a look that clearly means *get ready*. She's amazingly calm for someone brandishing a chair. "—a fat asshole!" Allison screams like a warrior as she smashes the chair with all her might through the office window. Glass shatters into a million glittering shards on the dull grey linoleum.

"Holy shit," I whisper.

Allison grins. "As my Aunt Ling says, when God closes a door, he opens a window."

Walt stares in shock at the gaping hole. "You son of a bitch. Son of a bitch!"

Before he can react, Allison pushes a cardboard filing box under the window as a stepping stool. "Go now. Backstage is to the left. I'll hold him. Go! Go!"

My heart thumps wildly as I climb over the jagged glass in the window frame. Allison races out of the office waving Walt's radio. He waddles after her screaming, "Gimme that radio! Gimme that fucking radio!"

I skitter down the hallway, slipping on broken glass as I turn a corner, hoping it leads backstage. Although I'm terrified, I've never felt so completely alive.

NIKKI

"Where are we supposed to meet after the concert?" Paul asks but I'm blocking him out. Don't let this be over. Not freaking now.

I know it's cheesy but it was like a waking dream. One that I've dreamt so many times it doesn't seem real. The moment Kurt Cobain stepped on stage, Paul took my hand. For a brief moment in time, we were like, a couple. Not like Jared Cole, who sophomore year asked me out to the movies twice and made me sweat with nerves and bit my tongue. Like happy couples who talk and laugh. We swayed and swung our hands. We yelled over the music, nodding if we understood. When Nirvana walked offstage, he started clapping and it was over.

He's repeating himself but I'm, stunned, totally re-living every second. "What?"

"Aren't we supposed to meet by the car?"

"Yeah, I guess."

The house lights are on, vivid white. People stagger to the exits, buzzing happily; deaf with music. Paul gazes at the crowd funneling out of the stage area. "I don't see Fran or Allison anywhere."

"Maybe they like, made it backstage."

He turns back to me and stops walking. "You didn't really think she'd talk to Cobain, did you?"

I shrug. "Yeah. I did. I do. Fran deserves a little luck in her life. She's had to put up with so freaking much."

Paul leans down, our lips are nearly touching. "You're a good friend, you know that?"

I don't know if he's talking about Fran or this screwed up thing where he holds my hands for twenty minutes in the dark. "Thanks."

He frowns, rubbing his forehead. "I just...well, I just want you to know that I really—"

"You really what Paul? Finish the sentence because I'd like to—"

Whatever I was going to say next evaporates as he plants his warm hands firmly on either side of my face before swooping down suddenly, covering my forehead and face with peppery little kisses that smell of Pepsi and Crest. Our tongues meet and it's metallic and bright, like lightening. My brain flies to the ceiling, seeing purple and black as we drunkenly press into each other, eyes closed, my hands pressing into his back, raking across his shirt while his fingers tug and press into my hair. We're pressed deep into each other for a minute, maybe it's ten before he pulls away, gasping for air.

"I'm sorry," Paul says, frowning, his hands still on my face.

"I'm not." I don't know what else to say. I'm kissing someone else's boyfriend. I'm not that girl and yet, at this moment, it's all I want to be. If only I could freeze this moment, rewind and repeat it. All my problems seem very far away, tiny.

The spell is broken by something crashing onto Paul's back. He staggers onto me, holding me at a distance to protect me from the impact.

Mike's head pops up over Paul's shoulder. "Yaaaaaaaaah! I found you! I thought I was totally lost and alone! Was that a fucking awesome concert or what?" Paul spins around fast. Mike lets go, crashing into a seat, laughing. "Dude, where's the lesbians? Stalking Kurt Cobain, am I right?"

"Mike, you're really freaking rude," I snap, wiping my bruised lips.

Mike nods at Paul. "Sorry dude. Got a little swept up in the momento. Plus, I'm totally lit."

I push Mike as he tries to stand up. "You shouldn't call Fran and Allison the like, lesbians. That's like me calling you The Hetero."

Mike beams. "Shit! I love it. The Hetero. For the rest of the year totally call me that. Okay?"

Paul rolls his eyes and pats me on the shoulder. "You alright?"

I nod. "Yeah."

Nothing could be further from the truth.

FRAN

The hallway I turned down is a dead end with nothing but numbered doors. There are footsteps coming up fast. I try one of the doors, praying it will open. It's locked. Thankfully the second door is open and I slip in, fighting the urge to slam the door. I close it slowly; holding the handle so the lock doesn't click. I'm in a dark conference room with a long table flanked by chairs. Heavy footsteps squeak past the door. He pauses so close to the door I can hear him breathe.

"Fuck this, man." He sounds older than me but not much.

This strikes me as unbearably funny. Shit. I'm going to laugh. Not funny ha-ha laughter. That horribly inappropriate laughter that wells up when I'm uncomfortable. It's nauseating knowing it's on its way and I'm powerless. The faceless goon will burst through the door, dragging me back to that horrible office. We'll be charged with destruction of property or some other bullshit charge. Some meaty female cop will pat me down and find the joints. She'll have watched one too many cop shows and say something stupid like, "Well, what have we here?" I'll lose my only chance to see Kurt Cobain.

In a last-ditch effort to stop my hysterical laughter I bite down on the fleshy part of my hand, near the thumb. Crouching down in the dark, I taste the metallic blood from the cut on my hand, praying he'll walk away. Sweat beads on my scalp, running into the gash on the back of my head. It stings. If God's listening, it won't do me much good cause all I'm thinking is: Fuck, fuck, fuck. Get this shithead away from me. It's not the kind of prayer you'd hear in Sunday school. Seconds tick by like hours.

Just when I think he's going to open the door, the footsteps recede. I crumple on the floor in relief.

My lungs explode as I breathe again. Now that my pursuer is gone I don't have the slightest desire to laugh.

I'm lost and tired. Every hallway is identically grey and institutional. There isn't any way to pinpoint my location. All I can do is avoid the squawk of radios and heavy footsteps and keep moving. I'm worried that I'll turn a corner and finding myself back at the Walrus' smoky office facing the shattered glass, handcuffed Allison, and some pissed off cops. Maybe Kurt Cobain is in a car driving away from the Cow Palace at this very moment.

As a worm of panic threatens to swallow me, I spot a sign ahead pointing to BACKSTAGE A-21. Nearly collapsing from relief, I slip inside, climbing a short flight of stairs to the backstage wings. Waiting for my eyes to adjust to the dark, I study the huge black boxes lining the walls and the antiquated stand lights bristling from dusty dark corners. One wall is covered in levers and buttons and huge pulleys that lead up to the dark black overhead. It's like entering a vast cave. A long-haired man in a black t-shirt and backwards baseball cap ambles past me with a fist full of cables. After he's gone, I creep to where he disappeared and catch a glimpse of the stage. Five roadies pack up and move sound equipment.

Two roadies exit the stage wheeling a huge speaker, six feet high, on a dolly. One pushes while the other directs.

"Slow down. Hang on." The roadie bends down to

move a cable sitting inches from my foot. "Ok. Anyway, he said the levels were all fucked up."

"That's why Cobain kept tuning between songs."

"Shit, he was pissed. He took off right after they got offstage. Wouldn't talk to anyone."

"Ain't our fault."

"Fuck, I don't know. They got here so late. I was throwing shit on stage so fast I was just praying I got it all amped in right."

I wave of disappointment crushes me. Kurt is gone? The two roadies disappear out swinging barn doors. A crack of daylight appears as they open a second door. I follow them at a safe distance, pausing as they wait in the hallway for a freight elevator. When it arrives, one guy helps the other position the speaker in the lift. As the door shuts, I smell cigarette smoke.

"You lost?"

He's in the shadows, slouched against a set of stairs climbing the wall to a fire escape. All I can see is the glow of his cigarette as he takes a drag. His jeans are ripped at the knees and the pale flesh pokes out. I know that voice. It's Kurt Cobain.

CHAPTER SEVENTEEN

"We remember Kurt for what he was.
Caring, generous and sweet."
Krist Novoselic

FRAN

M y brain is frozen. It looks like Kurt Cobain on a poster, or on TV, or on stage. But he's talking. To me.

My only thought - *he's smaller*. I need to get a grip. Now.

"Um, no, I'm not lost." *And by the way, wanna play at my prom?* I have rehearsed everything but the one thing I really need. *What a dumb shit.*

He takes another drag on his cigarette. It's hard to tell for sure if it is Kurt Cobain. My eyes don't seem to be working right. But I'd recognize that voice anywhere. "I'm looking for Kurt Cobain."

When he smiles I see his cleft chin and straight white

teeth. His sandy hair is darker than it looks on stage. "You and everyone else. Join the club man." He's hunched over, rubbing the bridge of his nose. "You know what I'm doing?"

I shake my foam-packed head.

He jerks his thumb towards a door. "I'm dodging another fucking interview." His eyes narrow as he holds an imaginary microphone. "So Kurt, where did grunge come from?" He pretends to ponder the question. "Well, it came from Mars in a giant spaceship." He grins. "I feel like if I said that, people would actually take it seriously." He takes a drag, lifting one eyebrow. "Sorry, it's not your fault. You're just a girl who snuck backstage."

I'm trying to concentrate through the sandstorm in my head. It doesn't seem right to request one more thing, at least not now. "How old are you anyway?"

"Eighteen." I need to lie down.

"That's when I started writing songs, when I was working as a janitor. You know? It helps, getting it out."

I lift my Nikon. "I take pictures."

He tenses up. When I don't ask for a photo, he sits up straight, relaxing. "That's cool. What do you like to photograph?"

I have to think about it. "Actually, people going into the food bank."

He looks over his glasses, interested. "Why a food bank?"

It just, sort of comes out. "When people walk in, they're kind of hopeless and—when they leave, they're a little happier, usually. Sometimes it's the people you'd expect but sometimes—I saw a teacher once but I didn't take her picture."

He looks up, grinning. "And you get this feeling, right? You've captured this raw emotion. Even if it's only for a moment."

I nod. "I couldn't describe it like that."

He sighs. "Did you like the concert?"

I can't help it. My eyes light up. "Oh my God it was amazing. I've been like a total fan since your first album. I had to buy *Nevermind* twice because my stupid Walkman ate it."

"That sucks," he laughs, as though maybe it's happened to him.

"Yeah. I have a job so, you know, I bought another one." *Why did I tell him about my dumb job?*

He flicks his cigarette. "That's cool. Where do you work?"

It's weird. We're talking like two people waiting for a bus or in line at the grocery store except one of us is Kurt Cobain. "Plaza Garcia. I wait tables." I add, "I'm still in high school."

"Yeah, we had a Plaza Garcia back in Aberdeen. I loved that place. Good cheap food."

He's eaten there? "That's the one. I'm from Aberdeen."

He shakes his head. "You're fucking kidding me."

I'm not sure if it's a rhetorical question but I shake my head no.

"My condolences, man. You go to Aberdeen High?"

I nod. "Yeah."

He exhales a long plume of blue smoke, watching it

drift up. "That place is a fucking prison. A holding cell before life actually begins, you know?" *Don't lie down Fran. Don't.*

"I just keep thinking that you made it out of there and so will I. You're like my inspiration or something."

Oh my God. I sound twelve. *Stop before you tell him that you've baked him a cake on February 20th for the last two years.* Funfetti. Happy Birthday Kurt in purple gel.

"You're not the first kid to get obsessed by a band, right? I used to hitchhike into Seattle for the new Pixies releases. Sometimes by the time I got there they were sold out." He shakes his head. "Crazy, you know?" He circles his hand through the cigarette smoke.

"Yeah." I can hear Allison saying *ask him, ask him now.* But it would break the spell.

But—I'm out of chances. This is *it.*

"I have to ask you—"

He interrupts. "So, is this like a senior road trip or something?"

"I guess so but-" Words gush out of me so fast they barely make sense. "I got nominated for prom queen and the parents at the school really hated the idea because-"

There is a loud bang as the double doors beside where Kurt sits bursts open.

"There she is!" Through my grainy vision I make out two uniformed security officers following Mr. Walter, bending over to catch his breath as he points. "That's her!"

Kurt stands, grinds out his cigarette. A security guard grabs my arm. "Sorry she got back here Mr. Cobain." He pulls me backwards. "You're in a whole heap of trouble young lady." He pulls me inside the freight elevator.

Mr. Walter joins us, punching a button. "We got your friend you know."

I'm dying to ask about Allison but I'm dizzy, concentrating on staying upright.

Kurt is joined by Dave Grohl. "Que pasa man?" They turn away, walking.

Kurt shrugs. "Fuck if I know."

In the last seconds, as the elevator door shuts, there is a burst of white light, maybe cameras or streetlights as Kurt and Dave slip out the door. As the elevator lurches downward, Mr. Walter cites all the rules I've broken, furious that I won't open my eyes.

I just blew it. I didn't ask the one question I drove eight hundred miles to ask.

And I'm still running for prom queen.

NIKKI

"The Jap one is a psychopath," Walt says to the two cops who just climbed out of their patrol car. Paul grabs my clenched fist.

The larger cop removes his sunglasses, pointing at his nametag: Fukohama. "Watch who you call a Jap."

Walt doesn't miss a beat. "She threw a chair through my window," he says for the eight-hundredth time. Moths flutter around the lampposts in the dusty parking lot.

I shake off Paul's hand, stepping forward. "Was that right after you like, called her a Jap?"

The other cop snorts as a small blur of red comes barreling towards us in the dusk.

"Who are you calling a Jap? Get your hands off my

daughter!" Allison's mom flies at Walt like a fighting rooster in slim black slacks, an elegant red jacket and high heeled suede boots. Her pearl necklace whips around as she confronts him, eyes blazing.

Walt jumps back, a terrified bowl of Jell-O, lifting his hands in surrender. "Hey, I didn't touch her!"

The cops try to calm her down, asking her name and relationship. She completely ignores them, talking to Allison in rapid fire Japanese.

Allison replies in Japanese and for a moment we're all silent. Allison's mom glares at Fran, pointing with a red nail, talking so fast I can't tell what language she's speaking.

I have no idea what Allison is saying but I do remember her mom's name. "Mrs. Kondo, I am so sorry. I'm the one that talked Allison into—"

Mrs. Kondo holds out a tiny hand, blocking my face. "You be quiet!"

She is freaking terrifying. If she were my mom, I'd toe the line. Paul puts his arm around me, rubbing my shaky arm.

Officer Fukohama takes control, flipping through his notes. "Your daughter broke a window ma'am. Threw a chair right through it."

Mrs. Kondo narrows her eyes, studying his nametag and face, boring a hole into him until he steps backwards, away from Allison. Mrs. Kondo spits out rapid Japanese. He nods. "Allison? Is what he says true?"

Allison would clearly rather dive into a pit of fire than answer. "Yes," she whispers faintly.

"Speak up!" Mrs. Kondo says in a clear, even tone.

"Yes, but the fat guy was holding us prisoners and-"

With a swift nod, Mrs. Kondo gets Allison to shut up as if slapped. She turns to the cops. "I will pay all the damages. Allison will come home with me. She will not spend any more time with her friends." She says *friends* as if we're vermin. She doesn't look at Walter as she talks to him. "She will be suitably disciplined."

"Mom, I'm staying," Allison says through gritted teeth.

"You have caused enough trouble."

"I blew off one day of classes to be normal."

"Normal? Worrying your father and me to death? Throwing a chair?" She raises herself to her full height. "Next year you will compete against thousands of kids who all want to be in the same medical schools. They skip nothing."

Allison glares back. "I don't give a shit about those other kids."

Mrs. Kondo freezes, watching the moths flutter in the dusk. Her jaw twitches.

Walt breaks the silence. "She's been smoking weed too."

"Oh my God, would you just freaking shut up?" I burst out.

Paul whispers. "Please don't. Just don't." He looks at the cops. "She'll be quiet. I promise."

Mrs. Kondo exhales as if willing herself not to lose her tempter. She turns to Allison. "We will speak of this at home."

"Ma'am, Mr. Walter is pressing charges. We have to—"

Mrs. Kondo turns to Walter. "I can write you a five-hundred-dollar check."

Walter nods. "Walt Walters. Want me to spell that for you?"

"No." Without looking, she extracts a leather covered checkbook from her purse.

"I'm staying." Allison's eyes fill with tears.

"Can I talk to Allison please?" The adults stare at Fran as if they've forgotten she exists.

Mrs. Kondo speaks to Allison very quietly but with such force, we're all riveted. "If you don't come, I will have you drug tested." She strides to her waiting cab. As she passes Mr. Walters, a check flutters to the ground.

Allison takes two steps towards the car, then shakes her head. Retracing her steps, she marches over to Fran, places both hands on her shoulders and kisses her hard on the lips. It doesn't last long but Fran looks like she's been hit by lightening. You can practically see her heart thumping through her shirt. Allison stalks over to the car, sliding into it with a sharp look at her mom that can be read for miles.

Game freaking on.

PAUL

After I unlock the car Nikki settles in beside me in the front seat, which makes me strangely sad and happy at the same time. I'm staring at her, wishing we could hang out here longer. What I should be doing is paying attention as I reverse the car but I'm trying to figure out what the hell I'm doing with her, why I'm smiling so much my face hurts. When I pull out, I hit a parked car.

Mike squeals, "I can't believe you hit a car! Jesus. We're doomed."

I twist in the seat, trying not to yell. "Do you want to drive?

"God no. I'm stoned out of my mind."

"Then shut up!" There's barely a scratch on the other car so I jump back in and slowly drive away.

"Tell you what. I'll shut up if you quit hitting cars," Mike says.

I'm about ready to say something but a siren grows closer.

"Slow and steady. Nice and easy," Mike says, completely paranoid.

"I'm going to kick you out. I swear to God." I go five miles an hour as we pass the ambulance near the entrance to the Cow Palace. Two medics pull out a stretcher.

"Okay everyone, look normal," says Mike.

"*We* didn't smoke a bonfire of weed today. So yeah, we're good." I pull into the lane exiting the parking lots.

Mike flips me off. "Screw you dude, at least my girlfriend doesn't keep my balls in her purse."

I can't help it. I let go of the wheel, pump the brakes once and launch over the seat, swinging punches. The car swerves, lurching over the median. Everyone screams as Mike and I exchange wild punches over the seat. There's not much contact thanks to Nikki, who pushed me back down into my seat as she tried to get to the wheel. As Nikki gains control the car lurches across the median into a patch of scrubby grass, rolling to a stop inches from a huge pine.

Mike and I flop into our seats, panting. The siren

grows louder. What if I'm the one to blow this whole thing? The ambulance speeds down the road, passing a few feet away, siren blaring, lights flashing. No one says a thing until it turns out of sight.

"Okay, we're done with the weed, the drama, and the fighting. From now on, we're all friends." Nikki's so calm and pretty I reach over and squeeze her hand without thinking. She pulls it back, looking away. What I want is an hour with her to talk.

"Just drive," Nikki says.

I'm backing the car up when Fran suddenly sits bolt upright in the backseat, clutching Nikki's shoulder.

"Nikki? Nikki!"

Nikki grabs her hands. "What's going on?"

Fran blinks repeatedly, looking from side to side. "I can't see."

Fran is the only one in the car not completely losing her mind. As we careen around the corner she slides into Mike. "Maybe you should slow down Paul."

"Maybe you fucking should!" Mike hollers.

"I am trying to get her to a hospital. Unlike you I'm not stoned out of my mind so shut the F up!" I snap.

"You missed the freaking sign!" Nikki points at a blue sign we just passed.

I slam on the brakes.

"Paul, what are you doing?" Nikki screams.

"I am trying to find the hospital. You are supposed to

be looking for the signs. Don't tell me when I've missed them! Tell me before you see them!" The cars behind us start honking.

"I can't help it. I'm worried," Nikki says, chewing one of her tiny red straws.

I take a deep breath. "Okay, alright. We're fine. Just help me find the hospital."

"Alright. Maybe just turn into this parking lot." I pull into the parking lot and turn left. "God I hope this is just temporary," Nikki whispers.

"I can still hear!" Fran says.

"On the upside, who wouldn't vote for a gay, *blind* prom queen?" Mike asks.

"Would you just shut up? Oh my God! What is wrong with you?" Nikki lobs a Big Gulp cup at Mike's head. He ducks as ice scatters over the back seat. No one says another word until we reach the hospital.

FRAN

"Even though your vision has cleared, we're going to keep you here for twenty-four hours for observation. You had a concussion that you should have sought medical attention for immediately. Concussions require close observation, rest and attention. In your case the dehydration, drug usage, lack of food, and poor sleep was a perfect storm for vision loss. Your brain is so smart that it shuts off increasingly larger systems until you pay attention."

I'm in a small hospital room lying in bed. My doctor is a young Asian woman who keeps pushing her red glasses up her tiny nose. "Honestly, I don't know how you lasted this long without something happening. That must have been quite a bump."

I nod, meeting Nikki's concerned stare. The doctor turns to my friends, asking them if we can have some privacy. Mike and Paul look eager to leave the room. Nikki is uncomfortable but lingers with her hand on my arm. If Allison were here she'd talk to the doctor and probably even impress her. How long have I been here? Is Allison home? When can I get out? I need to see Allison.

Nikki leans down to whisper in my ear. "We'll be right in the hallway."

As soon as they leave the doc crosses her arms, signaling Serious Talk. I hate serious talks. Since that December break in third grade when my teacher found out we'd been evicted, teachers, counselors, two social workers, and one principal have all launched into the same speech. They lower their voices and talk about my mom with fake sympathy in a superior, insulting tone. They say my mom is "doing her best" and "it's rough being a single mother." But they think she's an idiot. They never believe me when I tell them everything is okay. I never know exactly what I'm supposed to say but whatever comes out of my mouth is always wrong.

The semi-private room has a stale, air-conditioned chill. The other bed is stripped, making me wonder what happened to the previous occupant. I shiver in the flimsy hospital gown, dreading what's coming.

The doc pushes up her glasses, pretends she's not dying to glance at her watch. "You want to tell me what happened?" There isn't an ounce of fake cheer in her voice.

I shake my head, trying hard not to like her. "Not really."

"You know, we're supposed to report this kind of thing. Your tox report alone means I am cutting you major slack. That cut was infected you know. It could have been much worse."

I sigh. Clearly, she's not going anywhere. "Some guy at school pushed me into a locker."

She looks down at my chart. "In Aberdeen?"

I nod. "Yeah. He's been after me all year." Make that four.

"Did he sexually assault you?"

She pats my hand. "I have to ask."

I shake my head. "No."

She waits a moment to see if I'll elaborate. I don't. Thinking about it is bad enough. When I get back PC will be there with his Slim Jim breath and piggish eyes. But I won't say anything. It's my word against his and he'll lie his head off.

"Is there anyone you can talk to? Other adults? A social worker maybe?"

I shake my head before realizing my mistake. We could be stuck here for days, not to mention what would happen if she contacted the police. At this point, I can't imagine that telling anyone would make my life any better. School is almost over. "Um, I can talk to my friend Nikki's parents." *Right.* "Her mom is a nurse."

Bingo. The doc's pretty face relaxes. She can go home to her condo, drink chardonnay and feel good. "Hang tight." She's giddy with relief. "Someone will be here in a sec to take your blood."

"Yippee," I quip.

She squeezes my arm. "You're pretty tough. You'll be

fine. Just make sure you talk to your friend's parents. You shouldn't handle this alone. Okay?"

I nod, trying to look sincere as hell.

As soon as she leaves, I jump out of bed and locate my tangled clothes in a bedside table. My shoes are in a narrow closet sticking out of a blue plastic tub. My flannel shirt reeks of weed. My whole body aches as I get dressed, but my headache is almost gone. I must have slept quite a while. Ripping open a plastic-wrapped bag of toiletries at the tiny sink, I study my face as I comb my hair, brush my teeth. My skin has a faint trace of pink. My eyes have lost the deep purple rings.

More than anything, I need to go home.

Now.

CHAPTER EIGHTEEN

"The sun is gone, but I have a light."
Kurt Cobain

FRAN

"This is a bad idea," Paul says, looking out the hospital room window at the parking lot. "They're not discharging her until tomorrow at the earliest."

Nikki leans on my bed, ignoring every word coming out of his mouth, trying to explain her and Mike's convoluted plan. I'm afraid to ask where Mike is.

An hour ago, I was hustled back into bed. Although the crabby nurse made me undress, sniffing my shirt like a drug dog, I'm back in my clothes. The first hurdle, according to Nikki, is passing the nurse's station.

Nikki pokes her head out, peering down the hallway. "The coast is clear."

"This isn't a spy movie, Nik. There are no cameras."

She glares. "I'm not taking any chances. If we don't get home tonight my mom will find out we went to California and be one of those freaking people who everyone says was so nice, you never would have known until she stabbed her only daughter with like, a knitting needle."

"She doesn't knit," I point out.

"Okay, a soup ladle. Happy?"

Nikki gives up looking down the hall, shutting the door. "It's up to you. Obviously, your safety is more important than whether or not I end up buried in a shallow freaking grave."

"Nice guilt trip," Paul says with a frown.

"Thank you."

"I was being facetious."

"So was I, Mister SAT vocab." She turns to me. "We making a freaking break for it or what?"

I nod and she hugs me. "Yay." She's much happier without Allison. Her beaming face was the first thing I saw when I woke up.

I cannot stay in this hospital one more second. Although there have been genuinely sympathetic people, it feels like I'm hiding from real life. Nothing will get better if I stay here. Besides, I miss Allison. Although I've relived The Kiss a hundred thousand times, mostly I just want to see her.

"I am dead set against this," says Paul just as there is a knock at the door.

"Paul, I know you're looking out for me but I have to get home."

He comes over to my bed. "So wait a day."

I pour everything into two words, hoping he'll get it. "I can't."

A perky teenage girl in a candy striper apron wheels in a rattling cart loaded with books and magazines. She looks all of fourteen. "Hi, I'm Amber. I heard about your grandma. That is like soooooo sad."

"My grandmother?" I picture my grandma, a cigarette dangling from her lips, flirting with a logger who'd just won two hundred bucks on a scratch lotto card.

Mike slips into the room behind Amber, wiping away a fake tear. "Your grandma with the brain tumor? Hanging on to say goodbye?"

Surely Amber can tell he's lying but no, she's one of those girls who loves being in the middle of drama.

"Poor grandma."

<hr />

Somehow, through bodily contortions I didn't think possible, I have crammed myself into the bottom shelf of the cart. Amber will wheel me down the corridor, past the nurses' station and into the elevator. After that, things are vague. Candy stripers, Amber says, never take their carts outside. She's worried someone will stop her at the door. However, Nikki thinks we'll get caught if someone spots me climbing out of the cart when we're inside. After a lengthy debate, Paul points out that any minute a nurse is going to enter the room and bust us.

"Hurry up!" I squeal from my hiding spot. My left hip, shoulder and knee ache against the cold metal and my feet tingle.

"Okay," Amber says. There is a break of light as she parts the curtains. "You okay in there?" she asks.

"No," I snap and then feel guilty. She is, after all, volunteering to help me.

There is a light knock at the door. "Hello there." I recognize the nurse's cheery voice. "Where's Fran?"

Nikki whispers. "She's sleeping."

"Okay. I'll come back later. Hi Amber, very nice of you to visit the older kids."

"I was just offering them books. Nothing else. Nothing." Amber's voice is tense with nerves.

"Okay, fine."

"I have to go downstairs now," Amber says. "But not to the lobby."

"Alright." I can see the nurse's clogs through a gap in the curtain. "I'll come back later and check in."

The door shuts. "On my God!" Amber squeaks. "I could lose my job."

"Aren't you a volunteer?" asks Nikki.

"It's the same thing!" Amber hisses.

I can feel Nikki biting her tongue. "Uh-huh. Okay, let's go."

As Amber wheels the cart down the hospital corridor, my head bounces against the clattering top shelf. Various people say hello to Amber. She responds with a shrill, nervous "hello," pushing the cart faster. With every "hello" the speed increases until my head is bouncing like a tennis ball.

"Hey! Amber! Hold on! Wait up!" It's a man's voice. "There's something wrong with the cart."

The speed of the cart slows. "No there isn't."

"Yes there is."

"No. There. Is. Not." She pushes faster. My head jumps.

"No, no. It sounds like there's too much pressure on the wheels," he insists.

The cart stops. "There's nothing in the cart but books." Amber sounds like a mouse on helium.

There is a ding and the whoosh of an elevator opening. "Lemme just look-"

She wheels the cart halfway but from the bumping it feels like they're playing tug-o-war with the cart. "Let go!"

"No!"

"Ow! My foot!" Through the curtains I catch a glimpse of the man hopping on one foot.

Amber stabs the buttons as the elevator door shuts. "Shit. Shit. Shit."

Her face flushes pink as she leans down. "You've got to get out. That was Ivan. God he's so nosy. Hurry! We're only one floor up."

As she pulls me out I get really dizzy but it's good to stand. The headache is back. Amber stares at the illuminated floor numbers. "Come on! Come on!"

The doors open on a hallway flanked with windows and a reception area. "Go!" Amber screams.

I step out, unsure of where I should go. When I

arrived, I was blind so I don't have the faintest idea of the layout. A nearby door opens and Ivan bursts out.

He spots me. "Hey! You're the kid with the concussion!"

I take off running towards a larger reception area. Clusters of seniors rest on couches facing the wide glass entry. Paul's crummy car, looking surprisingly wonderful, waits at the curb. I race full tilt towards the sliding door, not far ahead of Ivan. His clogs squeak on the stone floor.

A little kid blocks my way. I hop over him and his mother screams. "Hey! Watch where you're going!"

The doors whoosh open. The heat is a blow dryer set on high. Mike pushes open the car door from inside, his lanky form stretching across the seat.

Mike drags me into the car. Ivan grabs a hold of my leg. "I saw that tox report. You aren't going anywhere!" He tugs my leg to pull me out.

"Go!" Nikki leans over the front seat swearing her head off at Ivan. "You son of a freaking bitch! Let go of her!" She turns to Paul in the driver's seat. "Drive!"

"Go man! I've got her!" Mike hollers. "Get this piece of shit moving!"

Paul guns the Taurus. It stalls with a high-pitched grinding noise before lurching forward. "Come on come on come on!" Paul whispers. "Don't do this now. Please."

Although I don't want to hurt Ivan or hit his face, I kick enough to loosen his grip. The car lurches forward with a sick squeal.

"Call the cops!" Ivan shouts at an orderly pushing a pregnant lady in a wheelchair.

"Why?" The orderly scratches his head.

"Oh for God's sakes call security. Call someone!" Ivan insists.

The Taurus gears find their groove. "Oh thank God," Paul whispers.

Mike keeps his hands firmly under my arms. Ivan's grip on my leg slips down to my shoe. It comes off in his hands. We speed off with the door open. We zip around the corner, flying into the street.

As his grip relaxes, I slide away from Mike, half slipping out the door. Mike grabs the fingers of my left hand.

"Owwwwww!" My fingers burn.

Nikki screams. "She's out the door! Shit! Shit! Shit!" Paul brakes and we all jerk forward. I land on the floor as the door slams shut.

"Everyone okay?" Paul asks, leaning over the seat.

Mike hauls me up to sitting position. I wiggle my fingers, nodding, unable to speak.

"You sure?" Nikki asks.

I keep nodding. Maybe I mumble something but I'm not sure. My brain is still hanging out of a speeding car with my butt four inches from pavement.

"That was intense." Paul puts the car in gear and hits the gas, speeding furiously with great control. The Taurus seems to understand that although it's ancient, badly maintained and hideous, this is its moment.

"Fucking A!" Mike screams as we squeal out of the parking lot. Nobody tells him to shut up. We all scream in delight at the first sign that says: to I-5 north.

"Nice job Paul!" Nikki says, scooting over to kiss him on the cheek. He looks at her for a long second before grinning happily.

"F-ing A!" he says. "Let's get out of Dodge."

And so we do.

Three miles into Washington, we're back in deep doo-doo.

NIKKI

Those last hundred miles with Paul beside me flew. I kept thinking about our Chapstick scented kisses, his smile and the way he slung his arm around me as if we like, belonged together. After we pass over the grey waters of the Columbia, it all drains away. A few miles later, Paul glances in the rearview mirror and bam, we're right back in trouble.

"Oh crap," Paul says as we pass a State Patrol. Mike and Fran are asleep.

"What?"

"He's got binoculars. He's reading our plates."

My stomach goes cold, churning like I drank too much Slurpee. "Shit."

Paul's fingers drum the wheel. "Could be nothing."

I know it's something before the lights start flashing. "Pull over Paul."

He keeps driving. "Could be someone else. We don't know it's us."

He pulls off the highway and I decide to tell him, whispering so no one else can hear. "I didn't get into UW."

He looks over at me. "What? Where are you going?"

I shake my head, wiping away a tear. "I was so sure I'd get in."

He puts a hand on my knee and I stare at it until he takes it away. "What are you going to do?"

More tears leak out. "I don't know."

After a rap on the window, Paul rolls down the window. A fresh-faced Officer Nance pokes his face into our car, his skin glistening under his Smokey the Bear hat. "Hey Nikki. Your dad said you'd be here."

He acts like it's a freaking football game and I'm with my boyfriend. "I'm not happy to see you."

He's on his radio, nodding. "Yeah. Most people aren't. You kids hang on."

God, he loves calling me a kid. Loved pulling me over as soon as I got my license, telling me he was going to let it go, this time. Next time he gave me a whopper of a ticket. Said it built character. Nobody says a word as he strolls back to his car. Cars whizz past on I-5 as I slump into my seat. "Shit. Shit. Shit. Shit."

"Nik—what the hell?" Fran says, wiping a crust from her eyes. "You know him?"

"He's my dad's Little Brother if you can believe it."

Mike, busy crushing unsold mini Tic Tac bongs, stops. "Thank God I smoked all the weed—wait, dude, your dad has a black brother? Is he like a half-brother or what?"

Paul's hand is over his face. "It's a mentoring organization you idiot. Big Brothers."

Of course Dad would totally call Bobby. The guy would cut off his foot for my father. In third grade, I'd hated him for taking my father's time. I dreamed of my father, who hated sports, coaching my soccer team. "My dad really wanted him to be a lawyer. He's still trying to talk him into it."

Paul's head is on the wheel. He groans, "I was going to shampoo the upholstery before my mom got home from work so she wouldn't smell weed. I'm supposed to be the good one."

When Bobby comes back, he isn't nearly as chipper. "Bad news."

I lean over the front seat. "I don't suppose I can get a pass because we're kind of related."

He shakes his head. "Sorry kid, strictly business here although, man, I thought I was just giving you a ride. This car's got an APB out on it. Your dad was worried but someone in California is not at all happy."

"Fucking Ivan," Mike groans. "That douche."

Bobby leans further into the car. "You watch your language."

Mike nods, giving him the hang loose sign. "Got it dude."

"Officer Nance."

Mike nods. "Yes sir."

Bobby shakes his head. "I've got to impound the car and drive your butts home, which I was planning on. But just you and your friend Fran here." He leans into the car. "You're Fran, right?"

She nods tiredly and I feel terrible, totally responsible. *What in the hell will Dwayne do when he hears about this?* "Yes."

"All of you out of the car on the passenger side. Nikki, you're going to sit in the front."

He glances at the boys. "Sorry but you're gonna have to find your way home. This car's impounded."

Half an hour later the tow truck arrives. Fran and I have spent ten minutes watching Paul and Mike with their thumbs out, arguing over hitchhiking techniques. Beat up old VW vans slow down for Mike, smelling free weed only to speed up when they spot straight-laced Paul. Sedans with families slow down for Paul until they notice Mike's drug rug and scraggly hair. Fran and I try talking Bobby into driving the boys. He finally turns around. "This isn't a state sponsored cab company. I'm a trooper. Every person goes in the log. The more people in the log, the more explaining I've got to do. Now hush."

Bobby returns to the car after a long discussion with the tow truck driver. I can't bear looking at the Taurus totally strung up. It's bad enough being delivered home by my father's little brother but knowing Paul's mom will end up paying a huge fee for her own freaking car makes me nauseous. Fran leans against me and I sling my arm around her. Tears slip from her eyes. She sighs and sniffles, trying hard not to full on bawl.

Bobby ends his discussion with the angry dispatcher, who wanted to know what he was doing so far south. After a moment watching the boys shake their useless thumbs, he turns. "She okay?"

"Not really." I'm close to freaking out myself. How can I face my parents after lying to them for so long? For humiliating them in front of their friends? For letting them go all the way to Seattle?

"You're that girl who's running for prom queen?" Bobby asks as he starts the car.

"Yeah." Her tone is flat, her face pale.

Bobby turns on his turn indicator, pulling onto I-5. I

look the other way as we drive past the boys. It's too sad. "I saw that on the news. Kind of a raw deal."

"Yeah," Fran says. "I'm gonna take a nap."

Five miles later her head rests heavy and warm in my lap. Bobby turns on his indicator but I don't say anything, thinking he's getting coffee or food. Instead he turns south, getting right back on I-5. Minutes later we pull up in front of the boys.

Bobby rolls down the passenger side window, beckoning to Paul. "If I give you a ride you can't ever tell anyone. Not a soul. I could lose my job."

"Not a word," Paul says, nodding. Hunching over the window, he turns. "Can you keep your mouth shut?"

Mike stares down the approaching cars. "Dude, we could get a ride."

Paul stands up. "So you can't?"

Mike thinks a long time, his hair blowing in his face. "Naw, I can't."

"Hang on a second," Paul says to Bobby. "You'd rather hitchhike?"

Mike shrugs. "I'm gonna smoke weed. I'm gonna talk. Thing is—I got one question."

"Shoot."

Mike darts past Paul, leaning into the open cruiser window. "Hey Nikki, you wanna go to prom?"

It's nice to be asked even though I know he wants to go with Hazel. My face lights up before realizing that Paul looks crestfallen. "Thanks Mike," I whisper, smoothing the hair on Fran's head. "I'd better make sure she has a date first."

"Gotcha." He winks at me and slaps Paul on the back before shutting the car door. Paul slides into a corner, watching me warily. Whenever we make eye contact, he looks away. Mike lopes out ahead of us on the freeway shoulder, putting out his thumb.

I keep waiting for Bobby to remind us that hitch-hiking is illegal but he keeps his eyes on his side view mirror before smoothly pulling out. Fran is still asleep.

PAUL

Welcome to Aberdeen. I don't know how many times I've driven past that green sign on the Olympic highway. Thousands. Logging Capital of the World is the next sign, although with so many mills shut down it's just a depressing reminder. As Officer Nance drives his cruiser into my hometown, I can't believe we've been gone for less than two days. It feels like a lifetime. Two days ago, I thought I was the luckiest guy in the world because Taylor was my girlfriend. I ran away to avoid my father, not her. Now my whole world is upside down because of Nikki. She was there the whole time and for some reason, I never knew it. Maybe I was too busy trying to keep Taylor happy. I even got jealous when Mike asked Nikki to prom. Now she's confided in me and I feel like I should be there for her. She's going to face her parents on her own. What's worse is that I want to be there. It's a serious problem and I cannot stop thinking about it.

When we get into town I give Officer Nance my address, hoping I'll have a chance to say goodbye to Nikki alone. Fat chance. What would I say? That I'm sorry? That I've spent the last two years with my head up my butt? That everything will be hunky dory with her parents, eventually. It doesn't matter anyway because when we pull up to the house I spot Taylor's early graduation present, a new white Jeep Cherokee, parked outside. She spots me climbing out of the cruiser and runs over, her blond ponytail bobbing.

"Well hey there, what a coincidence." She leans into the window of the cruiser, spotting Fran in the back, just waking up and Nikki beside Officer Nance. "You two look right at home there. Second home and all." She flicks her wrist a few times. "Bye!"

Officer Nance shoots daggers in her direction, driving off fast enough to unsettle her. As the car takes the corner, Taylor pushes her sunglasses to the top of her head, surveying my threadbare home, half-dead lawn, and buckled concrete driveway. Two days ago, I would have worried what she was thinking. Now I just wait to hear what she's going to say. It doesn't take long. "This better be one hell of a good story."

My dad opens the front door and things get ugly fast.

FRAN

Officer Nance drops me off at ten o'clock in the morning. Given that I slept the last two hours on the road, I feel pretty decent although it's hard to say goodbye to Nikki. I make a note to call her later because her dad always comes up with punishments he finds highly amusing: part-time work gutting fish at a local cannery or scooping poop at the Humane Society. After I woke up, Officer Nance asked me a few questions, making me promise to get my head checked out later with Fran's mom at the clinic. I made the usual promises.

"Yes, definitely. Thank you for the ride."

He doesn't hang around long, doesn't knock on my door, which is good. Maybe Dwayne won't find out. I wait a bit, watching the cruiser's taillights blink out of sight. The big exciting thing in my life is over. Allison's mom will have her on permanent lockdown. My second kiss, which is the movie running nonstop in my head, won't happen. There will be no once in a lifetime prom, just a depressing handful of diehard friends and misfits. Nikki won't want to go but then we'll get dressed up and say it doesn't matter, we can still have fun, except we won't. She'll watch Taylor drag Paul around and then drink herself into a stupor, reliving every second with Paul from kindergarten to the kiss in California.

My friends won't admit it but they'll wish they were at the other prom. There are no exciting college plans, just another summer of waitressing and this damp, sad town squeezing in until I explode. The only person I want to tell about the trip is Mrs. Garcia but I lied to her so I can't.

I say a little prayer hoping Dwayne and Mom are asleep or at least gone. Sometimes Dwayne works on Saturdays. The carport is empty, which is encouraging. Carefully I slide the glass kitchen door open, making sure it won't squeak. The kitchen is empty.

"You didn't fucking run away? You took my fucking money and went to a fucking concert?" It's Dwayne. He's sprawled in my mom's movie chair. It smells of cheap hairspray and burnt sugar from the days she's too tired to take off her uniform.

How do I respond? If I remind him that it's my home it'll lead to the ungrateful speech, extended version. "I'll pay you back." Maybe that'll appease him.

"You bet your ass you will. I gave you that money

so you could have a fucking head start in life. Not go to some dumb ass concert." He lifts his old Mariner's t-shirt, scratching his balls, encased in old cut offs. I look away.

He jumps up, kicking over a chair in his anger. He stares at it, waiting for something. "Pick up the Goddamned chair."

I'm about to tell him to pick up the chair himself when there is a knock at the door. We both stare at each other for a long time. "Well," Dwayne asks. "You going to get it or just fucking stare at it?"

Although every particle of my being wants to tell him that I do, in reality, just want to stare at it. If I can't go back to California, I want to go into my room. And, by the way, where is my mom? But instead I decide that it's safer and easier to get the door.

Standing on our wobbly front step is a slender man in a navy pea coat. He has a camera strapped across his body in a Canon case. His goatee has a well-groomed slickness that no native Aberdeener achieves. He grins and his face lights up. "Hi, I'm Nathan Steiner from The Stranger newspaper in Seattle. Are you Frances Worthy?"

I nod, staring at his extended hand before comprehending—duh, I am supposed to shake.

"There's a story on the wire that broke in a Fresno paper. They interviewed your friends in the parking lot of the Cow Palace after the concert. One of them was quite drunk or high or something at the time. Mike somebody?"

I nod, trying to comprehend. He talks very fast. "Yeah, that sounds about right."

We're still on the front steps. I'm nervous about letting him in. God knows what Dwayne will say. Also, in the two days I have been gone a layer of clutter has accumulated in the house making it look even trashier. I block his way.

Nathan Steiner is undaunted. Chipper even. "I was hoping we could chat a bit. Were you really hoping to talk to Kurt Cobain and have him play at your prom? I gather there's been some controversy about you running for prom queen."

I look behind the door at Dwayne, whose eyes have gotten huge. "Prom queen?" "Yeah prom queen."

"Now I've heard everything. That was a joke. Everybody knew it but you." Dwayne pushes past me, confronting the reporter. "Look, what kind of a faggot newspaper do you work for anyway? I never heard of The Stranger."

If I were Nathan Steiner I would have said adios and hurried back to my car. But he doesn't. He calmly pulls out a business card and presents it to Dwayne, who studies it in true caveman fashion, puzzling over it for a long time. "I also work for The Seattle Times and string for the Los Angeles Times. Maybe you've heard of them?"

Any normal person would be insulted but Dwayne cracks opens the door, pushing me aside. "I sure as hell have. Come on in."

There isn't room for the three of us in the tiny entryway so I move into the kitchen. As Nathan Steiner walks in Dwayne opens the fridge. "Beer?" he asks, handing a can to Nathan, who shakes his head.

"It's ten o'clock in the morning," Nathan points out.

Dwayne drains half his beer, burps loudly and pounds his chest proudly. "It's the weekend dude. Live a little."

Nathan studies me with a look that's hard to read. "Are you Fran's father?"

"God no!" I blurt out.

"Fran's daddy's been MIA since she was a baby. I'm the man of the house now." He thumps his chest as if he's been here decades instead of months, which makes me grind my teeth. "Do you need my last name for the article?"

Nathan shakes his head. "Thank you. I'll be sure and get it later." He turns to me. "Can we go someplace to talk?"

"Oh, I get it. You want to talk to Frannie all by herself," says Dwayne. "It's okay man. I'll just go in the bedroom. You can have all the privacy you want." He waits with bug eyes.

Dwayne will be sitting in his bedroom, ear pressed against the wall eavesdropping through the paper-thin door. "Can you give me a ride to work?"

"Aw those beaners don't need you to work today, do they honey?" Dwayne asks. "She works for these spics. They're nice as hell but still-"

Nathan ignores him. I'm ready to barf with all the Frannie and honey bullshit. "Yeah, I'm on at noon."

Nathan practically leaps at the chance to get away. We're already bonded by a mutual loathing. "Perfect. Let's go."

NIKKI

"I can't believe you didn't tell us. You had us go all the way to Seattle!" my mom says for, like, the millionth freaking time. "I bought a new dress!" She says this as though she had facial reconstruction for the event.

She and my dad were waiting, like twin freaking stones, standing on either side of the front steps when I got home. My dad clapped Officer Nance on the back, thanking him and then turned to me with a thunderous look. "Inside. Now."

Friday, they had pretended that everything was normal with all their friends until they could get away from the Freshman Welcome Party and come home. My ears burned thinking about that car ride back. It didn't take long to track me down, since Allison's mom had already gone to the principal. Now they keep repeating the same catchphrases on a theme. Or two themes, really. Mom wants to know how I failed her and Dad wants to know what the hell was going on in my head.

I keep telling them that I really and truly thought I'd get into UW, no problem. I kept meaning to tell them about the letter but there never seemed to be a good time. When my mom suggested that Dad make a few calls to his rich frat brother friends and see about a late admission, Dad shakes his head so hard I'm afraid it's going to fall off. "Oh no. Oh no. We're not going to make this any easier on her. No siree Bob." I swear to God my dad sometimes thinks he's in a freaking 1950s sitcom. "What are you going to do with yourself for the next year young lady?"

Young lady? I might be young but that's about it.

"So, you'd support me if I went to college but not if I'm at home?"

Dad again shakes his head, which I suppose I should be grateful for because clearly, he'd rather be strangling me. "If you think you're going to spent the next year lazing around, shopping and hanging out with your friends, you're sorely mistaken."

"My friends will all be in college," I point out. Kind of stupid to admit, I suppose. "Except Fran."

Which prompts my mother to cry out, "And you had the opportunity. Wasted. All wasted. Why didn't you apply someplace else?"

"I wanted to apply to Oregon but I knew how you felt about the Ducks."

They exchange a look that means that yes, if their daughter became an Oregon Duck it would truly be God's revenge for whatever crap they got into as teens but this is worse.

"Oh no," Dad snaps, "Don't you put this on us. This was all you."

Mom is actually crying. "It's the lying that kills me."

I roll my eyes. "Kills you, really?"

Dad slaps the arms of his chair really loudly. "That it. I've had enough of your smart mouth. Go to your room."

He hasn't said that to me since I was twelve and stares as if wondering if it's going to work. But it's a relief. All I want is to be away from these two psychopaths.

I don't know how I'm going to live with them for another year.

FRAN

"My faggot newspaper wants to run a story on this," Nathan says without cracking a smile. He looks down the narrow street at the boarded-up Aberdeen shop windows, the sex shop, the China Pearl restaurant and the food bank across the river. We're in his small, neat Honda, parked outside of Plaza Garcia. During the drive I kept sneaking glances at what he's wearing, trying to figure out what makes him so urban and cool. His Doc Marten's and black Levi's are ordinary but his gaunt frame and tortoiseshell glasses look radical and smart. He's in a place I'd like to be some day, mainly with a cool job in an anonymous city. He must think I'm such a loser.

"Sorry about Dwayne. He doesn't read much."

Nathan laughs. "No kidding?"

"He reads the sports page religiously."

Nathan's face gets serious, almost sad. "Yeah. That's okay." He fidgets with a pen, clicking it repeatedly. "So how would you feel about me writing your story?"

Inside Plaza Garcia Mrs. Garcia wipes down the tables. No doubt they're already clean. She doesn't trust anyone to get every crumb. "I don't know. I mean, it doesn't seem like much of a story. Kurt Cobain's not coming to prom."

He stops clicking the pen. "What? I didn't even know you got near him."

For a split second I think about telling him everything, before realizing in a sudden flash of clarity that I don't want to betray Kurt. Ever. Our conversation was private. If I give that away I'm just like everybody else cashing in on his fame. Or maybe I'm just doing it for myself. "I snuck backstage." No sense in telling him about the broken window. "I saw him but that was it."

"It doesn't really matter. I want to write about you going to the concert but this story is more about intolerance in a small town. I'd want to write about the atmosphere in Aberdeen, the tension at the school, the whole two proms thing." He starts clicking his pen. "I want to interview the parents in both camps."

"I'm sure the other parents have a whole lot to say. They had this PTSA meeting about it in March. Someone said it was the biggest turnout in school history."

"What do your parents have to say?"

"I haven't told my mom."

Nathan frowns. "She doesn't even know?"

I sigh, not wanting to share how Mom is completely checked out. "Not really."

"Does she know you're gay?"

"She and Dwayne made me go to this Teen Life thing. Pray away the gay, you know."

"And what was that like?"

"Well, I met a girl." It feels so good saying it aloud.

"That's hilarious."

I nod. "Not what they'd hoped for."

He reaches into the back, takes out a small black notebook and shows me, asking permission. I nod and he starts writing. "Do you know who's coming to the prom at the school?"

"Just a handful of friends. Maybe a couple teachers are okay with it. I never saw it being a huge deal. I just thought it would be super cool if we could get Nirvana to come. I never wanted to divide the school. The head of the PTSA announced that she was planning this other prom and people kind of went crazy."

He writes quickly in barely legible scratch. "Did you think if Nirvana did show up maybe you'd win?"

"Yeah, I guess. There is a five-thousand-dollar Rotary scholarship."

"Is that why you're doing it?"

I think for a moment, realizing I've changed. Nikki is right. Love is a drug and Allison drips through my veins. Her smell, her eyes hiding behind her hair, her hand pressed into mine. She threw a chair through a window for me, which makes me grin. It's not for the money. Not anymore. Even though it means PC will find me and beat the shit out of me. But that's not what I say.

"I'm doing it because I'd be an awesome prom queen." I don't really believe it. But it's important to say.

Mrs. Garcia has spotted us. I look at my watch which prompts Nathan to look at his notes. "One more question. How does it feel to be a lesbian in Aberdeen?"

No one has ever asked me anything like this before. The slumber party in sixth grade: sleeping bags in a circle, bottles of glittery nail polish and gossip. Nikki got me invited so I went. Each girl had to say what celebrity they were crushing on. All variations on a theme: Jonathan Taylor Thomas or Leonardo DiCaprio or one of the Backstreet Boys. Bored out of my mind, I was flipping through *Tiger Beat*, ignoring everything when Taylor pointed, barking "Who's your crush?"

"Winona Ryder," popped out of my mouth without thinking.

The chattering girls went silent. Nikki spoke through a mouthful of popcorn and braces. "We're not like, talking favorite actress here Fran. We're talking crush! Go again."

Taylor hissed, "You have a crush on a girl?" with such fascination and loathing, I knew instantly that I'd made a colossal blunder. Even Nikki couldn't save me. Those girls were a pack of wolves and Taylor went for blood.

The answer to his question gets stuck in my throat. Winona Ryder pushed me out of the closet. It sounds pathetic and campy. Something in Nathan's kind face dislodges the word in my throat.

"Lonely."

Nathan's eyes meet mine and I pray he's done. I've already said too much. He closes the notebook. "You know, I saw Kurt Cobain on Christmas Eve a few years ago, walking with Courtney and the baby." He looks out the window as a truck rattles past. "It was really cold, almost snowing. I was coming out of the office near Pike Place and they walked right past. Anyway, I thought it was kind of sad to be alone like that on Christmas Eve. Neither one of them are close with their families, I guess. So I've heard anyway."

"At least they have each other."

"Yeah." He drums his pencil on his notebook as if trying to decide something. "So, you're okay with me doing this story?"

I nod and tell him, "Yeah, go for it." When I'm out of the car, I bend over to thank him.

"Can I call you at home if I have any questions?"

"Sure." Just like any other Saturday I go to work. But

it's not. What I've just told Nathan Steiner is going to change my life forever.

PAUL

My dad comes strolling out of the house like he belongs here, which really pisses me off. "Hey kiddo, how's it going?" He yells, nodding at Taylor. She might not have a lick of sense sometimes but she knows bad news when she sees it. After a quick goodbye she jumps into her little white car and speeds off. I can see the whites of her eyes as she drives past.

"That your girlfriend?" Dad asks. He doesn't look half bad, considering the last time I saw him. His hair is neatly combed and his flannel shirt is tucked into his clean jeans. When he was on the junk his breath smelled like a dragon, He looked borderline homeless.

"What're you doing here?" I ask, walking around him towards the house. He follows me into the house.

"Can't a man see his own family?" he asks, standing awkwardly in the entrance. I'll give him this—he seems to be waiting for an invitation.

"Is Mom home?" I poke my head into the kitchen. It doesn't take long. Every room in the house opens onto this one room except the small hall that leads to the two bedrooms. Mom keeps it neat but years of boys and time has eroded any charm the old place once had.

"She went to the store. She'll be back later." He sits down on the couch, patting the chair across from him. The one Mom sits in to soak her feet after a long week at work. The worn carpet has stains from years of Epsom salts. "I thought me and you could talk a while. Man to man."

I shake my head. "I'm beat. I'm going to go take a shower."

He leans back. "I can wait."

"Wait all you want. I don't want to talk to you. Ever." He gets up as if he is going to stop me. "Hang on pal."

I turn around and look at him for a very long time. It is dark in the living room and I think of all the times I wished he was here. I wonder what would happen if I tried just a little. There would be awkward dinners at Arby's and fishing. We'd be one of those families you see on the weekends, the dad trying a little too hard, the kids wishing they were home, watching TV. All kinds of things roll through my head and I think about Nikki. About what might be happening with her parents, two people who only want the best for her.

And then I punch him.

CHAPTER NINETEEN

*"I started being really proud of the fact that
I was gay even though I wasn't."*
Kurt Cobain

FRAN

Instantly I know something is off. Mom's sitting at the kitchen table facing a dirty ashtray, tapping Morse code onto a butt. She never smokes inside, always puffing at a window or near a cracked door. "Hey baby, how's work?"

"Fine. Busy." She never asks about work. I slide the huge container of leftovers onto the table. Sometimes I think Mrs. Garcia makes up phantom orders just to give me leftovers.

Mom pushes the food with her thumb, taking another drag. "Smells good."

"Someone never picked up a party platter. I got the whole thing."

Dwayne pushes open the sliding glass door, loping inside, shivering. "'Bout time. I'm starving."

"I'm going to bed," I say to my mother, ignoring Dwayne. As I hurry down the narrow hall he asks her if she's told me.

"No," she says quietly.

"Well you oughta," Dwayne says through a mouthful of food. "Sooner the better. Damn these taquitos are cold. That's the thing with beaner food. It's lousy cold."

I'm too tired to worry about Dwayne's latest stupid plan. After I've changed into pajamas and washed the grease smell from my hands and face, I reach under the bed to grab my camera bag. Tomorrow I'll hit the darkroom and develop the film. I fish around for a moment before lying on the floor. It isn't there. A small shiver of fear runs down my spine. I must have hid it in the closet. My head still isn't working. That must be it.

A quick search of the closet confirms the worst. Shirts are knocked off hangers. Dirty clothes spill out of my duffel. Someone's been here. In a nauseating flash, it hits me. It's Dwayne. He took my camera. I stand up, hitting the hangars with my head, clawing at them trying to get out. I can see my beautiful little Cannon in Dwayne's ape hands. He'll fiddle with the lens and pry the film door open. He'll ruin the film.

My Nirvana pictures.

My face goes red with anger. My stomach curls into a tiny, pulsing knot. Maybe my mom stopped him. Maybe she saw him opening the case and told him to put it back.

I don't remember how I got into the living room but

I'm facing my mom, screaming and crying. "Where's my camera? Did you take my camera? Where'd you put it?"

Mom looks away from her movie, shaking her head as if she can't understand the question, whispering. "He didn't tell me he was doing it. He just did it."

"Did what?!"

Behind me the sliding glass door opens. Before I can count his thudding footsteps Dwayne spins me around with one meaty paw. "I sold your fancy ass camera. You owed me money."

"You gave it to me! You gave me the money!" No point in reminding him that he was drunk.

He points a finger at me but he's looking at my mom. "That's a load of BS. I gave you some ones. You know you took that hundred. Don't lie to me. You two'd be out on your asses if it weren't for me."

For a long moment we stand still with the black and white flicker of the television casting shadows across the tiny room. My head fills with pure venomous rage. Every rotten, stinking thing I'd love to tell Dwayne. Every shitheel loser my mom's brought home. Every moment I was completely on my own. Dwayne's hand clutches his Oly beer can like it's my throat. The aluminum crackles as he crushes it.

Mom's eyes squint with rabbity fear. "He didn't tell me," she whispers.

Eyes steady, I glare at Dwayne until he reluctantly drops his hand from my shoulder, heading for the kitchen. "We're fair and square now. I got seventy-five bucks for it down at Pete's Pawn but I'll spot you the twenty-five till you get paid." He leans into the open fridge. "We'll forgive and forget 'cause that's how I roll." The pale glow highlights his flushed cheeks as he turns to wink. "Okay? We got an agreement, right? Next paycheck from the beaners you square up."

He tosses his old can in the garbage, waiting for my reply. I wait until he's close enough to stink: stale beer, refried beans and sweat. "You gonna answer?"

I shake my head.

He takes a long pull on his beer. "You better say thank you."

Before I tell him to fuck off and end up with a broken jaw, I turn and walk down the hall.

NIKKI

I totally wasn't supposed to drive or leave the house except to go to school but that didn't freaking matter. It was almost midnight. McDonalds's was going to close and Fran sounded panicky on the phone. I rolled the car down the driveway in neutral and started it down the street. What was I supposed to do? Let her sleep at McDonald's? I don't freaking think so. Even if I was caught I think mom would forgive me for Fran's sake Having a friend over also breaks the rules but Fran will be here for a while, I suppose. It happened once or twice with each of her mom's boyfriends, although her mom used to call and we thought it was a fun sleepover. Fifth grade was very exciting because that boyfriend went to jail. We're tucked into my white canopy twin, butt to butt; my feet dangling off the side. We're totally too big for this but she won't let me sleep on the couch or the floor. As we're falling asleep, she thanks me for rescuing her.

I'm almost asleep. "No bigwhoop. There's only like, one problem."

"What's that?"

"My dad thinks I shouldn't see you for a while."

She's quiet for a long time. "How come?"

"I didn't get into UW."

She's quiet for a moment. "Oh shit. I'm sorry."

"And I didn't apply anywhere else."

I can feel her turn over to look at me. "What? Are you kidding me?"

Flipping over, I tell her about the whole alumni welcome party thing. She starts to laugh. "Holy shit. What were you thinking?"

"I don't know. I was scared."

She pats the back of my head. "Oh. You poor thing. You should have told me."

I snuggle back into my bed. The world has righted itself a little now that she knows. Nothing has changed and yet I feel better. "You had your own shit going on."

"Are you in trouble?" We both know this is a stupid question but I don't call her on it.

"Shit, it's bad."

"Go on."

"Painting the entire freaking house. Outside. I'm going to kill myself falling off a ladder and he like, doesn't care. Then there's the skin cancer from working all day in the sun." The bed shakes as Fran giggles. I bump her butt with mine until she almost falls out. "It's totally not funny. If I finish before the end of summer I'm supposed to start painting the basement and work my way up. You know what my reward is if I do a good job? A freaking internship for my dad's fat law partners who think I'm like, eight. One of them still pulls quarters out from behind my ear. My dad is a sadistic monster. Stop laughing."

"It's kind of funny."

"Screw you."

"Why thank you. Sweet dreams."

"If I have to be stuck in this town with anyone it better be you." She answers with a sleepy murmur.

I'm falling asleep when she sighs. "I've called Allison's house about nine hundred times."

"Did you leave a message?"

"No. Her mom answered one time. I didn't say anything but she knew it was me."

"What did she say?"

Outside an owl hoots. "Stop carring my house. Arrison has moved. She's gone."

"She's totally lying."

"Maybe."

"She's lying."

"Or not."

"She's so lying."

"Go to sleep."

Monday morning all hell breaks loose. My dad, angry that I didn't wake him up about the car is bellowing so hard he spills coffee. While he's changing his shirt, my mom, who is working from home today, hands me her keys, making me promise that we'll only go to school and back. My little shit of a brother Moyer dances around the kitchen chanting, "Spank her! Spank her!" as Mom convinces Dad that he was better off with a full night's sleep. He's wearing his lucky tie which means he's in court. Both parental units are super polite to Fran without actually asking why she's here in front of blabbermouth Moyer.

<hr />

As we pull into the student parking lot in mom's Volvo, we're greeted with a kind of pathetic picket line of five people waving signs chanting, "Keep our schools Christian! Keep our schools Christian!" They're led by a wobbling minister who looks about eight hundred years old.

Four fights have totally broken out over who is going to which prom. Every day Mr. P. has the same message during morning announcements. If we don't show some maturity and like, tolerance, he will cancel both proms. Taylor's camp burst out angrily saying he had no authority off campus. In homeroom Stephanie Calder passed Fran a note: Thanks for ruining my only prom bitch. Every time Fran walks down the hall people hiss, "prom queer." I've gone to the office twice for checking two girls like it's a soccer game which I have to admit was totally fun. One I locker slammed, the other hit the ground. Both times they called my mother who blabs on and on to me about Gandhi and Martin Luther King and productive non-violent resistance. Yeah well Gandhi didn't go to Aberdeen

High. Mr. P. finds out that I'm already grounded and waves me out of his office telling me to stay out of his office or he'll hold my final transcript. When I tell him that I'm not going to college he looks like he's going to cry. "But you're one of our most successful students."

Freaking tell me about it dude.

And now this.

Taylor's mom wears a hot pink velour jogging suit as she passes the minister, who seems blinded by her teeth. She waves her fist, shouting, "Principal P., we know you're in there. Come out and talk!"

"Holy shit." We study the spectacle from the car. "Taylor's mom looks like a giant piece of freaking Bubble Yum."

"I'm not walking past them," says Fran.

I climb out of the car. "It's like three moms, one homeless guy and a minister who dated Mary Todd Lincoln."

"I can't deal with this."

When she doesn't budge, I lean back into the car. "Just get out and we'll like, go in the gym entrance."

It would have worked fine if the camera crews hadn't found us. Just as we rounded the corner around the back of the school near the track, someone yells, "There she is!"

I stop and turn around. Running towards us in perilously high heels is Jean freaking Enersen, the King 5 newswoman. Her bright blond hair bobs up and down as she waves a microphone, balancing precariously on the gravel.

"She looks like an emu." I giggle.

"Oh my God she does!" We both break into helpless laughter.

"Should I talk to her?" asks Fran.

We both love Jean Enersen. On TV she's polished and warm. In Washington State, she's a genuine celebrity. And she's running towards us in heels.

By the time Jean catches us, she can barely breathe. She smoothes down her hair with a perfectly manicured hand. "Are you Fran Worthy?"

Fran nods, awestruck.

Jean tugs at her crisp navy blazer. "Can I ask you a few questions?"

Fran goes pale, raising her eyebrows at me. I mouth, "Jean Freaking Enersen."

"Okay." Fran clenches her fists, hiding them behind her back.

The cameraman arrives, lugging a huge camera on his shoulder, sweating furiously. Jean nods at him. "Okay, why don't we stand in the doorway like this?"

"I can't be late for school," Fran reminds her as Jean combs her hair.

"Of course not. Thank you for talking to me. I appreciate it."

"Sure." When Jean turns away Fran raises her eyebrows in astonishment.

"Would you rather be called gay, homosexual or lesbian?"

Fran glances at me and laughs. "What?"

A red light blinks on the camera and Jean perks up, suddenly all energy. "I'm here with Fran Worthy, the high school senior at Aberdeen High School in Southwestern Washington. We're in the back of the school because out front a minister from the First Church of Nazareth and some parents are demonstrating because of Fran Worthy's decision to run for prom queen. Their objection? Fran is gay. Today is when the seniors vote on their prom queen although the results will not be shared until the night of prom. Fran, what made you decide to run for prom?"

I'm worried that Fran will be truthful. *Good question Jean. Because my best friend is completely bat shit insane and talked me into it?*

Fran frowns for a second. "Maybe it was the scholarship money at first but then when people started to tell me that I didn't have a right to run or that they wouldn't even come to prom if I was in the running, it made me realize that I had a right just as much as anyone else."

"And if you could send a message to those parents and students who object to this, what would you say?"

My answer? *Kiss my ass. That's what I'd freaking say Jean.*

"I would say that we can all have prom together, no matter who wins. I didn't start this out thinking it would divide people. I was pretty shocked when the parents decided to do another prom off campus."

Jean nods. "Would you call yourself a gay rights activist?"

"Other people made it an issue. And it's made my life difficult because there is a lot of prejudice against people like me. Or anyone who is different."

"And that's why you're running? To pave the way for people who are different?"

Fran tilts her head and thinks about it for a moment. We talked about this on the road. She did it to make this world a little less shitty for anyone who is different. But that's not what she says. "Yes."

"And what about those rumors that Nirvana is playing at your prom? Is there any truth to that?"

I have no idea what Fran's going to say. She's so upset about Dwayne taking her camera and more importantly, the film inside; God knows what she'll say. She stares directly into the camera. "Well, we did go to a Nirvana concert and I did talk to Kurt Cobain."

Jean lights up. "You talked to Kurt Cobain? Did he make a commitment to be here?"

Fran totally goes all Mona Lisa and cocks her head. "I guess we'll all find out on prom night."

Jean turns to the camera. "There you have it. A small-town girl standing up for her rights and a small-town prom that could quickly turn into a global event. For King 5 News, I'm Jean Enersen in Aberdeen, Washington."

PAUL

"Oh my God! Turn on MTV now; right this second!" Taylor slams down the phone. Her voice is helium high.

"Now darling! Do not take the Lord's name in vain, right Paul?" says Mrs. Davis from the sparkling white kitchen.

"Now! Now! Now!" Taylor commands.

Taylor started talking to me again. For a week, it's been "Karen, can you please tell Paul that I'm busy?" "Caitlyn please tell Paul that I am still super pissed?" "Blaire, can you please tell Paul that I'd like a vanilla milkshake?"

Unfortunately, the first time she spoke directly to me it was a dinner invitation to her house followed by tutoring.

Taylor might flunk World History. Naturally, it will be my fault.

"Karen says we have to turn on MTV." Taylor gets up from the couch where she was pretending to snore while I asked her to outline the Marshall Plan, glaring because I've never figured out her dad's elaborate remote collection.

She turns on the TV and paces with her arms crossed. Kurt Loder is in front of the picture of Aberdeen they always show on the news, usually in conjunction with another story about the depressed lumber or fishing industry. Taylor turns up the volume so high her mother tells her to lower the volume.

"Shut up!" Taylor snaps.

Her mother comes running in, yelling, "Listen young lady, don't you ever speak to me-"

Taylor hisses at her to listen and miraculously, she shuts up. As Kurt Loder continues, we all watch in silence.

"It's the same town where Kurt Cobain and Krist Novoselic were raised and even the same high school they both attended. Parents of students at Aberdeen High have banded together in protest of a gay student being allowed to run for prom queen by hosting a different dance the same night at a local hotel. They have booked a band, sold tickets, and plan on having the majority of the seniors in this rural community attend. However, if the student in question gets her way, she'll have Nirvana playing at the school sanctioned prom on campus."

Mrs. Davis runs into the kitchen to get her wine,

draining the glass as she stands barefoot on the white carpet.

There is footage of Mike being interviewed in front of the school, looking surprisingly awake. In the background, a few protesters wave their signs. The camera stays tight enough to make it look bigger than it actually was. The interviewer asks Mike if he thinks they have a chance of getting one of the most famous bands in the world to play at their prom. "Well, sure man. I mean, if anyone knows what it's like to get the crap beaten out of them in Aberdeen for being different, it's Kurt Cobain. So yeah, she's hoping that he can do it. Show some solidarity and shit." The profanity is bleeped out.

Kurt Loder is back on the screen. "When contacted, Nirvana's label said they had no information about any arrangement with the band or its managers. Kurt Cobain didn't respond to our request for comment."

"Shit," Taylor says. "Do you think he'll come?"

I don't know what to say. I still can't believe Mike made it on national television.

Mrs. Davis pats Taylor on the shoulder. "Of course he won't honey. That boy's is clearly on something. Why on earth would anyone listen to a kid like that?"

Taylor ignores her mom, who picks up the phone and stomps back into the kitchen. A few moments later I hear her telling a friend that her sign and one of her hands were on national television.

Taylor pouts, crossing her arms. "You already broke my heart once by going on that road trip. Tell me the truth: is there any possibility that Nirvana could show up at school?"

"Honestly, I don't know. I don't even think Fran knows."

She flops on the couch revealing a slice of toned belly above her tight jeans. "So, nothing is for sure?"

"Not that I know." *She's gorgeous.*

She flips her hair, ready to fool around. Although I'm not ready, with her mom a few yards away, I obediently sit down. "She's just messing with my head."

She starts kissing me, rubbing my thigh and I can't think straight. "I guess so." Her tongue circles mine. She doesn't stop me as I slip my hand up her shirt. She's saving herself for marriage but she doesn't act like it, pressing herself against my hard-on as her mother yammers. Every time we've come close she says she's saving herself for prom, then laughs and says, "whoops, I mean marriage. No, I mean prom." It's driving me crazy.

Why am I thinking about Nikki?

FRAN

"Do you think she's like, home?" Nikki leans over me to look at Allison's house on a pretty suburban street high above the Wishkah River. It's nicer than Nikki's neighborhood, with huge old trees and rosebushes behind a neat white picket fence.

It's three days before prom. For the past five days Nikki and I have snuck in and out of the back of the school because the picketing parents remain although now it's only three people. Apparently they don't have jobs. There are rumors that the principal is seeking an injunction against them but every day they show up. Nikki is alternately sad and angry, thinking that what happened on the road with Paul actually meant something. Every night she dissects The Kiss, analyzing what's going on his head. What have I gotten everyone into? All this for a dance?

Rumors about Nirvana are rampant. All anyone talks about in the lunchroom and hallways is their choice of prom and Nirvana's possible appearance. Mike holds court during homeroom and at lunch, telling everyone about my conversation with Kurt Cobain, coloring outside the lines of truth to a captive audience. Whenever I try to correct the rumors nobody listens. Mike's story is landing a bigger fish, reeling the world's biggest band back home for a private concert. Wouldn't Mike know? He's been on national TV.

Tension floats over the entire town like a low pressure system making everyone irritable and snappy. *The Daily Word* and *The Aberdeen American* newspapers have published articles, interviewing dozens of people. At least three ministers have preached sermons about a town divided. Hazel said most people in her church think our principal should be fired. I've overheard Nikki's dad talking worriedly with her mom. At night he walks around the house checking the doors and windows. It feels like something is going to explode. Thankfully PC keeps it to a dull roar, leering in the hallways, adding to the Prom Queer comments but nothing more. Maybe my notoriety is keeping me safe. Who knows? The one person who doesn't mention it is Mrs. Garcia, although she did hug me on Saturday, which was nice.

I have spent days searching for Allison in the hallway but either she's avoiding me or she's now homeschooled by her mom. Every lunch hour I scan the cafeteria but she's not there. I even trailed Monica to her car.

She turned on me. "Leave Allison alone. You've already gotten her into enough trouble, alright?" When I asked her what kind of trouble, she slammed the car door in my face. I kept knocking on her window until she rolled it down.

"Nirvana is nothing special," she said, backing out so fast she nearly ran over my toes. "And neither are you!"

Out of desperation, I let Nikki talk me into showing up at Allison's house like some random stalker. Maybe I agreed because planning it in her basement, holding the twenty-pound boom box over my head made us giggle like fourth graders. A few years back Nikki's dad came home with it, saying a poor client had paid his bill. We both know I'm going to look like an idiot. I have nothing to lose. It is our "Say Anything" plan from the movie we both considered the ultimate in romance. If a guy or girl held a boom box aloft outside your window, not only were they in decent shape; they were a modern Romeo. Rain drizzles down my Juliet's storybook house with the blue shutters and creamy grey trim. On either side of her red door is a camellia bush, bursting with fat blossoms. A girl who lives in a perfect house isn't going to fall for someone like me. Allison is going to be a doctor. My future is serving enchilada platters and scraping change off linoleum tables.

I can't do this runs through my brain like it's on a loop. Or maybe I said it out loud.

"You can't not do this," is Nikki's argument. "You can't go through all of this freaking drama about prom and not like, have the date you want."

"If I go to prom with a girl I'm pretty sure all hell will break lose. Remember Hester Prynne from *The Scarlett*

Letter? Remember how well things worked out for her when she defied the angry villagers?"

"First of all, I read the *Cliffs Notes* and barely remember them and second of all, if you don't go to prom with a girl you're totally going to regret it for the rest of your life. I mean, if you're going to take a stand about not being discriminated as a gay woman you might as well go to prom with a girl. Your secret is like, out."

I wipe at the fog on the windows. A light goes on inside Allison's house. "What if I drop your dad's boom box? He'll kill me."

Nikki takes my hand and squeezes it. "You know he'll kill me. In case you haven't noticed, you're his hero. And right now, you're just a normal girl crushing on someone. So, go be a normal girl and get your crush to come outside, okay?" Normal. She called me normal. Which is just about the best thing anyone has every called me. Big fat tears well up in my eyes. "Suck it up baby, before her mom gets home."

She reaches across me and opens up the car door. Before I can think about it, I get out of the car, lug the boom box from the back seat and walk across the street to her front yard. Those seventy-five steps feel like a thousand miles.

PAUL

"You shouldn't have hit your dad." Mom faces me in the dark living room, a cup of decaf cradled in her hand.

"I should have done it sooner."

She tucks her hair behind her ears. She's still pretty young. She could meet someone else. "I never meant for you to get into the middle of all this. I just thought a boy needed his father, you know?"

I shake my head. "Not one like him. Listen Mom, I know we've given you a run for your money but you've been fine. We always knew you were there for us. We don't need anyone else because we've got you."

Tears stream down her face and she wipes them away. "Oh, wow. You've turned into a young man while I wasn't looking."

I get up and put my arm around her. "Mom, you were here the whole time." We stay there on the couch until there isn't any light left in the room. When I stand up, I somehow feel taller.

CHAPTER TWENTY

"Wanting to be someone else is
a waste of the person you are."
Kurt Cobain

FRAN

Twenty pounds of boom box is heavy and slippery in the rain. I'm doing my best to hold it over my head like Lloyd in the movie except it's nearly tipping me over. I'm blasting "Smells Like Teen Spirit" at full volume when Allison flies out the door.

"What are you doing here?" She's panicked, glancing around the street like she's worried that someone will see that infamous lesbo on her doorsteps.

"Jesus Fran, you're going to drop it."

She helps me steady the boom box and get it to the ground. My finger keeps slipping off the button. Music continues playing until I jab it a few times, finally shutting it off. "Sorry about that."

The tiniest of grins lights her face as she wipes her hair off her face. "Say Anything?"

"Yes." *What if she despises the movie and thinks John Cusack is an asshole?*

"Great movie."

It's all I can do not to hug her; I've missed her so much. "I haven't seen you since the concert." *Since the best kiss in the history of the universe.* "I just want to talk." The words stick to my throat. She doesn't want to see me. I've caused enough trouble.

"Mom grounded me. If I see you they'll send me to my aunt in Chicago after my last final."

"Because of the concert?"

Allison pushes her hair off her face, looking up at the drizzling sky. "Look, this is more complicated than you think."

I frown, getting a sick feeling. "That doesn't sound good."

"When we lived in San Francisco I got involved with someone a lot older. She was in college and my music tutor. My parents hired her from Berkeley and when they found out, it really freaked them out. They felt betrayed by her and just shocked at the whole situation. So, when my dad got offered this job my mom finally agreed to move." She waves her hand around. "This was supposed to be a fresh start for all of us."

"I don't suppose dating a girl is part of that?"

"It's not just that, it's that I skipped school and lied. It feels like the same betrayal to them. Back then, I think the worst part was the dishonesty. Maybe not. We didn't talk about it."

"That sounds familiar."

"Now my mom thinks my sister is rebelling. She wants to quit piano."

"And what do you think?"

Allison looks miserable. "If I don't listen to her she'll talk my dad into cutting off my tuition. I'll spend next year working some lousy job and hearing about all her friends' kids who are pre-med and pre-law and spending their summers interning at hotshot Seattle firms."

All the air is sucked from my lungs. "So that's it?"

She rolls her eyes, throwing out her arms. "I don't know what you want me to do Fran. It's not like I can just go, oh well, screw college. This is my life."

"It's your future, not your life."

Her eyes flash. "They're the same thing."

"No, they're not. You have no idea what's going to happen in your future. You could change your mind about medical school. You could stand up to your parents and see how they deal with it."

"God you make it sound like it's easy."

"It is easy!" I'm yelling and crying a little through the rain on my face. "Every day I go to school and face people who despise me. People who tell me I'm worthless because I'm gay. I came here because I thought when you came to the Nirvana concert it actually meant something. I thought you cared about me and were willing to risk something. I thought we were on the same side."

She looks down at her feet. "We are but this-" she gestures between us, moving her hand back and forth. "-is too complicated."

I study the winding inky river at the foot of the hill.

"I want you to go to prom with me." It hangs between us like a grenade.

She's crying. "I can't."

"You don't want to be seen with me in public. Is that it?"

She reaches out, puts a hand on my arm. "It's not like that."

I jerk away my hand. "It's exactly like that."

She won't meet my yes. "I'm sorry."

"No you're not. You're a coward."

Her eyes flash. "I'm just the one with something to lose so don't blame me if I don't throw it away."

"You're right I'm just some piece of trash from the wrong side of the tracks who's never going to make it college. But at least I'm not afraid of who I am."

When I turn around Allison says "wait," but I keep going. She isn't going to change her mind. I'm not even sure I want her to.

NIKKI

That night when Fran and I get home, there is a police car parked outside of my house. It's not Bobby. Neither one of us says anything as we hurry up the stairs and into the open front door. My parents are in the dining room with a uniformed police officer. As we enter, my mom snatches a piece of wrinkled paper off the table, folding it into her arms.

"What happened?" No one mentions that I'm grounded or that I took the car, again.

The police officer explains that while Moyer was home

alone someone threw a rock, shattering the front window. While he talks I study my parents. Mom keeps scratching the same place on her arm leaving red welts. Dad is about ready to totally explode. There is a tic popping in his jaw that makes me so nervous I wince. After we learn about the location of the broken window, Fran and I step back, staring down the hallway into the living room. Sure enough, the large plate glass window has a freaking hole surrounded by spidery cracks that we didn't notice in the dark. I wonder if the lights are off in the room to prevent anyone from looking in. The officer asks Fran if she has any idea who did this.

"No." Fran studies the carpet before forcing herself to look him in the eye. He's thick-necked and reminds me of Dwayne.

"There's no one at school you can think of who's been belligerent or mean?" Dad asks.

Fran frowns. "His name is PC. He's on the football team. It's him."

The officer nods. "What makes you think it's him?"

"He's been threatening me all year. He said if I didn't drop out of running for prom queen he'd get me. It's him."

I get an icy feeling down my spine as my dad and the police officer exchange looks. The cop hands Fran his card, telling her to call if she thinks of anything else. "We're gonna have a little chat with PC."

Fran nods, staring at the tic pulsing in my dad's jaw. He totally looks like a cartoon character right before steam blasts out of his ears.

After the officer leaves, Fran tells Mom that she's really sorry. She can't even look at my dad. "I should go home."

"Don't be silly. We're happy to have you." Scratch, scratch. Mom's poor arm.

Dad's mouth is a tight line as he frowns at Mom. He would shit an entire freaking brick if he knew his boom box was soaking wet, possibly broken.

"I should go home," Fran insists, knowing home isn't an option. My dad opens his mouth to say something but Mom shoots him a look and he changes his mind. This is how their marriage works. I've seen entire conversations where neither of them have said a word.

"Fran, you can stay here for as long as you need to. And if this kid bothers you, please tell me," My dad says, a little too loudly. "You're not the only one involved in this now. Moyer is really shaken up. He's just a little kid."

I step forward. "First of all, he's almost thirteen. He reads your Playboys." I do air quotes around reads. "And Fran didn't do anything wrong. PC is the one who did this, alright?"

"That's enough Nik," Mom says.

"Of course she didn't do anything honey but the fact remains that your brother got very scared tonight. I just want her to be forthcoming with us, that's all."

"Which she has been so leave her alone."

Dad says something under his breath. "Your turn," he says to my mom who nods her head. He goes to the fridge, cracks a beer and goes onto the back deck.

Mom squeezes Fran's arm. "He's just worried. He'll be fine. Why don't you girls go find some cardboard to put over the window? It's in the garage."

I dig around the ice-cold garage while Fran collects the boom box from the car. Rain drums on the roof as she enters, sheltering it with her body. Her hands shake as she dries it off. I study her in the half light. Her cheeks burn pink as she repeatedly presses the on button.

"It's broken."

"Maybe not. Let it dry overnight."

She stays crouched, hand on the rag. "Okay."

"PC won't bother you anymore. You know that right? He's a big freaking chicken."

She stands up, looking away as she hangs up the rag. "I know. Look, I'm fine."

She's lying.

That night I can't sleep. I go into the kitchen for a glass of water and spill some, wiping it up with a paper towel. When I open the garbage, I discover the wrinkled note that must have been wrapped around the rock. It's on the back of a ripped-up paper grocery bag, brown and creased with blue printing on one side. I hold it in my hand for a moment, not wanting to know what is says. But I'm going to open it. There's no freaking way I can't.

There are two words scrawled in angry pen: DIE BITCH.

FRAN

Two days before prom, PC shows up at my locker with his stupid friend Rog. When I turn around their beefy frames block my view. "You told the cops I threw the rock." PC sneers. "Good thing I was with Rog."

They both snicker. This is the closest we've been since he slammed me against the locker. His acrid sweat stings my nostrils. His pulse throbs on his neck like an angry toad.

"Whatever. If you bother me again, I'll tell Nikki's dad."

"Ooooh. A dad, now you're in trouble!" Rog snickers.

"He's a lawyer," I snap.

Rog and PC frown as though they're not quite sure what this means. I let it sit, not knowing exactly what it means myself.

PC's has lost a little steam but plows on. "Drop out or you'll be really fucking sorry."

Rog bumps my elbow and I drop my books. PC snorts with laughter. He kicks them smoothly down the hallway. People jump out of the way, rushing to class. Rog stomps my three-ringed binder and papers explode out. Snickering, they disappear around the corner.

I'm sitting on the floor against the lockers waiting for the hallway to clear out. A shadow falls over me. "You wanna tell me what happened?"

It's Paul. He's got my binder and a handful of papers. I wipe my nose on my sleeve and shake my head, taking the papers from him when he squats down. "Okay, then, do me a favor. Meet me in the gym after third period."

"Why?"

"Just do it." The bell rings and he's gone.

When I enter the gym all the lights are on so it takes a moment for my eyes to adjust. Except for Paul the gym's empty. It stinks of Pine-Sol and BO. "Over here!" His voice echoes.

Paul's in the corner, dressed in grey sweats. When I reach him, he takes my backpack. "Take a lap."

I roll my eyes. "Um, no."

"Come on, I'll go with you." Soon we're jogging side by side around the empty gym, our sneakers squeaking on the floor. It's nice to see him, after the trip. I have to bite my tongue not to ask about Taylor.

"You wanna tell me what we're doing here?" I ask after the first lap.

"Sure." We've reached the mats and he sprints ahead, boxing into the air. "Just do what I do."

I stand there, limp-armed. He encourages me by dancing around like he's in the movie *Rocky*, punching the air. "Come on, it's fun."

Except it's not. "Paul what are we doing?"

He throws a few jabs. "Teaching you how to fight."

"Me?" *What?* "That's probably the sweetest thing any guy has ever said to me."

"If you're not going to tell me who's messing with you then I'm going to teach you self-defense. Put up your dukes."

When I hesitate, he demonstrates a stance: arms up, feet wide. "Come on. I know what I'm talking about. My mom's last boyfriend teaches this stuff in Olympia. Don't you want to learn how to defend yourself?"

After two hours we're tired, sweaty, and resting on the floor on some mats. He's taught me to dodge a punch, where to hit (face, groin, knees,) how to get out of a hold, and how to use my own weight to inflict damage. Although I'm not very strong, I work hard. I'm panting so Paul hands me a water bottle.

After I drink, I wipe my mouth, staring at Paul a long time. "Hey, I don't mean to get personal or anything but why are you going out with Taylor?"

He throws himself backwards on the mat. "Oh no, that's not personal at all." He focuses on the fluorescent lights humming on the ceiling. "Why wouldn't I want to go out with her?"

"Because you two are very different people." I measure my words out carefully. After all, he is dating her.

"Hey, that's not nice." He sighs like he knows exactly what I mean. "I don't know. I mean, I've had a crush on her since freshman year and when she acted interested in me last summer it was, well, shocking I guess. I just never thought it would happen. Do you know what I mean?"

Here goes nothing. "Nikki is in love with you."

The gym grows deadly quiet. An outer space vacuum where no sound has ever existed. Paul sits up, gripping his knees, his mouth hanging wide open looking genuinely shocked. "Come again?"

"Has been for ages."

"Nikki?"

"Yes, Nikki."

He sits up even straighter, blinking like a robot making millions of calculations. "You mean like Nikki, Nikki?"

I wipe the sweat off my brow, staring at the dusty beams running across the ceiling. "Oh for God's sake Paul. The girl who flirted with you for 800 miles and back for a grand total of 1,600 miles of flirting. Are you completely blind?"

"I thought she hated me."

"If that's what you got, you are the world's stupidest boy."

PAUL

Apparently I'm the world's stupidest boy. I wave absentmindedly at Fran as I stumble into the boys' locker room, thinking about how Nikki is actually the idiot. How one minute she kissed me and the next we were arguing over something dumb like who's going to take the FIFA Cup this summer. Brazil. Italy. Brazil. Italy. How she gazes into my eyes and then won't talk to me. When she kissed me it felt real and fantastic but then again, she was high and so how could I be certain it meant anything?

Right now, I'm not certain of anything.

But Nikki.

Wow.

This changes everything.

Right?

While I'm in the shower I think about how Taylor is my first real girlfriend. Maybe all girls show you their best side and then bam, you're their lap dog. Maybe Nikki would order me around like Taylor. I can't really see it. Nikki argues with me but if I'm perfectly honest, I like it. It makes it feel like we're on equal footing, instead of me being another lap dog to Taylor.

Taylor, who is my prom date.

Yes, Taylor.

By the time I'm toweling off I'm back to Taylor my super-hot girlfriend. More importantly I'm not the kind of guy who dumps his girlfriend right before prom. My dad was disloyal.

I'm not.

I'm the good guy.

Right?

FRAN

Taylor and her minions have gone into overtime squashing rumors that Nirvana will play at prom. She glares at me in the hallway screeching "As if!" every time she sees me. Hazel and Nikki take turns chaperoning me from class to class, providing a buffer although Taylor doesn't bother me. PC is my biggest worry. No one seems to believe that I don't know the answer to their question: will Nirvana show up? After all, it's prom. Nobody wants to be in the wrong place.

Two days before the prom Nikki and I part ways as she hurries into Calculus. World History is two doors down but I have to go to the bathroom. When I come out of the stall two girls named Donna and Lareese block me at the door, telling me they are going to beat the shit out of me if I don't tell them the truth about Nirvana coming to prom. When I tell them I don't know, I haven't heard anything they get even angrier, waving their long nails like weapons. If I am from the wrong side of the tracks, Donna and Lareese are from the side of town where people aren't just poor, they are crazy, either from meth or lack of fear or both. Both girls started dyeing their hair in fourth grade and probably carry knives too.

"Well then I don't know what the hell to do," says Lareese, the smaller of the two. A ponytail spouts from the top of her head like a fountain. Piercings run up her ears like braces. "My boyfriend says he's not going to the lesbo prom. His dad would go after him with a baseball bat but shit, it's Nirvana." She pronounces it Nearvana.

"Tell us!" says Dana, who flunked sixth grade and is nineteen. She wears purple sparkly eye shadow. The acne sprinkled across her forehead is spackled with yellow concealer.

"I swear to God I don't know. It's not like I even know Kurt Cobain."

"Then how'd you ask him to play at prom?" Lareese twirls her bleached hair around a finger.

"I didn't. I don't even know if they've heard about it."

Lareese looks happy. "So that stuff about you talking to Kurt Cobain in California is all bullshit?"

Would it piss them off further to know that yes, I did talk to him? My head is finally clearing from my last concussion. I don't want to get knocked against the dirty tile walls. The bell rings so we're definitely late but neither one of them budges. I'm bone tired of all the gossip and frenzied speculation. What the hell. "I did talk to him. But not about prom."

"Why the fuck not?" Dana explodes. "I mean no one's going to come to your pathetic lesbo prom. It was your one chance to get some people there. Know what I'm sayin'?"

"Shit Dana, whose side are you on anyway?" Lareese shoves Dana into the sink. "Don't go queer on me."

Dana turns to Lareese like they're on some kind of

demented afternoon talk show. "If she drove all the way to California to talk to Kurt fucking Cobain, she should have asked him to play at prom. Am I right or am I right?"

Lareese shrugs and applies watermelon Lip Smacker.

I'm trapped in a bathroom with two psychopaths. I keep waiting for someone else to come in the door and distract them long enough for me to dash out but everyone sane is already in class. "You're going to make me late."

They both reek of the Southern Comfort they carry around in their backpacks, which is sad because I'm pretty sure that bump poking out of the fringe on Dana's cropped t-shirt means she's pregnant. Aberdeen is full of angry, bored girls. Being trapped in here with two of them makes me realize that Allison is right. I desperately need to get out of Dodge.

"Just tell me why you didn't ask him?" says Dana. "'Cause now I seriously wanna know."

Lareese is looking at her like she's crazy, which I think she is. And pregnant. Maybe if I tell them they'll let me out. "It just seemed like too much to ask."

Dana throws up her hands and steps aside. "God you are fucking stupid." She digs in her purse, locates a pint of Southern Comfort and takes a long swig.

I dart out of the bathroom thinking that maybe she's right. Keeping my mouth shut would have been so much easier.

CHAPTER TWENTY-ONE

"If it's illegal to rock and roll, throw my ass in jail!"
Kurt Cobain

FRAN

"Fran, can I talk to you for minute?" Principal P. sticks his head into third period. The entire class makes an "Ooooohhh," noise as if I've been busted. I give Principal P. a deer-in-the-headlights look which annoys him. "Just bring your books." There are only a few minutes left in class.

He shuts his office door and collapses into his squeaking chair. "I just got the strangest phone call." He grabs a hand strengthener off the desk, squeezing it as he gazes out the window at the rainy street. "From someone at DGC records." He turns to me. "Have you ever heard of them?"

My heart starts beating a mile a minute. "Yes. It stands for David Geffen Company."

"I take it they record or represent the Nirvana band."

I nod, wishing he'd get to the point. "Nirvana. Just Nirvana."

"Isn't that what I said?" The muscles in his forearm stand out as he squeezes the gizmo. I nod again to avoid further delay. "The Nirvana band wanted to respond to all the media hoopla about prom and to say that the band is completely sympathetic to your situation and-" He locates a sheet of paper on his desk and finds his reading glasses. "They are one hundred percent supportive." He puts the paper down, looking at me over the top of his glasses. "That's what this woman, Irene Gellar said. One hundred percent. I took notes."

I want to scream at him to get to the point before I pee my pants from excitement. I'm bobbing my head and clenching my jaw, praying that they're coming.

"She said that their touring and recording schedule won't allow time for them to come here and show their support. And they're not going to make a statement to the press at this time."

They're not going to make a statement? Whoever asked them for a statement? I can't help it. I'm so disappointed I want to scream. *Don't make a statement. Just come. Just show up.* That would be the statement. My eyes well with tears.

"I'm very sorry Fran. I was hoping it would work out." He's so sweet which makes it worse.

I nod, numb with disappointment. "Can I go now?"

"How about this one?" Hazel holds up an

off-the-shoulders blue cocktail dress that reminds me of Shelley Winters in *The Poseidon Adventure.* The old me would have tried it on and held my cheeks, pretending to scream at an imaginary wall of water before boring Hazel to death with the entire plot summary of the movie.

The new me is dragging. "Maybe not." I paw through the formal wear section at Goodwill. It reeks of mothballs and musty old fabric. The front windowsill is a collection of crispy dead flies on dusty stacks of magazines. We've been here for forty-five minutes and I have hated everything. The new me is sick of prom, sick of school and sick to death of living in someone else's home. Nikki has been awesome but with her moaning about her punishment, her future, and Paul, I'm ready for a break.

Hazel is the only person pushing this prom forward. She's rallied with a Goth Theme, draping the gym in miles of black tulle with black cardboard chandeliers and twinkling purple fairy lights from Party On in the Aberdeen Mall. She's thrilled, even giddy about prom in a way I haven't seen since she came to school on painkillers from having her wisdom teeth pulled. She's even hired a punk band called the Wastrels. In their photo, they look like dubious meth heads but I'm not going to burst Hazel's bubble. We're going to wear 1950s thrift shop dresses with combat boots and ripped black tights - if I can find a dress. Although I've tried faking enthusiasm I feel like a reluctant groom to Hazel's bubbly bride. She shares every development and detail. I nod and pretend to listen.

"How about this?" I show her a turquoise silk monstrosity with oversized green rhinestones sewn around the high-necked collar.

"Are you serious?" Hazel wrinkles her nose.

I grin and she's relieved. We both keep digging through the overstuffed racks. All of Aberdeen has been depositing their prom dresses at Goodwill since 1930 with very few going back out the door. It's a graveyard of style, the end of the line. Like everything else, this strikes me as depressing.

"What are you going to do about the whole prom date thing?" I ask, trying to be nice. I know Hazel isn't going with anyone because she would have told me.

She keeps pawing through clothes, flushed and bright eyed. "Wait, you're going with someone?"

"Yes!" She's barely able to contain her glee.

"Who?"

Her face goes suddenly somber. "Don't laugh."

"What? Why would I laugh?"

She moves around the clothing rack, looking suspiciously at the volunteer biddies whose collective age is a thousand years as if they're going to turn up their hearing aids and eavesdrop. "Just don't. Okay?"

"Who is it?" I am wracking my brain but Hazel hasn't mentioned a crush or a boy or anything all year.

She smoothes down her skirt. "Alright, it's Mike."

"Mike who?"

"Mike Mike."

I frown. "Who?" And then it dawns on me. "Dirty Mike? Are you freaking serious?"

"He doesn't like to be called that anymore." She's angry, raking through the clothes quickly.

"He loves being called Dirty Mike. Are you kidding me? He prides himself on having the dirtiest mind in

Grays Harbor County. You didn't say yes, did you?" When she doesn't answer, I know I'm in trouble. "Look, Hazel, I'm sorry. I knew he liked you. I just didn't think you'd go for him."

"Why not?"

"It's just-"

"It's just what?"

"I mean Hazel, he's a total stoner and you're like, the Christian girl who works at a daycare."

"So, what?"

I think about it for a minute. "You're right. He's really funny. And on the trip, he was really sweet."

Hazel relaxes visibly. A glowing smile lights up her face. "I know, right?"

Holy shit. Mike and Hazel. I mean if you take away his dirtball behavior and brushed his hair he could, technically, be considered good looking. Not to mention that Hazel is the one girl I know who is actually excited to be going to prom, which feels so right, so all-American apple pie normal in a deluded but hopeful way that I decide to jump on board. "So, what are you wearing?"

She collapses with a giddy squeal, so elated she looks like she swallowed the sun. "I don't know. I want something really amazing. Will you help me look?"

And I do.

"Isn't it wonderful to have our friends Frances and Allison join us for our last meeting?" Don beams. The soggy carpet and potato chip smell of the South Aberdeen Baptist Church basement reminds me of the first time I saw Allison, passing notes back and forth and even getting in trouble. It's like rewinding a favorite movie to the parts you loved instead of the shitty ending where your favorite character dies of cancer.

It's the night before prom. Rather than mope around Nikki's house feeling like a sleepover kid who never got picked up, I've returned to the scene of the crime, hoping Allison would too. Now that we're sitting next to one another, I'm not sure if it's such a good idea. It's like tearing a Band-Aid off a too-fresh wound. We're both awkward and unsure of what to say, staring at one another when we think the other isn't looking.

While Don passes the box of Costco assorted potato chips, and drones on about the life choices we'll be facing as adults, the temptations we'll be up against, and the importance of maintaining our Christian faith in the face of evil, Allison slides a note in front of me.

I HOPE YOU WIN

I write back. I WON'T.

THAT'S THE SPIRIT, she writes back.

I write back: HAZEL IS GOING TO PROM WITH MIKE

WTF?????

SHE THINKS HE'S ADORABLE

She replies: IF YOU LIKE EAU DE BODY ODOR MIXED WITH WEED

MAYBE IT'S HER KINKY THING

This is the note that Don grabs. "Ladies, I'll see you in my office after class."

Once again, I don't get to talk to Allison because her mom storms into Don's office, all red lipstick and glowing pearls. She glares at her daughter sitting next to me, spits out a few words in Japanese and hauls her out of the room. "Arrison will not be attending any more of these crasses."

Don shrugs because they left so fast they didn't hear him remind her that it was the last class anyway. "I hope you got something out of this class," Don says to me after the classroom door slams and we're alone.

"I don't know." I shoulder my backpack, strangely sad at this ending. "I guess so." I hope he won't ask me for specifics.

Through an open window I hear Allison speaking Japanese. Two car doors thud and the engine starts. She's gone. It all feels so inevitable and sad. Knowing what I know about San Francisco, I have more sympathy for Allison's mother. Maybe it's not the relationship but the lack of trust. Either way it doesn't matter.

"Good," Don says in a way that makes me suspect that he knows the truth, which is that he gave me a place to fall in love. And have my heart broken. And feel, perhaps, closer to God, even if it wasn't Don's God. I wish there was a way to explain all this but there isn't. So I just say goodbye.

<hr />

I hate my dress. Not just mildly disapprove or dislike but outright despise it. After Hazel told me about Mike at the Goodwill store, I grabbed the first dress that fit, convincing her that I loved it. Even she had a hard time getting enthusiastic but she was due back at the gym to finish the decorations. The dress, a boring 1950s house-wife's idea of a dreamy cocktail dress (safe neckline, long hem, loud flower print,) lies on Nikki's bed like a bad mistake.

Nikki comes out of the bathroom smelling like a field of flowers, already dressed. Her dress is new, soft cornflower blue, and strapless, flattering her graceful shoulders and cleavage. It's the kind of dress that is going to make Paul eat his heart out because Taylor will be in some over-the-top nightmare.

Nikki's sick of my complaining. I've tried on every dress in her closet.

Nothing works.

"Just put the freaking thing on," Nikki says, her head angled to put on an earring. She straightens up, flushing with a deer-in-the-headlights gaze over my shoulder. "Um, whoops."

Her mom is at the door, frowning. "Fran, there's someone here to see you."

Nikki raises her eyebrows, meeting my eyes. We're thinking the same thing. Allison? Could it really be her? If she escaped her dragon mom for Teen Life, maybe she found a way out for prom. A quick spark of energy shoots down my spine. If it's her I will never cuss or smoke pot or do anything bad. I'll dedicate my life to helping people, rescuing animals and visiting old people. I'll be the Mother Teresa of Aberdeen or, better yet, someplace I'd actually want to live, like Seattle. Floating on a cloud of hopefulness, I'm about ready to walk out the door in my bra and underwear before Nikki's mom clears her throat, suggesting I might want to put something on.

"Oh, right." Nikki and I both laugh as she tosses me her robe.

I hurry down the dark hallway, so excited I can barely breathe and, oh no, my mother, in her white bakery uniform. Her arms are crossed and she's facing away, studying the broken window, still crisscrossed in duct taped cardboard.

"Mom?"

She turns, giving me a shy smile. It's weird seeing her in Nikki's living room, which makes me realize that Mom and I don't really see each other out of the house. She seems unsure of herself.

"Fran! Hey. I'm glad I caught you." She crosses the room with a garment bag, holding it gingerly. She offers it to me, squeezing my shoulder in the process. It's a surprisingly tender gesture. I can tell she wanted to go in for a hug but she's really awkward and weirdly formal. "I bought you something. It's a dress. I thought you might need a nice dress."

I hold the bag up, staring at it, unsure of what to do. *My mom bought me a prom dress?* I can't even remember the last item of clothing she bought me. Sixth grade? The garment bag is imprinted with the Nordstrom logo, which doesn't mean anything. It's probably an old bag from the Goodwill Store. My mother can't even get herself to a Nordstrom, let alone afford anything in the store. She claps her hands together like a little kid. "Open it. I hope it fits."

I stand there, awkwardly holding the garment bag, wanting to throw it back in her face for letting Dwayne pawn my camera. I don't want any part of this lousy dress. Nikki's mom is in the doorway, eagerly clasping her hands.

My mom beckons her into the room. "Come see."

Nikki's mom is so excited, holding her breath and biting her nails. Does she have anything to do with this? Did she call my mom? Although I'm furious at my own mother, the last thing I want to do is hurt the woman who has always taken me in without question. She paid for soccer camp, saying I won a scholarship so I wouldn't be embarrassed. If I turn my back on Mom and throw a tantrum, that's exactly what I'll do. Slowly I unzip the bag and get a glimpse of pale silvery material that glows in the dark room.

"Come on honey!" Mom says.

Nikki's mom wipes a tear from her cheek as I pull the dress from the bag. It's a gossamer light silver slip dress with delicate black beading on the straps and across the chest. "Oh gosh, it's beautiful."

My mom nudges me. "Oh I really hope it fits. Go try it on."

There are tags, real Nordstrom tags dangling from it. "Seriously? I mean—where you'd get the money? This is like a really expensive-"

"Go try it on!" Nikki's mom pushes me towards the hallway.

There is some drama. My cotton bra won't work so I borrow one of Nikki's, which is a bit small but gives me cleavage. After Nikki zips me into the dress, she turns me towards the mirror.

"Wow!" Nikki gasps. "Like, I mean, wow!"

I can't believe the girl in the mirror is really me. The dress hugs my hips, falling gracefully to the floor. I look like the kind of girl I've always wanted to be. A girl from the right kind of family. A girl without money worries and a bright future. I look, well, normal.

PAUL

My brother lends me money for my share of the limo. Ever since I hit my dad, Owen's been really nice. We haven't said anything but there is an unspoken solidarity. We've all made a clean sweep. We've started eating together a couple times a week. Mom's even talking about a vacation, something we've never done.

I wasn't happy about the limo but Taylor told me how much we owed so I paid it. It's putting me even deeper in the hole. I'll spend the entire summer working on my uncle's boat just to pay Mom back for the impound and towing fees on the Taurus. If there's enough left over, I might have some spending money at UW. Maybe. I keep wishing that Nikki was going to be at UW next year. I have picked up the phone to call her dozens of times but hang up, unsure of what I'd say.

When the long white limo arrives at Taylor's house I feel like a jerk. Everyone else is whooping it up, pretending to be movie stars, rolling down the windows and screaming but I just feel stupid. Driving around in a limo in Aberdeen seems like a jackass move. Although Taylor knew exactly when we'd arrive, I have to wait in the living room, trying not to pit out the over-starched shirt. Of course I didn't pick out the tux myself. The ridiculous looking cummerbund and matching bow tie coordinates with her dress: sparkly white. My brother pronounced the whole ensemble "pimptastic."

Awesome.

Mrs. Davis asks me to sit then goes to get her husband. He clears his throat about nine times before sitting down.

"Have a good time." Mr. Davis stares at his wife like a dog begging to go outside.

"You two have a nice chat." Mrs. Davis pats his back. "I'll go hurry up princess."

After she leaves Mr. Davis chews the inside of his mouth. "Sequins on your tie?"

My face flushes. "I didn't pick it out."

He laughs, flashing white teeth. "I know." He frowns again. "Look, Taylor made a promise to us that she'd stay pure until she's married." I nod. "So I'm asking you, man to man, to make that vow to me."

Blood pounds in my ears. *What in the hell?* "You want me to stay a virgin?"

He throws back his head, laughing. "Lord no, son. Keep my daughter intact."

"Intact?"

He leans forward, breathing into my face, his eyes narrow and intense as if ready to rip off my head. "Don't have sex with her!"

I straighten up. "Yes sir."

Mr. Davis jumps up, all smiles, opening his arms. "There she is, doesn't she look lovely?"

My terrified body responds to her beauty with a full salute. Turning away from Mr. Davis, praying that my hard-on isn't visible under the tux jacket, I nod my head thinking that Taylor looks like a wet dream. How could I be turned on by the challenge of screwing his daughter? Life is so freaking unfair. "Beautiful."

Mrs. Davis makes everyone get out of the limo for a group photo. She has no idea why I'm wrapping my arms around her daughter, leaning my head on her shoulder. Taylor knows and grinds into me, making matters worse. The whole time Mrs. Davis snaps away, calling us adorable and precious, I'm sporting a woody, thinking about what exactly is going to happen at the beach, when I finally get Taylor alone.

NIKKI

We're all piled into my mom's Volvo with the radio totally blasting Nirvana. Although I'm grounded, I get one night out for prom. I keep thinking about the trip to California. How I thought it would all magically work out and I'd be with Paul. How freaking deluded and lame. You'd think by now I'd know that nice girls come in last.

Fran and I keep cheering each other up, telling each other how amazing we look, how lucky we are to have such fabulous dates. After dinner at Plaza Garcia, where Mrs. Garcia fussed over us like a mother hen and refused to let us pay, *Oh no, chicas, por favor! This one is like my granddaughter. Your money is no good here tonight!* we stop at Morrison Park on the river to kill time. Although Hazel wanted to get to school early to check on the decorations one last time, I informed her that only losers arrive early.

Mike and Hazel set off on a walk down to the river-front dock casually holding hands as seagulls swoop overhead. They are so freaking cute it makes me barf. Fran and I remain in the car, silent in mutual discomfort at seeing our friends on a date.

"You missing Allison?" I ask.

"Yep."

"You missing Paul?"

"Yep. He doesn't freaking deserve me."

"Nope."

We agree that although the moment is sad and kind of pathetic, we'd rather be sad and pathetic together. I produce a bottle of rum I've stolen from my parents. Fran half-heartedly takes a few sips. It burns going down and although we'd both happily ditch Mike to get some Coke mixer, we agree, we can't leave Hazel.

When Mike and Hazel return with wind whipped hair and chapped lips, he pounds the front seat. "Let's do this bitches!" Hazel frowns and for once, he pays attention. "I meant ladies. That's what I meant."

I offer him the pint. "Yeah, I can see you meant that. Bitches and ladies sound so much alike."

Mike opens the bottle, looking self-consciously at Hazel. He screws the lid back on, passing it back.

"Mike, it's like Hazel. She knows you. You can have a drink," I point out as Nikki pulls out of the empty parking lot.

Mike gives Hazel a nervous glance. "It's okay," she says. "Seriously. Go ahead."

I pass him the pint. He takes a long drink, smacking his lips. "Okay, bitch ladies, let's do this!"

FRAN

The warm glow from Nikki's house and the beautiful dress has leached out of me, replaced with a panicked dread that grows as we approach school. I keep thinking about the movie *Carrie*. Mom and I watched it together. I felt sorry for Carrie, even though she ended up killing so many people at her prom. Mom said her crime was that she overreached, which is exactly what I've done. A girl like that would have done better to keep her head down and mind her own business. Both of us should have just skipped prom.

As we turn onto Wishkah Avenue I plead with Nikki. "Why do we even have to go? We all know I'm not going to win. Everyone will be there to hear the announcement for prom queen and king and then they'll go to the other prom. Why don't we just go someplace else?"

"Because we're going," says Nikki, her jaw set in a way that I've come to recognize. Nothing short of a natural disaster will stop her.

"I don't see why we have to." The enchilada I ate for dinner is threatening to make a reappearance.

"Three reasons," Nikki says, going all courtroom drama on me. "First, you look totally amazing and you have to show off that kick-ass dress. Second, Hazel worked like, really hard on this prom and the gym looks totally awesome and three, I voted like thirty-five times so you might actually win."

"How the hell did you manage that?" I ask, shocked and somewhat horrified.

"I voted like ten times," Hazel says.

"Eighteen," says Mike.

"You guys cheated for me?" I'm not sure if I'm happy about it or not.

"I was just kidding." Hazel says. "And you guys are all going to Hell by the way."

"Well that was a given," says Mike. "I knew that in like, third grade."

Nikki whips around a corner, hitting a mailbox, flattening it without comment. I look out the back window at someone's mail fluttering white in the wind. "Did anyone else see that?"

Nikki, as usual, gets the last word. "Stop trying to distract us. We're going to prom whether you like it or not."

PAUL

As much as I want to hate the limo; it's not that bad. It's a self-contained mobile party unit. Dance club music pounds against the windows. The three other couples drink tequila and sway, yelling to each other over the music. There's some kind of weird lighting running along the floor and ceiling. It reminds me of a runway because even though I've never been on a plane, I've seen movies of what it looks like, landing at night.

Taylor drinks Kahlua and milk. Every time she leans into me her breasts lift in her dress. It's like when I was a kid, turning the page on a pop-up book, excited to see the next page, except this is a million times better. She keeps kissing me, telling me to try her drink, shoving it at me. I'm sipping a beer and don't want anything else but I'm worried the brown liquid will spill over the rented tux. So I drink.

"It's delish, right?" Taylor gushes.

"Tastes like coffee."

"No shit Sherlock." She licks a drip off my chin like a cat.

I want to shove her away but she climbs into my lap,

squirming and wrapping her arms around me, grinning happily. "Hey baby. Having fun?"

I sip my beer. "Uh-huh."

Underneath all the glittery make-up, her eyes narrow. Her breath is hot and boozy. I'm not fitting into her storybook prom and it pisses her off. "Don't look so sad baby, tonight might be your lucky night, if you know what I mean." She kisses me forcefully with tongue, knowing she's guaranteed a reaction, raking her hands through my hair. As if to seal the deal, she wiggles her ass against me.

Everyone in the limo starts screaming. "Get a room!"

My face flames as I take a long swallow of beer. Taylor grabs the beer bottle from me, waving it within arms distance. "Come on, take it from me."

I have to lean into her to get it back, my face practically buried in her cleavage. The guys cheer as I retrieve my beer, taking another long swallow. Taylor kisses my neck, whispering about how this is going to be the most amazing summer. She has a new bikini and her dad is going to let us use his new boat for waterskiing. My mind wanders. I stare out the window at the passing lights, drinking my beer when I realize that someone is making a group toast about this being the best moment and we'll all be friends forever.

I lift my beer, clink it with Mark, a guy I barely know. "Forever!"

FRAN

Nikki was right. The gym is packed with people spilling outside onto the steps. Music floats into the parking lot as we pile out of the car. My stomach is doing flips so I hang behind. Nikki grabs me, dragging me by the arm towards the gym. "Come on. It's not going to be so bad."

"You're right. It's going to be worse."

"When did you become such a freaking pessimist?" Nikki drags me toward the door. People stare and point.

"When my mom's boyfriend told me there was no Santa Claus." The one who went to jail.

"Everyone is totally checking you out," Nikki says.

"Because it's my big gay prom."

Although we're close to the ticket table, where Mrs. Harder and Mr. P. are waiting expectantly, Nikki pulls me aside. "Do you know why they are like, staring?"

I shake my head. "That's a rhetorical question, right?"

"Listen to me. Just stop with the self-pity and pay attention. There might be a lot of kids who are here tonight to see you lose and go to their own stupid fucked up prom based on hatred and insecurity but right now those people are looking at you because you're beautiful. Now pull your head out of your ass and take some credit. Okay?"

I clap my hand on my heart. "That was a beautiful speech."

She beams. "Screw you."

"Thank you."

She takes a deep breath. "You ready?"

"Nikki, you know what?"

She shakes her head. "Now what?"

"You look amazing yourself."

She's not listening because Paul shows up at the door with Taylor, resplendent in a glittering cupcake of a dress. They hold hands as Taylor's minions flock towards her, gushing over her dress, reassuring their queen that the decorations inside are absolutely scary horrible, like a funeral instead of prom. Paul's eyes are glazed, like he's drunk, which is weird.

"He doesn't deserve you," I whisper under my breath.

"Probably not." Nikki winces. "But it still hurts, you know?"

"I know." Boy, do I know.

"Roy-al court! Roy-al court! Roy-al court!" The chant in the over-heated gym grows louder as students join in, trying to get Mr. P. to announce the prom king and queen. They shout over the punk band, The Wastrels, who are loud and pretty decent although the lead singer thinks he's Sid Vicious. Mr. P. is at the back of the gym near the punch and cookie table, shouting over the music with Mrs. Harter and Mr. Yusilitch the math teacher. Kids start whistling and stomping their feet. Mr. P. waddles to the corner of the stage and climbs the steps, huffing and puffing. The small cluster of kids on the dance floor stop dancing. Mr. P. reaches the Wastrels. They stop playing except for the skinny little drummer, who is in his own world, jamming a drum solo as though he's with Aerosmith playing to a stadium crowd. The drummer plays for what seems like eternity, finally throwing his sticks in the air. He looks up, finally aware of his band, the students, and principal eyeing him. He goes dead still.

"Oh shit." His mike echoes into the gym. *Shit. Shit. Shit.*

Everyone laughs and cheers. Mr. P. clears his throat and motions for us to calm down. "Okay, okay students. We've all heard the word before." He waits for everyone to be quiet. "Normally we don't announce the prom king and queen until later in the evening but since you all have requested this, I'm going to go ahead and announce it now. I just want to say that despite this being a fractious race, which threatened to divide the student body, the results were very close."

Out of the corner of my eye I can see Taylor rolling her eyes. "Yeah right."

Her idiotic friends giggle and whisper, their dresses catching the low light, glimmering. Taylor's snow-white dress offsets her fake tan, making her smile hover above her dress like the Cheshire Cat. Paul, stiff and uncomfortable in a black tux and stripper dude sparkly white tie studies Nikki. She catches him and scratches her cheek with her middle finger. He cracks a lopsided grin. It's hard to despise him when he looks so pathetic.

"Roy-al court! Roy-al court!" starts up again. Everyone wants to hear the winners and go outside and get blasted. The air is thick with tension, waiting to roll outside and explode. Principal P. waves his arms, trying to calm everyone down. "Okay, okay. Come on now people."

"I need more rum," Nikki says.

I pull her arm, desperate to get away. "Let's go now."

She grabs me firmly. "No way. You're staying."

Principal P. opens an envelope. "The Prom Queen and King for 1993 are Taylor Davis and Paul Cazek."

Taylor doesn't bother acting surprised. She screams and hugs her friends, who hop around, squealing excitedly in their poufy pastel dresses. Watching them is so much worse than I thought it would be. It's acknowledging that we can never, ever win. They're going to a better party, with better booze, a fancier venue and a much, much better band. The thing that scares me the most is this feeling of wanting to belong. To be part of a group that wants nothing to do with me. This dance is a distant second. Hazel worked so hard for nothing. We all did. We drove 1,600 miles, put up with the scorn and pity of the entire school and for what?

I am never, ever going to fit in.

The worst part is that I want to. I do.

It's horrible.

Nikki, who has dropped my arm, watches Taylor and her crew with disappointed resignation. It's seeing Nikki like this, the girl who never gives up, who doesn't believe in lost causes or unwinnable battles that makes me realize that this really is over. We've all lost. I'm not going to be prom queen. I'm not going to get that scholarship. I'm never going to escape Aberdeen or spend the summer with Allison. I'll be stuck here forever, jealous and resentful when my friends leave for college. I'll have the same narrow life as my mother.

I thought I was different.

I'm just not.

All this comes crashing down, sucking the air out of my lungs. I can't breathe. I can't stand everyone studying my face, waiting for my reaction. A few people have come up to me and said something but I can't hear them.

Taylor manages the stairs in her ridiculous heels to the stage. Paul trots after her like an obedient puppy. Nikki tries hard not to cry but her lips quiver. I should stay. I should be the one to comfort her as she watches Paul beside Taylor as she preens and poses and makes some dumb speech about being surprised and how the other couples running were so amazing. But I can't. The sensible heels Nikki's mom lent me pinch my toes. Everything in my body is shutting down.

I have to get out of here.

Now.

I blow past the teachers and parents milling by the gym doors. They turn their heads. I don't stop. Some of them call out but I run so fast I can't hear a thing. I just want to get away. I'm tired of everything and everyone. Nothing will be clear until I get away. Space and quiet and time are what I need. The ground is slick with rain and I'm afraid of falling. I dash around the corner of the school to the side of the gym in the shadows, stopping to take off my shoes near the solid brick wall, grateful for the obliterating dark.

"Please tell me you didn't buy those shoes."

The voice is vaguely familiar. Looking up, my heart skips a beat. Maybe it's the rain. Maybe it's wishful thinking.

"They were free."

"They look like it."

"Why are we talking about shoes?"

"Because we're girls." Allison smiles.

She's in front of a red car a few yards away in a halo of streetlight like some perp in a cop show except she's amazingly beautiful. What happens next is inexplicable because time stops. We're both absolutely still, watching one another, waiting for the other to make a move. A fine mist settles on my lashes. I blink. The pale streetlights illuminate the airborne water. We're in the middle of a glowing cloud, suspended in time. Shivering slightly in a long- sleeved white t-shirt and jeans, she gazes at me for the longest time as if making up her mind. It could have been hours or minutes. I'm not sure. I hold my breath, waiting. She walks across the parking lot until she stands a foot away.

"What are you doing here?"

"I wanted to give you this." Reaching behind her, she produces a black camera case on a strap.

It's a plain black case. The strap is festooned with the Nirvana buttons I bought at the concert. It's my camera. "Where did you get this?"

"Dwayne doesn't have much imagination. I went to the pawn shop closest to the hardware shop. Easy Pawn. What a dumb name. As if pawning stuff is ever easy."

I take it out of the case, checking the body to make sure it's in good working order, putting it up to my eye and framing Allison. Her face is lightly beaded with rain, hair falling into one beautiful eye. Her beauty makes it hard to breath. I frame a shot, trying to think straight, bending my knees to get a halo effect from the streetlight over head. The mist glows around her, magnifying her shadow. I lower the camera, overwhelmed with gratitude. "I don't know what to say. This is amazing."

Allison shrugs. "Thank you works."

"Thank you. I can pay you back."

"It's a gift. Although I don't know if getting back your own camera can technically be called a gift."

"It's the best thing anyone has ever given me."

"I'm sorry I'm not dressed up. I climbed out a window. Almost broke my neck."

"You walked here?" The school is at least five miles from her house, maybe more.

"Being locked up gave me lot of time to think and I realized that you need your camera. When you have as much talent as you do, not having a camera is criminal."

I have talent? "You've never seen one of my pictures."

"Yes I have. Mrs. Harter framed some of your food bank pictures and put them in the library. They're amazing."

My eyes sting with tears. "She did that?"

She nods, taking my hand. "Is it too late to ask you to prom?"

"Kind of. It's half over."

She picks up my shoes and hands them to me. "What if I wanted to dance with you?"

"In public?"

"Yeah."

I slip my shoes on. "Are you sure you're ready for this?"

She offers me her hand. "No." Then she pulls me into her and kisses me. A long kiss that blots out anything I've ever thought about kissing. She holds me with both arms and it's the happiest I've ever felt. It's like running full speed with the wind in my hair and jumping. Unlike so many things that just never work out, this is the perfect moment with the girl I want. It's everything that a kiss should be and although I've missed out on a lot, I know that most people will never be kissed like this. I'm the luckiest girl in the world. Then it's over and she's staring at me with sparkling, happy eyes.

"Now I'm ready!" She beams.

Allison and I walk hand in hand towards the gym. Although my head spins, I feel amazing. "Where'd you get those pumps anyway?"

"Nikki's mom." Is she ready for what will happen when people see us together? Has she thought this through?

She squeezes my hand. "They're very sensible. Thank God you didn't pick them out." She holds me back for a second. "By the way, you look gorgeous."

We've reached the steps. My throat tightens. My pulse thuds in my ears. "You really don't know what you're getting into. Do you want to bail?"

Her hand tightens on mine. "Ask me tomorrow."

Students stream out of the gym as we walk up the stairs hand-in-hand. PC lurks in the distance with a group of thugs, drinking out of a paper bag. The exiting crowd parts and gawks. Some spit nasty comments as we pass. Words wash over me like water, not paint. Instead of feeling polluted and sick, it's thrilling. I'm not afraid. Although it's surreal and temporary, it's like the foggy memory of my dad pushing me higher on the swing. Clear blue sky and one perfect moment. Yesterday strolling into gym holding a girl's hand was inconceivable, impossible even, but tonight as Allison pulls me through the door I'm invincible.

So this is what courage feels like.

Amazing.

Hazel has done a terrific job making the gym a Goth wonderland with sweeping black tulle wound with neon green streamers. Giant purple flowers with a laughing white skull in the center, sparkling with glitter, spin from the ceiling between twinkling black stars. Giant sparkling Tarot cards fan out near clusters of black balloons for a photo backdrop. A photographer in a top hat and skeleton t-shirt snaps portraits against a backdrop of twinkling stars in a field of purple velvet. Huge vats of neon green punch and trays of cookies rest on a tabletop supported by large garden gnomes.

Thirty remaining kids mill around in couples and clusters, arguing about whether to check out the other prom or stay here.

"This band sucks." Michael Crawly says. "My cousin is in Skinny Lizard. Let's go."

His date, Andrea Sanchez says, "You ain't even danced with me once yet. If they play the chicken song I'm gonna drag your butt out there. Or the YMCA. God I love that one."

"You think a punk band is gonna play the chicken dance? I don't think so babe."

"Leanna is staying and so am I. If you don't dance with me, Carlos will."

A few people watch Allison and I as we stand there awkwardly. "This is nice." I say, not meaning it. I'd rather be somewhere in the dark, kissing Allison.

"Want to dance?"

"The band is on a break." I point to the empty stage.

"So?" She drags me out onto the dance floor.

I resist. "There's no music."

"There will be."

"Can't we just wait?"

"Nope." She keeps dragging me out with both hands, her eyes warm and sparkly.

A dull buzz of conversation rises as we stroll into the empty space. A few kids point at us and jump up and down. In a few moments, something bad will happen. I can feel it.

Sweat trickles down my armpits into my dress. "Let's wait until the band comes back, okay? They're not even a dance band. Punk is really hard to dance to."

"I don't care. I love dancing."

"I'm a lousy dancer. Can we just—"

She shakes her head. "No, we can't."

"Come on Allison. Please?"

She's shaking her head and sort of laughing. I don't get it. She seems perfectly happy and carefree standing here on the dance floor. I want to dive into the darkest corner. We're arguing when I hear something familiar. The first few notes of a song. Those two familiar notes played by a guitar are perhaps the most famous two notes in the history of music. Then comes the drums. The fast beat of the drums from one of the best songs of all time. A song that has more meaning to me, will always have more meaning, than any other. They are the first notes that pulled me out of despair two years ago in the Aberdeen Mall. Notes I've heard so many time they're etched in my brain.

The band is covering "Smells Like Teen Spirit." It's so cool. Allison is really beaming now and people are spilling onto the dance floor excitedly. What the hell? I take both her hands.

Then the vocals. "Load up on guns, brings your

friends. It's fun to lose and to pretend. She's overboard and self-assured. On no, I know a dirty word."

My feet don't move. My hands go all tingly. I am rooted to the spot. People are saying things that don't have meaning. Allison grins with tears in her eyes. It doesn't make any sense. "They're covering Nirvana." That must be my voice. It sounds like my voice. There's a lot of movement around me. Why am I having this out of body experience?

The voice is so familiar. I know it from my bedroom but it doesn't make sense. Nothing makes sense. "Hello, hello, hello, how low. Hello, hello, hello."

Then all the instruments start up. Something wet runs down my face. Tears? Am I crying? What is happening? Which is, I guess, what I said to Allison because her eyes fill with tears as she points. "Look up on stage."

I don't look. I'm just staring at Allison until she gently takes my shoulders and turns me. "Look."

"I don't get this."

"They came for you Fran."

I still can't believe that Nirvana is here. On stage. Now. "How?"

Allison shrugs. "They just came."

In a puddle of soft purple light, Kurt Cobain sits down on a stool, letting his hair fall into his face. His face is much more relaxed than at the concert. He looks younger, happier. He wears black jeans, a striped turtleneck and ripped Converse. He plays the second verse of "Smells Like Teen Spirit." Dave Grohl, in a grey t-shirt and jeans sits at the drum set. Krist Novoselic moves out of the shadows fiddling with his bass strap.

Kurt shields his eyes from the spotlight, looking out at the growing crowd. "God, this is surreal. You know that me and Krist went to school here. So yeah, this is kind of our first prom. We're here to support Fran Worthy and make sure that she has an awesome prom." He pushes his white plastic sunglasses to the top of his head, squinting. "Fran are you here?"

I'm stuck to the ground like gum, unable to move. Allison lifts up my leaden hand and waves it. "She's right here! Over here!"

Kurt squints into the lights, pushing his sunglasses over his eyes, bobbing his head, hair falling around his famous face. "Okay Fran—is it short for Frances?" I nod like a bobble-head. "My kid's named Frances too. After Frances Farmer who was institutionalized not too far from here for being a little bit different. Anyway, Fran Worthy—this one's for you."

There are maybe twenty kids left in the gym. They swirl in eddies, rush the stage, chattering excitedly. Many dash out to the parking lot to catch their departing friends. One kid screams, "Is it the Grays Harbor Hotel? We have to call the hotel and tell everyone!"

"Holy shit!

"It's happening."

"Nirvana is playing our prom."

"Oh my God. How long are they staying?"

"Is this like a full-on concert or what?"

"Should I go get Karen?"

"No, let's stay here! The hell with Karen!"

Krist Novoselic leans into his mike. "All right you little fuckers, let's rock!"

Kurt jumps into the air. They launch into the rest of "Smells like Teen Spirit." Kids laugh and clap and scream. Allison takes my hands and we dance madly through the entire song, swaying and singing along. Allison mimics me, trying to fill in the words she doesn't know, sometimes breaking into "la-la-la" or nonsense words. I'm so caught up in the music that it feels like a half second later the song ends. They launch into "Lounge Act." Dave Grohl pounds out a melody on the drums, Krist beckons to someone in the audience while yelling into Kurt's ear.

"It's you." Allison tugs me toward the stage. "Come on!"

While the rest of the band plays, Kurt kneels on the edge of the stage, cradling his guitar. "Hey, nice to see you again."

"Oh my God, thank you so much. Thank you so much." *Shut up Fran. Act cool.*

He grins like he's having a good time. "Sorry you didn't win prom queen. I guess your life is kind of over, right?"

"Totally! On the other hand, now I can die happy."

He's back on stage singing the next verse, bouncing around from one side of the stage to the other.

Allison bumps me with her shoulder. "Wanna dance?"

"Did you know that they were going to be here?"

Allison shrugs. "No. But I wasn't going to miss this either way."

"Aren't you worried about your mom?"

She shrugs. "She'll get over it in about a hundred years."

"I still can't believe this is happening!"

She pulls me into the dancers crowding the floor. "You did this Fran. You made this happen."

They play thirteen songs.

Song after song, time blurs into one big joyful moment. Prom is an elastic ball of joy that stretches, spitting me out at the end. Misery crawls and happiness flies. Allison spins me on the dance floor and then I twirl her, forgetting everything except how much fun we are having. How the world is one big bubble of joy and I'm never, ever going to forget this moment. I'm having an unforgettable peak, teetering between wanting to remember every detail and throwing myself headlong into happiness. Each frame clicks into place in my brain, slowing down time, imprinting the memory of Allison tossing her hair, throwing her arms, sweating, pink-cheeked and thrilled. I want to remember every second.

After the fourth song, Krist grabs Kurt's mike, talking to Principal P. He thanks him for letting them come in at the last minute and taking over. "I've heard you've been really cool supporting our girl Fran." Dave does a fancy little drum roll, finishing off with a tap of the cymbals.

"So, here's what we'd like to do," Kurt says. "We weren't exactly model students and gave your predecessor a lot of grief."

"There might have been bottle rockets," Krist says to a round of applause. "And a little booze."

Kurt lowers his sunglasses. "We kind of feel bad about

it. Someone told us that you like our music and we want you to come up here and sing along and do your thing."

Dave leans into his mike. "Just don't do too much of it."

"Yeah, it's like the record execs tell us. Be yourself but like not *totally* yourself," Kurt adds.

"PG-13," Dave laughs.

Mr. P. shakes his head, refusing but not seriously, as if one part of him is dying to and the other half knows it would be undignified. The teachers around him, who seem a little goofy, like maybe there was an adult pre-party, egg him on. The next thing we know our principal is up on stage with Nirvana, clapping his hands and dancing (well, sort of throwing his butt around like he's having a seizure) and really getting into it. What should be embarrassing and awful because it's a forty something chubby man dancing and thinking he's cool—isn't, for some inexplicable reason. Maybe the goodwill Nirvana showed by coming here has suffused the crowd. It is like that old timey AP English word—bonhomie, is in the house. Everyone except Taylor, who bitches about how her mom spent so much money and *you are all a bunch of ingrates and Nirvana sucks.* No one listens.

The Goth kids groove with the emo kids who thrash with the jocks. The artsy fartsy types drape the pie-eyed druggies with black crepe streamers. Until this prom, someone like Hazel would have never considered stoner Mike a legitimate option. Now they're dancing. Or she is anyway. He's, well, I'm not sure what he's doing but it's not dancing. Hazel doesn't seem to mind as she happily sings along. Boundaries have blurred, if only momentarily, in the mass Nirvana hysteria.

Kurt and Dave and Krist are getting a kick out of the whole thing, laughing and playing to Principal P. who mouths the lyrics to "School," clapping and fist bumping the air. "You're in high school again! You're in high school again!" When it is over, he straightens his tie, shakes their hands and thanks them for coming.

Kurt grabs the microphone. "I just want to say that when I heard about the parents protesting and getting all pissed off about a girl who got nominated for prom, I felt like even though I personally, had never aspired to be prom queen, I knew what that felt like. If you're the slightest bit different, Aberdeen is a rough place. High school is kind of a fucked-up time. The thing you don't know is that everyone else feels as lonely and scared as you are but no one talks about it. It's one big hierarchy of acting cool. Fran, you're not alone and you will make it out of here. Life after high school is anything you want it to be. I mean, look at us." He waves his hand around the stage. "If we made it, anyone can."

Dave stands up from the drum kit, doing a little curtsy. Krist crosses his eyes, pretending to pick his nose.

Kurt continues amid cheering. "So keep fucking doing your thing and don't let anyone tell you that you can't do something because of who you are, okay?"

And he launches into "About a Girl."

I don't keep track of the remaining songs or their order. I'm wrapped in boundless energy and bliss. There is a sense that as long as they keep playing, everything will be fine. Perfect harmony will rule as long as Nirvana is here to provide the soundtrack. It is the best feeling in the world. No drug could ever give me this kind of high. And the very best part of it is Allison, singing along, spinning and enjoying this every bit as much as I am. Or almost. I don't think this epic concert could ever mean as much to anyone else because Nirvana has been so much more, I realize, than music. Nirvana has been my path out of the dark.

When the last song ends, Kurt takes a bow and waves at me. "Good luck kid! Stay strong." He salutes everyone else with two fingers. "Class of 1993, be fucking cool, alright?"

Dave Grohl leans in to his mike. "And wear condoms."

They both laugh as they walked off stage. Krist follows, offering a peace sign.

Everyone cheers, screams and yells, begging them to play one more. Pleading with them to return but there is no encore. The stage is black. Everyone reassembles into their own groups.

"Can you fucking believe it?"

"Nirvana played prom."

"God that was awesome."

Allison and I grin at each other, eyes locked, reveling in the moment.

"Fran, go get a picture of them!" Mrs. Harter holds out my camera. "It's loaded. I checked. Go!"

I hesitate for one second but Allison grabs the camera and thrusts it at me. I run towards the gym's side door, throwing myself against the metal bar, hoping the security alarm is turned off. Luckily there is no alarm. As I get my bearings in the dark, the night air clears my head. Three figures disappear through the fencing bordering the large parking lot near the baseball fields. I chase after them, which is tough in my heels but there isn't time to kick them off.

I'm panting by the time I get close enough for a possible shot. Kurt, Krist, and Dave are in the empty back sports field parking lot, walking towards two shiny dew-speckled black Suburbans with blacked out windows. Kurt carries a guitar case. Krist totes his bass. They laugh. It's just the three of them on the vast blacktop, chatting. The contrast of the white lines on blacktop with these three iconic figures is stark and ethereal. The hulking new Suburbans remind me of hearses. They are between two pools of street light that casts long shadows.

"Can I take a photo?" I yell.

Kurt turns around and waves without stopping. The air around him is suffused with a backlit mist. It's so beautiful I'll take his wave as a yes. I snap the shot, then a few more. Maybe five total. Interior lights appear in both cars. Two drivers get out, opening the doors. A few seconds later they drive off, disappearing out of the parking lot around the corner. I wait until they are gone, staring at the black, empty street, lined with small sleeping houses. This is the best feeling in the world. I could chase this feeling for the rest of my life. I'm hooked. I could plan an entire life around finding the perfect shot.

I walk slowly back to the school through the parking lot caught up in my dreams, swinging my camera, so happy to have it back. Allison will be the first person I show the pictures. If I've captured what I saw in the lens, it's going to be incredible.

In the parking lot closest to the school, a hulking figure steps out of the dark.

"Those guys are a bunch of faggots." It's PC. Even in

the dark I know he's drunk but he's not a drunk like my grandma who gets sloppy and sentimental, he's the knife-pulling variety. Booze takes every shitty molecule in his body and distills it into a weapon.

He blocks the path back to the gym so I step around. He grabs the camera strap roughly, yanking it with such violence that my teeth chatter. The strap breaks and he tosses the camera like garbage. It clatters on the pavement. We're face to face, so close I can smell the rank whiskey on his breath. His eyes disappear into his red, puffy face. "Not so fucking easy lesbo."

Junior year I volunteered at Hazel's pre-school for Honor Society credits. The lead teacher taught us that when you're dealing with a three-year-old in meltdown, the best strategy is distraction. "How come you're not at the other prom?"

"Because no one is there." He takes a swig from the bottle he's clutching. "You fucking ruined that too. There is no one there. Everyone heard about Nirvana and left. You fucking ruined both proms and now you're going to pay."

My pulse throbs in my neck. *Stay calm. Don't panic.* "I didn't ruin them. I didn't even want to be nominated for prom queen."

"The joke is on me because I nominated you. I thought it was funny. You know—lesbian weirdo trying to run for prom. You made me look like a total jerk wad."

"Nobody knows. Nobody knows you were the one who nominated me."

He throws back his head, howling. "You are the dumbest cunt. Everyone knows."

My voice quivers as cold darts of fear run through me. If I scream, no one will hear. We're too far away from the front of the gym and there isn't another soul in sight. We're fifty yards from the houses across the field. "Let me go inside PC."

"Fuck you bitch. I should have clocked your ass the first time I had the chance. You're going to get what's coming to you and then some." He drops the bottle, ignoring the shattered glass. He rolls up his sleeves with some difficulty. "You know how you rehabilitate dykes?" His thick tongue fumbles around the long word. I take a careful step back and he moves forward with surprising speed, grabbing my hair. "You make them suck dick."

"Fuck you PC. I didn't report you to the cops last time but this time I will and you'll go to jail." He lashes out with surprising speed, punching me hard in the face. My head explodes in white hot pain. A warm gush flows down my face. For a second, I think about running but if he caught up with me he could knock me down. The ground is the last place I want to be.

"Who are they going to believe? You're just a low life piece of white trash. Do you think the cops are going to care about some fucking deviant?"

Grabbing my neck, he chokes me hard until I'm light-headed. He kicks me in the knee, hard but I stay upright by widening my stance in my heels.

One hand unzips his fly while the other forces my head down to his crotch. The pressure of his huge hand is impossible to duck. I'm going down, choking on blood. "Let me go you son of a bitch! Let me go!"

I'll fight.

I'll die.

My eyes shut. Jaws clench. His hard, hot flesh jabs my cheek. "Here's what you need baby. Do it right or I'll pop you one."

Newton's third law jumps into my head: every action has an opposite and equal reaction. My fury rises up to meet his hatred. I might be half his size but I'm sober and I remember what Paul taught me.

Grabbing his forearms, I yank them down with all my weight. His arms release. He grabs my hair, keeping me anchored to him. Yanking my head with all my might, I free myself, leaving him with a handful of bloody hair. Blood runs into my eyes. The moment I'm free, I jump up and kick off my heels, wiping my face with my arm.

Steadying myself, I step backwards. Pain shoots through me as a piece of glass cuts through my heel. My adrenalin has kicked in, bringing with it a plan: fucking annihilate him. There is no plan B, just red hot, unfiltered rage that blocks my ears from all the vile spitting from his mouth. I don't have to listen to know he's repeating the same vicious words. Crouching, I pull my right haunch back, turning to the side to gather the full force of my weight behind my kick. It lands on his thigh. He's off center.

"You fucking bitch!" He doubles over, staggering drunkenly on the path, trying to remain upright.

My eyes sting. I can't see. It must be blood mixed with sweat. If I can just clear my eyes, I'll have a chance. I bend down to wipe my eyes on my dress.

Thwack! I look up to see PC's head snapping back, his eyes rolling in terror. Thwack! He staggers backwards, lifting his arms to fight, waving blindly, roaring in anger. There is a small shape spinning in the dark. It's far too fast for PC. The shadow kicks hard at the back of PC's legs. Thud! Thud! Thud! PC is bent over, breathing hard, holding onto his knees to stop himself from toppling over. There is a great whoosh of air followed by more thudding. It's a soft smacking noise, like a beanbags hitting cement. Each time PC gasps, grunting as if the wind is being knocked out of him. He staggers sideways, batting at the air. He can't find his assailant who dances around him, always out of reach. It's all happening very fast. The other fighter moves with lightning speed, breathing timed precisely with the punches.

PC says, "What the fu-" before he's knocked down.

He goes down quickly, crumpling onto the pavement with a heavy groan. A second later there is a series of soft thumps as someone kicks him. The figure is small and dark and impossibly fast. Graceful.

"You rousy son of a bitch. You don't hit the girls. You don't hit anybody!"

I'm sure I'm seeing things but my vision has cleared. It's a woman with a ponytail. Oh my God, is it? Yes, it's Mrs. Kondo. She's pushing PC like she wants him to get up. Allison grabs her mother's arms. Mrs. Kondo is crouched in a fighting position, wearing a down puffer coat, white tennis shoes and black pants. Her pearl earrings glint in the dark. PC's moans and rolls on the ground, holding his face. Mrs. Kondo's arms are out like a martial arts expert.

Allison drags her mother away. "Mom! Stop it. He's down."

Mrs. Kondo kicks PC again for good measure, muttering in Japanese before coming over to me, suddenly all business, very much the mother. "You okay? My husband is good doctor. We'll tell him to meet us, okay?"

I shake my head that I'm okay but Allison is indicating that her mother won't listen. "She's not really asking Fran."

Mrs. Kondo grabs her purse from the pavement, pawing through it for something. It's the weirdest thing. One minute she's an avenging angel knocking over a thug and the next she's a suburban mom digging through her purse. "He's going to meet us." She bobs her head as she unearths her inhaler. "Ahhhh." She breathes in a few squirts, shooting a couple at PC as if he's an insect she'd like to kill, smiling at herself.

Paul is among the cluster of people who come forward, asking me if I'm okay. After they are reassured that I'm fine everyone wants to know how Mrs. Kondo took down PC, who has now puked.

"She's a black belt in taekwondo," Allison says, as if this explains everything. "She's like, sort of famous for it."

Everyone is staring at Mrs. Kondo, who doesn't seem to notice. She jingles her car keys, asking me if I can walk.

I insist I'm fine. PC yells that he's hurt. He was minding his own business and I attacked him.

"If you say one more word I'll let Mrs. Kondo finish you off," Paul says, which makes PC moan even worse.

"Where's my camera?" I repeat it three times while Allison wanders around the dark, looking for the camera, carefully stepping over the glass. Nikki's arm is around me.

Allison brings me the case and the dented camera separately. The old cases have zippers that no one uses backed up by lousy latches that sometimes fail. "Did you close the film door?"

"What?"

I can't lose this picture; I just can't. "Was the film door open? If it was open the film was exposed."

"Your film is fine, okay? Your nose is bleeding." Nikki kicks off her shoes and slips off her stockings, telling me to hold them to my nose. When I study them, slightly grossed out, she rolls her eyes. "It'll stop the bleeding."

She takes the camera, zipping it safely shut. "I'll look after it. Stop worrying about the film."

"What's he doing here?" I ask Nikki about Paul. It's not what I meant to say but my brain isn't really working. Adrenalin courses through my body making everything look super sharp and clear and oddly surreal. "Where's Taylor? What happened to the other prom?"

Nikki shakes her head as though I'm asking the wrong question. "I have no idea. Paul came with me. Are you okay? Hold that tighter on your nose. Wait, your head is bleeding. We really need to get you to the hospital."

Mrs. Kondo grabs my arm, taking charge. "Walk on your toes. Like this. See? Okay. Come on. Dr. Kondo is meeting us there. We'll take my car." She turns to Allison. "Good thing you have such a good mama who chases you down."

Allison kisses her mom's cheek. "Good thing."

Mrs. Kondo pats Allison's cheek. "You're still in big big trouble."

Allison takes my hand, leading me to the car. "I know. I know."

CHAPTER TWENTY-TWO

"The duty of youth is to challenge corruption."
Kurt Cobain

FRAN

The yearbook's dark room is nothing more than a couple of long closets with clotheslines and chemical baths swirling with possibility. Mrs. Harter stayed late so I could wait for the final developing bath of the Nirvana pictures. In the red light, I can just make out the first photo. This is my favorite part. The moment of truth when I'm finally able to see if I've captured what's in my head. I remember that night so clearly, how I was feeling right when I took that shot. Of course, a lot of it has been tarnished by what happened right afterwards. Life can hand you a silver-plated miracle one minute and slap you in the face the next.

Nikki wonders if Paul would have left Taylor if PC hadn't attacked me. We went down this whole road wondering if I would have gotten together with Allison if we hadn't been chasing Nirvana. Life is one big flow chart. You take one turn and it branches out, again and again.

I know it before I even pull the photo out of chemical bath. There's a place in my gut that knows what makes a good or even a great photo. This one sends shivers down my spine. I nailed it. It's the best picture I've ever taken. It belongs in a magazine. My lens captured the feeling of these three men living on the world's stage being whisked off in shiny Suburbans by waiting drivers to destinations unknown and also, their isolation. The camaraderie between the three of them is unmistakable and yet, heartbreaking. I'm not sure why. Maybe I'm reading too much of myself into it.

I work for another hour developing the rest of the roll from the Cow Palace. By that time the first shot, the best one, is nearly dry. I limp out of the dark room and show Mrs. Harter.

When I lay it on her desk, she studies it for a very long time with her chin on her hand. It's my favorite time of day, when the crows head across the purple sky. The gloaming. "This is wonderful."

"Thanks." I'm relieved that she thinks the same thing although, if I'm honest, I know I've captured something unique. I lean back in my chair, resting my foot on a chair. Nikki's mom said elevating my stitches will help them heal faster. They tend to ache at the end of the day. I stayed out of school for a week until I could hide the black eyes from my broken nose with make-up. Nikki styles my hair every morning to cover the scab where my hair was ripped.

"You could make a lot of money selling this. There are magazines and photo stock companies that would pay really good money for this Fran." She looks at me with hopeful eyes.

"Seriously?"

Her smile crinkles right into her eyes. "Seriously. It's an arresting image. Very soulful and stark. It's not your typical rock and roll fan photo. It's a very serious portrait. You've got some chops young lady. I'm looking forward to saying I knew you when."

I'm pretty sure I flush down to the tips of my aching feet but it's a joyful embarrassment. Instead of being annoyed by Mrs. Harter's optimism, I'm floating on top of it, letting it go to my head until I'm in a helium bubble, a few feet above the pain.

"I don't think I'll sell it." I surprise myself and yet know, in my heart, that this is right thing to do. This photo is part of my history. Selling it would be exposing myself and selling out Nirvana when they went out of their way to help me. Everyone else in Aberdeen is talking to anyone who will listen about the night Nirvana came to town. It's all over the news. But I'm staying quiet.

"At least use it in your portfolio when you go to work for other photographers." She starts packing her things into the backpack she has stored under her desk.

"What other photographers?"

She zips up her backpack, straps a Velcro tab around her right pant leg and walks to the bike she keeps in a corner of the classroom. "Professional ones. Journalists. Worse photographers than you have gotten jobs going on tours with famous rock bands. There's a whole world of possibility out there but it's not going to find you unless you show people that photo." She waits with her bike while I open the classroom door for her. As she wheels her bike out into the hallway she stops. "And Fran," she says, tilting her head like a wise old auntie. "It's not going to find you in Aberdeen."

I stand in the hallway watching her as she steps on one pedal and lifts herself, pushing off the shiny floor, letting the bike carry her down the hallway into the light.

Do normal people stand at their own front door, wondering if they should turn around, jump on a bus and move into their best friend's basement? I'm weighing my options when Mom opens the door in her bakery uniform. "Don't just stand there like a stranger, come on in."

Offering an awkward one-armed hug, she flutters around like a butterfly with a broken wing, trailing me into my bedroom, fidgeting as I unpack. Pacing nervously, she unpins her nametag from her apron, studying it like an understudy moments from walking onstage in a play called "Whoops, I'm a Mother." Just to keep busy, I hang up the empty garment bag, unsure of why I kept it and put away my clothes.

After staying at Nikki's, I realize how young my mother is compared to Nikki's mom. If she hadn't had me would she have gone to college or done something with her life besides drift with the tide like my barfly grandma?

"Well Dwayne took off," she says, settling down on my creaky bed. "I guess that means we'll be getting an apartment or something."

Wanting her out of my room, I hurry into the living room. A black and white movie flickers on the TV. She winces when I shut it off, pressing stop on the VCR. "Hey! That's Claudette Colbert in *It Happened One Night*. The one where she plays the spoiled heiress who runs away from home. First time she appeared with Clark Gable. He's this reporter looking for a story 'cause he got fired. They meet on a bus. Imagine that—meeting a millionaire on a bus. I ride the bus all year and all I ever meet are drunks and losers. Did you ever see it?" She drags a chair from the kitchen, patting it. "Come on, sit down. We can watch it together." All my life she's been shushing me. *Shhhhh, baby. No talking. This is the good part.*

"Mom, I'm dating a girl named Allison."

She walks backwards into her chair, flopping down without looking. "I don't get it."

Moving to the sliding glass door, I draw squiggles on the condensation. "What's not to get? You've known I was gay for a long time."

She rocks in her chair, which isn't a rocker but is so decrepit, it moves like one. "Yeah. It's just I don't know what to do."

"Maybe you can go to the library and see if there's a Guide to Raising Your Gay Kid."

Agitated, she jumps up. "You're not being helpful." Grabbing her little plastic spritzer, mom sprays the African violets on the windowsill. "Well okay then. You can have her over here I guess." Three energetic little squirts for a dying violet. "When I'm gone."

With swooping letters I scrawl Allison's name on the window. "Will that help you pretend like she doesn't exist?"

"I just can't believe there's another lesbian in this whole town."

"There is and I found her." The little hearts I trace around Allison's name drip down the glass. Perversely, I want to talk about Allison to the one person who doesn't want to listen. It's like I want to jam her existence down my mom's throat. Show her that someone beautiful, funny and smart would want me. "She moved here from San Francisco."

Mom sits back down in her chair, massaging her always tired feet. My childhood in two words: I'm tired. "Figures. Dwayne says it's full of fags and dykes. Lesbians, right? Isn't that what you want to be called? A lesbian? What an ugly word."

The creaking of her stupid chair makes me want to flip the whole hideous thing through the slider with her in it. Maybe we were close when I was tiny enough to hold hands crossing the street. When she took me to the park and lifted me onto the swing. My dad pushed me the highest. That moment when my feet hit the sky was with my father.

She gets the basin from under the sink for soaking her feet, pours in Epsom salts and runs the water until it's hot. "How come you didn't call me when you were at the hospital when you got beat up? I'm the one you're supposed to call. I bought you that dress."

She's so defensive it confirms what I already suspected. Nikki's mom wanted my mom to look good so she drove two hours away, bought the dress and handed it to Mom with a ready-made fairytale story. "I was staying at Nikki's."

"You're just mad because I don't want to meet your girlfriend. There. I said it. I said girlfriend." Mom pivots away from me, slipping on the worn linoleum. For a moment, I worry that she's hurt but she's just a little wet from the saltwater. She lifts her hand, wanting help. Gritting my teeth, I soften my tone, lift her up.

"You okay Mom?"

"No. No I am not. Thanks to you my boyfriend moved out. I just want to soak my feet and watch my movie. Is that okay with you?"

In my mind, I run over to the battered old TV, grab it with both hands, lift it over my head and violently smash it to the ground. Parts would fly and clatter around the room in a burst of sparks. She'd stand to face me, shocked and trembling. Amid the smoking parts we'd stare at one another for the first time in years. I'm not sure what we'd say to one another. Either *fuck you* or *I love you* or quite possibly some variation of both. A Pretenders song flits through my head. *It's a thin line between love and hate.* Those words are what stop me from picking up Mom's beloved TV. Love and hate. As much as I despise Mom right now, I can't. She'd kick me out. I can't go crawling back to Nikki's. Sleeping under a bridge isn't an option. Not tonight.

"Fine." I press play and sit on the chair beside her, trying to get into the movie. But I can't. After ten minutes, I give up and escape to my room, lying on my back studying my Nirvana posters with my Walkman firmly embedded in my ears. Tomorrow is graduation.

NIKKI

I'm visiting Paul at the University of Washington, trying not to feel like a total loser among all the other college students. My internship is surprisingly okay. Mr.

Waites, who works with my dad, gives me tons of research but I like it, especially when I get sent to the UW law library. I feel awkward sitting in the HUB food court by myself amongst the streams of chattering students so I grab an old newspaper sitting on the table, *The Stranger*. Flipping through the pages for something to do, I see a photo of the demonstrations at Aberdeen High School with the caption "Gay Prom Queen Nominee Divides Small Town." It's Mrs. Davis and other parents brandishing signs. Keep Our School on the Straight and Narrow. Parents for Family Values. There is another sign with two female sex symbols in the center of a circle with a line drawn through it. God. What shitheads. I don't have time to read the article so I stuff *The Stranger* into my backpack to show Fran later.

Paul left town first for UW athlete orientation and training. We spent a lot of time in my freaking backyard because I'm still grounded. Although it made me feel about five, we ended up talking a lot. Paul says he really had it out with his father, which has let him move on. He doesn't have anything to prove to anyone anymore. He seems more relaxed. Hazel and Mike both enrolled at Aberdeen College because she plans on running a daycare (barf) and he's going to become a pot-smoking diesel mechanic. Since I'm re-applying at UW and also University of Oregon, Fran finds it depressing to be the only one without big plans. After Allison left for Seattle, she was a total zombie. Every time I call her she isn't at home. What is she doing? I'm worried about her.

PAUL

My mom has filed for divorce. Turns out she never really got one, which is shocking. I guess at some level we thought Dad would walk back in the door and become his same old self. When he showed up, it turned out we'd all changed. Nobody wanted to go backwards except him. The weird thing is now there is more breathing room in the house. Mom calls it closure. She's going to a divorce support group and comes up with all kinds of goofy sayings. Although I make fun of it, I'm glad she's going. Who knows, maybe she'll meet someone.

I look back at my time with Taylor and wonder what the hell was going on in my mind. Nothing. Absolutely nothing.

FRAN

Nathan Steiner forgot to send me *The Stranger* article but Nikki brought it back from Seattle. I've read the article several times, re-living my time with Nathan Steiner. The article is exactly what I want the world to think about my stint as prom queen nominee, including the road trip and prom featuring Nirvana. Nathan also interviewed Nikki's mom, who told him about PC. Nathan didn't share the details of my assault, only that I'd been bullied and tormented in high school, something that Principal P. and Mrs. Harter confirmed. There is a vague statement about scars that will last a lifetime.

My finger traces the thin pink scar on my cheek while I study the business card embossed with *The Stranger* masthead and Nathan's name and phone number. My mom or maybe Dwayne left it tacked to the side of the fridge under a Domino's Pizza delivery magnet. I've picked up the phone about a hundred times to call him, rehearsing my speech, wondering if he has a secretary, if he'll remember me or return my call. Dwayne has moved back. If he answers the phone, I'm toast. Either way when he sees the phone bill, he'll bitch. I have to pay one third of every bill: rent, utilities and food, although I never see the actual bills. I'm sure he's gouging me, looking for me to talk back or complain. He's itching to kick me out. I'm working hard not to hate my mother. It's not going very well.

After wrapping and un-wrapping the phone cord around my wrist a hundred times, I dial the number. It rings three times. "Nathan Steiner."

My throat closes up. "Um, hi Mr. Steiner this is Fran Worthy."

"Fran?"

"Um, yes, you came down and visited me in Aberdeen last spring?" My voice squeaks.

"Oh, sure. Right. Hi Fran. How's it going?"

"Good. Good. It's going fine. I've actually gotten a photography portfolio together and I'm wondering if you know any photographers in Seattle." I squeeze my eyes shut, spitting the words out fast.

"I know freelance people. I didn't know you were a photographer."

I take a deep breath. "I am. I have a portfolio and I could do dark room or scheduling or whatever needs to be done." I lie down on my bed, looking up at Kurt Cobain's face for reassurance. Mrs. Harter walked me through everything I should say, rehearsing a few times so I wouldn't babble. She's even given me a few people to call, a photographer and a couple gallery owners. I started with Nathan because he was nice. He'll reject me painlessly, with kind words.

"Okay kiddo, listen. Lemme make a few phone calls. I'm working on something right now but I'll get back to you in a couple days. Give me your number."

It takes me a minute to reply because the words on my tongue: *That's okay, no worries. Thanks for your time,* aren't needed. I give him the number to Plaza Garcia because that's where I spend all my time these days. I thank him and hang up the phone, shaky and so full of excitement I jump up, spinning until I'm dizzy, falling flat on the bed..Silently I thank Kurt Cobain for writing songs that made me feel less lonely. While I'm at it, I thank Nikki for pushing me. I thank Paul and Mike for going along for the ride. I thank Hazel for making prom an unforgettable Goth wonderland. Allison I save for last because saying goodbye was so painful. Maybe she's still my girlfriend. No matter what she'll always be my first kiss, my first everything. It's easier to think about all this because I have an inkling of a plan. Maybe, just maybe, if I make enough phone calls and knock on enough doors, and drag my portfolio around, I do have a future in Seattle. Maybe I'll sneak into the Crocodile Cafe and get another shot of Nirvana. Stranger things have happened.

ABOUT THE AUTHOR

Ellyn Oaksmith is the USA Today bestselling author of four books including the Kindle bestseller Chasing Nirvana and 50 Acts of Kindness. She lives in Seattle. Luckily she's waterproof.

**If you'd like to read another
Ellyn Oaksmith book
visit EllynOaksmith.com.**

Made in the USA
San Bernardino, CA
18 January 2018